The Child Who
Walked on the Sky

Pierre PELOT

The Child Who
Walked on the Sky

But What If
Butterflies Cheat?

translated by
Michael Shreve

A Black Coat Press Book

Visit our website at www.blackcoatpress.com

ISBN 978-1-61227-107-1. First Printing. August 2012. Published by Black Coat Press, an imprint of Hollywood Comics.com, LLC, P.O. Box 17270, Encino, CA 91416. All rights reserved. Except for review purposes, no part of this book may be reproduced or transmitted in any form or by any means, electronic or mechanical, including photocopying, recording, or by any information storage and retrieval system, without permission in writing from the publisher. The stories and characters depicted in this novel are entirely fictional. Printed in the United States of America.

TABLE OF CONTENTS

Introduction
The Best Place to Escape[1]

I was born in this valley cramped into worn, round uplands.

These summits and valleys are not and have never been for livestock or crops, but for a long time, and for lack of anything better, destined to small farmers and artisans before the textile mills set up house. Today they figure on changing the mountains of the Vosges into tourist attractions. Not even one winter resort: the snow is no longer bound to keep its appointments.

Pierre Pelot (born Pierre Grosdemange, aka Pierre Suragne, aka Pierre Carbonari, aka Pierre Pélot) was born on November 13, 1945 in Saint-Maurice-sur-Moselle, a small village in the middle of the Vosges. He continues to live there.

He began writing westerns and in 1966, at the age of 21, his first novel appeared, *La Piste du Dakota* (The Dakota Trail). At a madcap rhythm he published seven novels and a collection of short stories before creating the character of Dylan Stark in 1967 for Belgian publisher Marabout, and winning the Grand Prix des Treize that year for *La Couleur de Dieu* (The Color of God), the second Dylan Stark novel.

---

[1] The text in italics is by Pierre Pelot and translated from the "Identity Card" on his *tanière* (i.e. in his lair): http://www.pierrepelot.fr/pierre_pelot_la_taniere/carte_didenti te.html

After a number of "social" novels, often dark and violent, in the early 1970s, the promising young writer broke into science fiction and horror under the name of Pierre Suragne for Fleuve Noir's famous *Anticipation* and *Angoisse* series.[2] His first science fiction novel was *La Septième Saison* (The Seventh Season, 1972), inspired by legends of the Hopi Indians against a background of colonial massacres and pollution, but where Nature unites with the despoiled people for recompense.

Pelot wrote fourteen science fiction and seven horror novels for Fleuve Noir before 1980 and has gone on to write around 200 works covering all genres: westerns, science fiction, speculative fiction, dark fiction, crime novels, horror, thrillers, children's stories, young adult fiction, prehistoric fiction, screenplays, stage plays, and literary fiction. His books have been translated into twenty or so languages. However, this is his first translation in English.

So, here is the fledgling Moselle, a fragile river that glides between the humps and hills, lazes around, in no hurry, far from the men and women who govern us and say they speak in our name, with their drooling, honeyed lips, their sharp, hungry teeth, singing the same old lying song that disguises the profit of a few under the tawdry rags of so-called public interest.

Those who are proud of their cheap work became those who built the concrete and the metal frames. Soon just the pictures in our memory will be all that is left. The industrial zones and the supermarkets, the invading

---

[2] *Anticipation* and *Angoisse* published works by G.-J. Arnaud, Richard Bessière, André Caroff and Kurt Steiner, also trandlated and available from Black Coat Press.

highways and byways are now electoral platforms for the pot-bellied deputies and conceited senators, objects of their base proud groveling, masterpieces bearing witness to their inability to hold onto (for everyone's sake, they say) the fate of "my valley" that they are shamelessly mutilating.

In addition to *L'Enfant qui marchait sur le ciel* (The Child Who Walked on the Sky, Fleuve Noir, 1972) and *Mais si les papillons trichent* (What If Butterflies Cheat?, Fleuve Noir, 1974), presented in this volume, some of his other notable early works of science fiction include:

Transit (Robert Laffont, 1977) which was awarded the Graouly d'or and Grand prix du Festival International de Science-Fiction of Metz in 1978. Carry Galen lives in amnesia, lies and a false life. He lives in two, parallel, radically opposed, irreconcilable worlds, which lead him to… utopia? An astonishing play with multiple realities and a keen socio-political critique.

Delirium Circus (J'ai Lu, 1977), which won the Grand Prix de l'Imaginaire, also in 1978: Citizen is famous for his role as Zorro Nap, army commander. Except the role that he plays is always the same, imposed by the God-Public, an entity that no one can see but that every actor must be ready to sacrifice their life for so as not to end up rejected. Citizen decides to discover the hidden face of the God-public. Here also, two universes oppose each other—the rich and poor, the real and unreal. A strangely, surprisingly contemporary novel, reeking of reality TV, with real deaths on screen, and with one of Pelot's favorite designs: to denounce the shams of our society and unveil the "doctored décor".

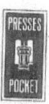

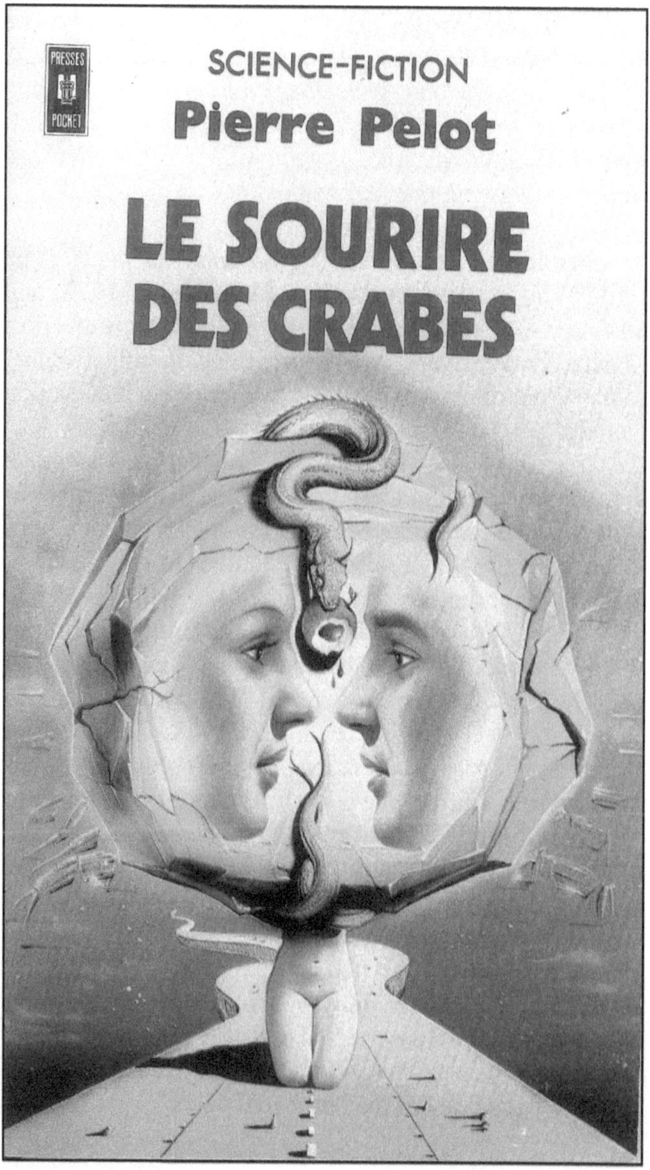
PRESSES POCKET
SCIENCE-FICTION
Pierre Pelot
LE SOURIRE DES CRABES

Le sourire des crabes (The Smile of the Crabs, Presses pocket, 1977): A love story between brother and sister, both schizophrenic, who take a last joyride sowing death and destruction in their wake. Violent, nihilistic, desperate, a cry of rage, an explosion of anger, a bloody, hallucinating ride down the highways of power where Fear pushes the individual to take refuge in the worst of traps—blind violence or insanity to escape insupportable reality. But is any of this real?

Les barreaux de l'Eden (The Bars of Eden, J'ai Lu, 1977): describes a society divided hierarchically into three classes A, B and C where a drug, ANC X, lets you speak with the dead. But a society founded entirely on lies and servility and an Eden that does not exist. A dystopist puppet show as disturbing as it is discerning.

Foetus Party (Denoël, 1977): The Holy Director's Office checks overpopulation, recycles waste and recuperates corpses to feed the huge population. Couples have three tries to procreate and their fetuses are surveyed, interrogated in the mother's belly to see if they want to live and then to snuff out any anti-social or borderline cases. Something between *1984* and *Soylent Green* to describe the horrors of an absurd system where the technology to preserve life develops into an unnatural selection to eliminate people.

La Guerre Olympique (The Olympic War, Denoël, 1980): every two years an Olympic War is declared between the white camp of the liberal confederation and the red camp of the socio-communist federation. Doped up, super champions, modern-day gladiators face each other in mortal combat with no holds barred. Penalty for losing—10 million dead in their camp, chosen among the delinquents, subversives and deviants whose brain has a mini-bomb set to explode on the announcement of results, which are televised for all to see. The media moguls and politicians, of course, make good use of this ideal solution.

Kid Jesus (J'ai Lu, 1980): On Territory F a colony of Searchers lives in gigantic bulldozers digging the frozen ground in search of traces. Julius Port finds a cassette that speaks of a certain Jesus of Nazareth and gets the idea of becoming a spokesperson of the "rats" and "shit-diggers". When he dies in an explosion, young Alano henceforth passes for him until the day when he accepts to speak the truth, which will be fatal. Was Kid Jesus a false prophet, hungry for glory and money? Or a puppet in the hands of hidden, pitiless powers? Is safety in escape or in hard-won lucidity? Unless it is in the difficult search for an identity that is threatened, doubled or lost.

Pelot also embarked on writing series like *Les Hommes sans futur* (Men Without Future), six volumes published between 1981 and 1985 that portray the history of the end of Mankind, with no drum rolls or fanfare, supplanted by his own children, the Superiors, just like homo sapiens had formerly ousted the monkey; and *Konnar Le Barbant* (Dumbass the Bore), five hilarious volumes published between 1981 and 1991 that parody the heroic-fantasy.

Among Perlot's diverse works should be mentioned the prehistoric novels written with the anthropologist Yves Coppens, particularly *Le Rêve de Lucy* (Lucy's Dream, Editions du Seuil, 1990) which won the Grand prix de l'Imaginaire pour la jeunesse in 1990 and *Sous le vent du monde* the Prix Spécial in 2001.

Much of Pelot's current work is classified as "mainstream" literature, but there's very little "mainstream" about it, like his brilliant coming-of-age novel *Méchamment Dimanche* (Héloïse d'Ormesson, 2005), winner of the 2005 Prix Marcel Pagnol, where the eyes of a child recount the lives and relationships that are as dark and tumultuous as the rivers of the Vosges.

With my ass on my slope, I remember a time not so long ago when this valley, protected by mountains sitting like big, quiet dogs, was beautiful. The village square was, in large part, shaded by trees that were more than 100 years old, surrounding the monument to the dead with their venerable wisdom. They cut down the old trees on the pretext that they were not pretty, twisted, not clean, not straight.

And today the serrated roofs of the textile mills sit on top of empty buildings, for the most part.

This country is the country of stories with which the lives of human beings are built. I'm here to relate them.

Stories—this means human beings passing through existence as best they can. That's what interests me. I went to search them out in their burrows, these stories, poaching them, without a license, in my way, nobody taught me. Just use the way that's right for you; that's how we learn to catch them.

Pierre Pelot is first and foremost a storyteller. He writes original stories with simple (not simplistic) ideas in a devastating style. Efficient and intelligent works that make the reader think and reflect but not get bogged down in heady constructs.

His earlier novels are fast, nervous and radical, brushed with beautiful lyric passages. Though often violent, they are capable of extraordinary tenderness. Pelot is a master architect who builds a story with expert handling of different styles to paint his narrative and illustrate his ideas.

In general, Pelot's novels are subtle reflections on power and the individual, the economy and ecology, especially the manipulation of such: the abuse of power and injustice, the corrupt foundations of society, the problem of individual freedom and self-identity among the masses, the devastation of nature.

Pelot's fiction is a questioning of reality as perceived by the social being in the face of others and oneself, often manifested in a revolt against a dehumanizing society that is more preoccupied by economic conquest than the well-being of its citizens. It is the refusal to submit to an authority, a conscious revolt against authority. Rebellion. It is anarchy, but his own type of anarchy. He criticizes the concentration and centralization of power and knowledge through a constant opposition of the individual with the different avatars of authority. But in stigmatizing the evils of society, he does not preach, does not deliver a message. He expresses himself, says what he thinks.

Man is caught up in a world he did not choose and sometimes when he believes he is wriggling free, he is only falling deeper into the trap. Sometimes when he has to fight his way out or flee from the darkness, he is never sure of escaping. Thus his heroes often end up dead or insane, reduced to silence, imprisoned or buried. But he does not choose the stories, they chose him and the stories are in the struggle.

One winter evening, "they" asked me to give an author's name to put on the cover of what would, then, be my first book. Being a writer is to break yourself in order to better accept yourself and what you give to your writing. It's being hollowed out day after day, getting lost trying to represent yourself in the only way you know how without annoying others too much. Both inside and out, with and without.

It's being an outlaw whom nobody's tracking, who has no price on his head, no wanted posters slapped on the walls. Hiding among the people here who never stop escaping so that they, too, can survive, here or elsewhere.

Michael Shreve

ANTICIPATION

FICTION

Pierre SURAGNE

L'ENFANT QUI MARCHAIT SUR LE CIEL

FLEUVE NOIR

THE CHILD WHO WALKED ON THE SKY

CHAPTER I

The world itself has a name. The world is called Zod.

They say that the machine, pulsating and silent, is in the belly of the world. The Machine. Since the beginning of time, the Machine has counted and calculated. Since the beginning, the Machine has copied and translated time and made it something vaguely comprehensible to the minds of men. It is the Machine that calculates the slow succession of years. One year is a cycle of well-defined time determined by the mechanism and revolutions of transparent spheres in the belly of the Machine.

The child was eight years old. Eight is sometimes very old already, very desperate. Sometimes it is old enough to die.

He was eight years old and his name was Horan. That was an additional crime—but he was long past just one crime, he was past counting his revolts.

In the world of Zod, the children do not have a name. The adults who make up the class of Subjects do not have one either for that matter. The Prime Master has a name. The Teachers and the Directors, too. But especially not the children.

They yell them out by a number.

Before, his number was 47. He was 47. The forty-seventh student of the class of Maladjusted in the world of Zod. He was barely born when they had placed him in this class of "specially" controlled education.

He had learned life; he had received the teaching like the other children with him. There were hardly more than a hundred in each "special" education class. There was a natural turnover; some entered, others left. Those who left had become subjects of Zod: they had cured their sickness, they had modeled them correctly and they had wiped out the harmful traces of revolt. If the teaching did not bear fruit, after a certain number of years, the maladjusted still left the class. For somewhere else…

The classroom was high-ceilinged and cylindrical, like a big tube stuck right in the middle of Zod's flesh. The ceiling was dome-shaped, pierced in the center by a ventilation grill. At ground level the corridor crawled up the wall, in an even spiral, opening onto the individual student cells all the way up to the vaulted ceiling. Horan's cell was practically at the top of the corridor, almost under the grill with its steady breathing of fresh air.

He was stretched out on his bed, his hands crossed under his neck, his eyes lost in the tightly woven mesh of grill that covered the air vent. In this position, looking toward the door of his cell, he could see nothing else, nothing but this grill.

Horan was small and slim. Fragile limbs and skin so white, so thin and delicate that it was almost transparent. In certain spots, under his skin, you could see the bluish network of glassy veins, especially in his temples, and in his wrists, too. His face was round. A small, round child's face. Big, colorless eyes, too often hardened by some terrible inner inferno. And then the mouth, like a pink line, blunt, determined, more often closed than open. On top of his round, fragile, disturbingly firm face, a black shock of hair sticking up, in constant battle.

For a long time Horan lay there without moving, simply stretched out on the cozy bed, staring. All around him the confused murmur of thousands of words strung together, hundreds of confused conversations swirling softly. For an hour yet, maybe more, the lights of the classroom would stay on, then it would be dark and the signal to sleep.

The muffled sound of a footstep suddenly drew Horan's attention and he stopped staring at the ventilation grill. His eyes fell on 23, standing frozen in the doorway. Horan propped himself up on one elbow, smiled faintly, and nodded. 23 entered and looked around for a chair. He did not find one.

"Come and sit here," Horan invited, pointing to the foot of his bed.

23 smiled and sat down. He was eight years old, too. He had come out of the Birth Machine on the same day as Horan. A little taller, maybe, pretty stocky, and with dark red hair. The synthetic fiber shirt was stretched tightly over his short trunk.

"He won't come tonight," 23 said. His voice was deep, almost husky. He was scared, certainly.

"What makes you say that?" Horan asked.

The other shrugged, twisted his smile. "The time," he said. "He usually comes earlier."

That was wrong. The instructor could show up at any time. Sometimes he burst in just a few seconds before the signal to sleep.

"He can come at any time," Horan said. "And he'll come tonight, for you and for me."

23 fidgeted on the bed, buried his fists in his coat pockets. He was pale and trembling.

"Are you scared?" Horan asked.

"Of course you're not scared!"

An astonished gleam flashed briefly in Horan's eyes. Scared?... No, it was certainly not fear.

"I don't think so," Horan said. "They won't have me."

This time the astonishment was in 23 and he stared at Horan for a long time, trying to guess, to understand what was hiding behind this idiotic... and decisive declaration. After a while, he nodded his head and said, "They forbid us to talk to you and we're punished when we do. They forbid us to listen to you."

"So, what are you doing here?" Horan shot back angrily.

"I really think you're crazy," 23 said softly. "You're not scared... You say you're going to escape."

"And you accept it, don't you? Arg, the instructor, will come soon. He'll call 47 and 23 to tell them they have to die tomorrow, that they're incapable of becoming subjects of Zod. In front of everyone he'll yell out the sentence and you'll accept it? You'll accept walking to the Death Chamber tomorrow? You'll accept that this is your last night of sleep?"

"47!" 23 was aghast.

Horan calmed down, smiled. He said, "I have a name now. I'm called Horan. It's an old word from the language of the Ancients. It means rebel."

Shocked and trembling, 23 stood up, took three steps back. He looked at Horan as if he were the most terrifying monster that could come from above the sky. "A name, but... but you..."

"I don't want to be a number anymore," Horan said ferociously (he was gritting his teeth, looking at nothing). "Yes, I took a name, this morning. I gave myself a name. I'm called Horan."

"Names," 23 said, "are reserved for Teachers and Instructors. Only for them and the Prime Master... And you..."

"I don't believe in the Instructors or the Teachers," Horan said. He did not shout, was no longer furious. He suddenly looked very unhappy, weary, shattered. He was an eight-year old child and his eyes glistened with tears. "I can't believe in them," he continued in a croaking voice. "I can't. I never could... Since always. Since forever. I know they're lying to us, they're lying to all the Subjects. I know it's false. Everything they teach us... They told us that we have to believe in tomorrow. The Hope Religion! Me, I can't. Not in that way. For thousands of years it's been like this and millions of subjects have died, for no reason, for nothing... For nothing."

"But death," 23 risked, "is also a form..."

"I can't believe in it!" Horan cut him off. "I can't. They also invented legends for death... for afterward... I know there's nothing in what they say. I know." He did not finish. All of a sudden his shoulders shook with sobs. He was silent on his bed, became a little heap, a little thing, a knot of tears.

Without saying a word, 23 stepped forward and after a short hesitation put his hand on Horan's shoulder. They stayed like that for a moment, in silence. Then, when the sobs died down, 23 spoke softly, "You see, you're scared, too."

Horan shook his black shock of hair from left to right. He said, "It's something other than fear. I don't want to die for nothing. They won't have me."

A long time afterward, he raised his eyes, wiping away his last tears with the back of his hand. He noticed that 23 had left. Horan felt vaguely relieved. 23 was nice. He, too, was not destined to become a perfect subject. He, too, was bound for destruction. Waste was not tolerated in Zod.

But Horan preferred to be alone. Alone with his eight years of life, with his sickness of maladjustment.

But he had tried! To hear and understand and swallow quietly this teaching that was supposed to make a number out of him for life. Yes, he had tried... But total failure. It was deep down inside him, stronger than him, stronger than all the drugs and all the machines. Refusal. The bitter need to refuse.

He had quickly become one of those taboo subjects, headstrong, with a mind that was more rigid than the oldest of metals. He had become, almost despite himself, almost without knowing it, one of those who had that talent for always asking the questions that should not be asked, if you did not want to sow the seeds of doubt; one of those extraordinarily gifted in spin and the perpetual need to know more; one of those who are always asking "why"?

Why this? Why that? And why not like this or like that...

He had become a waste.

They told him: a long time ago the people of Zod lived in the sky and they were happy, learned, they knew everything, they were the masters of all sciences. They knew too much and one day the sky exploded. A handful of survivors, a meager handful, took refuge under the wreckage of that murdered sky—for, they had foreseen this catastrophe. They took refuge in a shelter that became the world of Zod. And they still live in Zod the buried land, as they have for thousands and thousands of years. For more than 22,000 years. They wait for the sign. And the sign will come, one day, and then the chosen people of Zod will once again be able to take possession of the sky because it will be forever rid of the monsters that inhabit it.

They told him this. They told everyone this.

But Horan had answered, why? While the others accepted. Horan—he was still just 47—had expressed doubts. Doubt, the desire to always know more, was in him from the time when, still a five-month old fetus, they had wrenched him from the belly of some female to stick him in the accelerated incubators of the Birth Machine. It was in him.

He did not believe in the sky inhabited by monsters or in the sign that was supposed to come.

They had told him: The Prime Master of Zod is eternal. He is the God of Hope. He is the guide of the people of Zod.

And he, Horan, without even trying, without any effort at all, asked why. Why give names to Teachers and numbers to Subjects? Why should the Instructors and Teachers live so long when the Subjects die after thirty years of life? Why? He had said naively, "I want to become a Teacher."

It was, of course, a huge mistake. In the first place, a psychologically maladjusted had no chance of becoming a Teacher or Instructor. Horan less so than the others. And the guide of the class had understood completely. "I want to become a Teacher" in the mouth of this curious 47 might certainly mean, "I want to become Prime Master".

They rarely came across rebels in Horan's class. Of course, there was no meanness in him, or hatred or anger. He was just a child. His defect was even worse than anger or hatred: it was called dissatisfaction, curiosity. Need for the absolute… it had countless names.

Some Teachers, talking among themselves, claimed that they saw these tendencies to rebel against the teaching more and more often. The percentage of waste was rising higher and higher as time went on, in Zod. The Teachers claimed that some kind of frustration complex was at the heart of these psychological defections. A mental shock occurs in the fetus' unconscious and the aftermath just intensifies it in certain subjects. So, what was needed was love and tenderness. The Teachers said that some people might require these things… They said this among themselves and in whispers, feeling a blasphemer's shame. Love and tenderness were very old words that were of no use at all in the current language. They served no purpose in Zod. They were not needed because, well, the remaining survivors could very well disappear in just two or three generations.

Of course, Horan could not know what the Teachers said when they talked among themselves, in their distant cells deep in the heart of Zod. He did not know. But he knew the two taboo words.

Love. Tenderness.

And others besides. Like "Father" and "Mother".

He had learned them recently. Only a few days ago. He had to steal one of those old, fascinating books from the highest shelves of the room of antique bookcases. The books were unbelievably old and dusty. They looked like they came from some kind of bottomless pit and when you touched them it was like you were putting your finger on the dawn of time. The covers were hardened, wooly, and the plastic pages were yellowed and stained.

Horan had stolen a book. Its writing was one of those ancient writings he had wanted to learn in the first years of teaching—another point against him because students ordinarily did not choose to violate the dead languages.

The child had been able to keep the book for one whole day and night. At night he read in the dark—he often wondered if all the other children, like him, could see in the dark when the lights went out. He could. He had never spoken of it, out of fear of revealing another, as yet unsuspected defect.

He had read. He had arduously deciphered part of the book and he had learned the words. Father, mother, tenderness, love. And others, which were more or less connected to them. He was able to understand the gist of them, but he found no comparison or translation in the language of Zod. They were really new words, unique words. He had vaguely felt some incredible sense of wealth in them. But also danger. A dreadful danger.

The words were not made for Zod. Maybe they were magic, or evil... But he was not scared. He started to love the words.

Like he loved the little noise, the weird little noise that he had been hearing above his head every night for the past three or four days. Higher than the bulging vault of the classroom. Higher than the ventilation grill. It was there in the magma of the collapsed sky, a little sound of life passing by...

The breeders—or more precisely, the Subjects in the mandatory breeding period—of Zod could have called themselves "fathers"... The bellies of the women could have been the bellies of "mothers"... No. It was really something else. It was really a secret, it was magic.

It was for elsewhere.

And that noise, high up, in the sky of steel and rock? That little noise…

Brutal, the voice suddenly thundered over the loudspeaker and startled Horan. And yet he was waiting for it. He couldn't not help but wait for it: he would be eight tomorrow and the wastes in special teaching never got past that age. That was the limit. That was the first thing they taught: "Be worthy and capable of becoming Subjects before you're eight years old."

He was waiting for it, but he was startled. He felt tears rising again. But he was not scared. He was determined.

He jumped out of his bunk and walked through the door of his cell. He was in the bare corridor, on that spiral ramp that sloped all the way down to the floor of the classroom. He leaned over the rail at the very moment when the metallic voice pronounced his number.

"47… 23… 45… 37…"

A few away feet from Horan, 23 had left his cell as well and was also leaning on the plastic railing. He was very pale.

"56… 78… 13."

There were nine of them in all. Nine who, tomorrow, would turn eight and who had not been able to learn, who had not been able to swallow the teaching like a sponge soaks up any liquid whatsoever. There were nine, incapable of becoming satisfactory subjects. Nine with a conscience too twisted, too complicated, with too many rebellious tendencies, eyes too open not to become dangerous down the road.

Nine wastes.

At the bottom of the classroom, at the end of the giant spiral, the Teacher standing there was the size of a

26

pea. But his voice, like thunder, his inordinate voice, rendered even drier by the amplifiers, went on, "...tomorrow when you wake up. You will be guided to the exit of this classroom and into the Death Chamber. Thus the law of Zod demands. Thus the law of life demands."

Then, miniscule, he left.

There was not a sound in the classroom, except, again, for a few split seconds, the booming echo.

But Horan had chosen not to accept the law of Zod; he was made in such a way that he could not accept it. He had chosen to put his hope in a different law of life. He was convinced intuitively that the teachings of Zod were hiding marvelous mysteries.

He avoided looking at 23, alone and frozen on the ramp, and went back into his cell. As he was sitting down on his bunk, the lights went out. But it changed practically nothing for Horan.

CHAPTER II

In the world of Zod the "times of night" and the "times of light" were not always the same duration. They increased or decreased according to an immutable and regular cycle. It had been like that forever, throughout the years. There was certainly a reason for this—they taught the children from their earliest years that the gods who regulate time are not required to reveal their secrets to men.

Whether the times of night were long or short, they were, in any case, always the best times for Horan. He had never trusted sleep, that false death, that terrible shifting hole in the consciousness. He had always fought against the numbness, the irritating lead weight that suddenly fell on your eyelids, that enveloped you.

At night, Horan was finally alone and he could dream, let his thoughts wander wherever he wanted, totally undisturbed, without having to worry about upsetting some rite of the austere teaching. The night belonged to him and he belonged to it.

To make this complicity even more valuable, there was this acute and blessed night vision that Horan "suffered" from. During the day, in the classes and corridors and all the lit up places in Zod, the child squinted, screwed up his eyes, almost closed them completely. One thin line for his colorless eyes to fight against the brightness, to keep this artificial light, this enemy, from entering him and hurting him.

Despite his efforts and his diaphanous eyelids drawn as far as possible over the trembling visions, despite the brutal pain at the end of some days, the child never went to the doctors and never even whispered a complaint. He had the nights to himself, alone, and it was a fantastic treasure. It was the only treasure—he had to defend it tooth and nail.

It was during these nights that the doubts came. On this bunk while he let his thoughts drift endlessly, he could, all alone, compelled by some indefinable force, find and patiently enlarge the first cracks in the all too solid, too compact wall of Zod's teaching. Doubt was already a victory, even though it had to be the cause of this decision by the Council of Teachers who were sending him now to death, banished forever from the society of Zod.

At night objects looked different. He was the only one to know them like this, almost immaterial, with almost no consistency or volume, devoid of shadow and relief. There was no one else in the entire world of Zod to know, like Horan, this face of things in the night. And it was, yes, really, a great and beautiful gift.

He had not moved. He was lying there on the bunk, hands looped behind his neck. He had not closed the door of his cell and his wide-open eyes stared at the ventilation grill above.

Either way, whether he carried out his plan to escape or waited for tomorrow and death, it was his last night in the place. But he had decided. He knew that he would not wait for death. Only, he could not leave just like that, all of sudden, at the risk of waking up the whole class. He had to have a little patience.

Maybe it would have been preferable for Horan to focus his mind on something, some specific subject—his plan to escape, for example. But he let his mind roam free, and that is how he thought of 23. He saw his face again, thin and shattered, his red hair. He saw his profile and his hands gripping the rail while the Teacher's voice echoed through the loudspeakers.

Why think of 23? It was certainly not a good thing. But it was too late to stop and move on to something else. He did not really know 23. In Zod, no one really knew anybody—what's the use? 23 was simply the child who occupied the cell next to his. He had been placed at the same time as him in the Birth Machine and just like with Horan the Machine had not completely succeeded in its pre-modeling. 23 had red hair. A sentence of pariah pronounced on his eighth birthday. Nothing more.

Nothing?

23 was scared—he was scared and Horan, with his thoughts moving to a faster rhythm, almost managed to convince himself that he was the cause of this fear, that he was at the heart of this tragedy that fell upon 23 to-day. Hadn't he shared his doubts and his unthinkable hopes? One sentence, one word was enough. And 23 was maybe congenitally, psychologically predisposed to revolt. Horan himself had pronounced the word, the sentence… Hadn't he sparked the process?

He tossed and turned nervously on his bunk, irritated. No, he should never have thought about 23.

Not to think… Not to think… But rather think, for example, about what he was going to bring with him on his flight. And then, what good would it do to think about it? Everything was ready. Everything was already in his student's bag. There were dried vegetables that he had managed to steal from the horticulture class, in that huge round room where fruits and vegetables grew at fantastic speed in their glass tubes.

…But 23 was scared.

After a long, long time, he had to admit, very quickly, that maybe he, too, was a little scared. There on the brink of escape. All alone…

He got off his bunk, heart pounding, hung his bag full of treasures from his belt and took one last look around his cell drowned in darkness. Then he left, in pitch-black silence. Overhead, above the ventilation grill, the little noise could be heard again. If I still hear it, Horan had told himself, it'll be a signal. He heard it. Maybe it really was a signal.

23 was sitting on his bunk, hugging his knees, his head buried in his arms. Horan saw the child's shoulders shaking with jerky, dried out spasms. When he came into the room, 23 bolted up, lifting his tear-stained, frightened face. He fell back against the wall and muttered, "Who's… What is it?"

"Shh," Horan whispered. "It's Horan. Don't be scared."

"Horan?"

"47," Horan said. "Don't be scared." He sat down on the bunk and put his hand on 23's arm, which shuddered at the contact.

After a couple of seconds 23 seemed less scared, "What do you want, Ho… Horan?"

"I came to get you," Horan said. "If you want, we can leave."

"Leave?" 23's tortured face no longer showed surprise or fear, but a kind of totally bitter, totally sour disappointment. It was better than fear.

"Listen," Horan spoke in one breath. "If we wait here, they'll come and get us tomorrow morning to take us to the Death Chamber. I don't want that."

"But no one's ever tried to escape the sentence!" 23 objected feebly, shaking his head in desperation. "They'll catch us and they'll…"

"No one. Maybe that's true," Horan cut in, "but I will. Even if they catch us, even if they bring us back to the Death Chamber, it won't change a thing. If we have to die anyway… Me, I want to try to escape them."

23 nodded two or three times, sniffled again, and dried his nose on the back of his hand. The black veil over his watery eyes slowly lifted. "How do you want to do it?" he asked. "Where do you want to go? The Subjects will denounce us—it's their duty. They won't want to hide us."

"I don't want to hide with the Subjects," Horan said. "I want to leave Zod."

The most absolute bewilderment was slapped onto 23's face again and the hope that was rising in him once again faded away. But before he could utter a sound, a single word, Horan continued, "Listen, I've never told this to anyone. I see at night. In the dark, right now, in the deepest, darkest black, I see. I don't know why, that's how it is. We can leave right away and get away easily—I see. I'm the only one who can see and even if they notice we're gone tonight, we'll still have a big head start."

23's round eyes became even rounder, then they squinted, trying to see, to make out Horan in the dark. "For real?" he finally shouted, almost smiling.

"Shh! Yes, for real, I swear to you. You're sitting there… your hands are here… Your nose, here…"

"How do you want to leave Zod?" 23 pressed him.

And Horan felt himself becoming warm, pleasantly warm, at the simple sight of 23's smile in the darkness of his cold cell. He said, "We're going to get away through the sky. We're going to leave Zod and escape into the sky."

"You're crazy," 23 said. (But as amazing as it sounded, he was already almost ready to accept the madness). "Who can walk on the sky? Up above there's the land of monsters and evil. Up above are the souls of the dead who didn't know how to make the most of their lives. The time hasn't come yet for men to inhabit the sky."

"That's what they teach us, yes," Horan admitted, "but..." He paused. "I don't think it's true." He decided to ignore 23's astonishment and continued, "Zod is buried in the sky of earth and rocks. Above the sky, maybe there's something other than what they tell us. Maybe there's something other than these monster people they talk about. Maybe it's not true that the souls of the dead... I want to leave Zod and walk on the sky, alive. Listen, there's got to be something else and the air we breathe is pumped in from above the sky. The land up there can't kill us."

"How... How can we get there... above the sky?" 23 stammered. He was not saying it was crazy or unthinkable anymore.

"In the middle of Zod," Horan said, "there's the Machine that inhales and exhales the air from above the sky. I know where it is. We visited it one day, remember?"

"I know, but I didn't know..."

"Me, I know. I remember. I'll be able to find it again. I see in the dark... The Machine breathes in the air and pipes it all over Zod, into all the rooms. We just have to slip into a ventilation duct and follow it all the way up above the sky."

23 was pale. But it must have been exciting. He said, "How can you be sure that we can do it?"

"I'm not sure. I believe I can do it. Others did it, or are doing it."

"Others?"

"A few nights ago," Horan said, "I heard a noise, up above. In that duct that must run over the classroom, over the grill. A sound. A sound of life. Someone is already in one of those ducts. I'm sure of it. It's like the sound of little footsteps."

"Someone?"

"Maybe one of those "monsters" who live above the sky and who fell into an air vent, I don't know. Maybe... no, I don't know. I only know that it's proof for me that someone can move inside the ducts. That's enough."

23 did not say anything. He was still hesitating, by reflex. Then all of a sudden, "I'll follow you, Horan."

And Horan let out a little cry of joy. "Well," he said, "find yourself a name. I don't want to call you by a number."

"Of course... My name is... My name's Lem."

"Okay, Lem."

He helped Lem get up and off the bunk. He took him by the hand and led him to the door. On the threshold, Lem stopped and in a strange, vibrant voice said, "Why are you doing this, Horan? Why are you doing this for *me*?"

"I don't know," Horan said. "Come on."

In total silence, the two children went down the spiral corridor that led to the floor of the classroom. The one guiding the other, without a sound, in the pitch-black that was Horan's ally. Then they were at the bottom. Still dragging Lem along, Horan headed for the door and opened it. The doors are never locked in Zod. Why would they be and who would want to shut themselves in one of these tube-rooms? Who and why?

All of Zod was shut in under the hard sky.

CHAPTER III

Somewhere in the earthy, mineral universe, the universe of rocks, sand and gnarled roots, somewhere, Zod is there and Zod is watching.

The grueling, lost world, the world of Zod the Survivor. The remains of a very great population of men. What the gods spared. And they hang on, they struggle, they fight endlessly for that coming day, that day like a pale star in the invisible future when time will finally change. That day which will explode over the reign of man.

Zod is waiting.

Zod is waiting for the chance, the moment of *its* chance.

There was nothing stranger than the structure of Zod. In fact, no one knew the exact shape of the whole complex. Some people simply knew that at the heart of it was a huge, round room, like a knot, like a void, and that this room was the domain of the machines that translated time. In fact, the Machine is maybe not exactly in the center and there are other rooms adjoining: rooms of the Birth Machines, lab-rooms for certain crops, the areas of the First Master and the other Senior Teachers, etc.

It forms a knot, the heart of Zod. And out of this throbbing heart come dozens, hundreds of tubular corridors. They lead everywhere, in every direction. They go up and down, radiate straight out or at an angle. They form a huge network linking all the rooms and cells that house the life of Zod. These rooms, these cavities, all cylindrical and vertical, are like a fantastic organ console with scattered, fragmented, sporadic tubes. Like a brilliant explosion forever frozen, inert.

In Zod they no longer remember who constructed the world, who erected this demented universe crushed under the rock of the heavens. They no longer remember why. They know that the world is 22 or 24,000 years old, maybe more. They know that those who built Zod have been dead for 24,000 years. Maybe more. That's all.

But there are some who remember, who believe they know. Or who really do know. They are not part of the population of Subjects who live and die at regular intervals in a cycle of around 30 years. Those who know the secrets of the gods are infinitely fewer, in Zod the Survivor.

His name was Agaran. They also called him the "First Master" and he ruled Zod.

He was 8,304 years old.

Sometimes his subjects called him "God".

In the break room of his armored den Agaran was not sleeping. He rarely slept. And when he did… well, it could hardly be called sleep.

This time of night was no different from the hundreds of thousands of other times of night. Agaran was alone, leaning over an old calculation game. Sometimes he raised his head to let his strange eyes wander over the walls of the room covered with abstract, decorative panels in superb colors. The room was lit soberly, cleverly bright. A lamp casting a soft beam on the game table and a few globes artistically placed so as to bring out the reliefs of wood and metal on the decorated panels.

It was never day or night in the space where Agaran lived, but instead this permanent (for almost 8,500 years) half-light, soft and friendly.

Agaran was tall, maybe taller than most of the men in Zod. His face was long, symmetrical, without a wrinkle, without a crease in the skin. This face alone, framed in smooth, black hair, made one want to call him God. He wore a long, light-colored tunic, with no ornamentation, no embroidery. Hands and feet bare. The hands and feet of old men are usually twisted, chapped and shot through with knobby veins. This was not the case with Agaran, at 8,304 years old.

At one point Agaran looked up from his game and stared at one of the decorative panels. For a long time. Too long for his mind to be simply sorting out some mathematical enigma. The silence was like a limp, living, tense presence. No, Agaran was not thinking of the game.

He was thinking of Zod, his universe, his world saved from the great disaster. He told himself that the time was still far-off, damn far, if you believe the memories of the gods, before he could finally enjoy the life of the Golden Age. Damn far.

The people of Zod had held on for 24,000 years, unfailingly. And life had been hard, the law brutal and implacable. And the natural selection, in the beginning, had wrought havoc, real massacres. But they had held on. They were still holding on, still blind, still clinging to hope. It was he, Agaran, who had been able to make a kind of religion out of hope. It was necessary to keep them blind: it was the primary condition.

Since the beginning of time—the New Beginning— the chain had unwound its generational links endlessly, endlessly. The long chain. And only the last link will see the light and find life again. Thus it was; that's how it was. There was no question of it being otherwise. The last link would have a chance of knowing the truth.

It was necessary to invent legends and religions to protect the chances of this destined last link. It was necessary to lie and hide the secrets. To reveal them to the mass of Subjects would inevitably be throwing Zod's future on the ground and trampling it.

The chain had held. Would it hold until the end?

Without really knowing why, doubt was entering Agaran's mind. An ugly impression. More and more frequently, for example, the student subjects were producing an ever-increasing number of wastes. They wanted to know, *to know* more, always. They did not hide their laughter when they taught them the old religions, when they mapped out their program for life. When told of the future age of the chosen ones, they lost patience and wanted it immediately, shamelessly, and they bared their sharp teeth. They wanted everything, right away. They no longer wanted to sacrifice themselves; they no longer believed in death. Something was changing.

Should they revise the religions? Should they destroy them?

Something had to be done. For the moment, the change was not yet so dramatic or very important, but it was threatening to become so quickly. You have to seal the crack in a dam when it is still just a crack. The chain had to last 2,000 more years. It could not break before then. And for some time Agaran had the feeling that it might very well break beforehand.

He leaned back in his suction-shaped chair and his eyes fell upon another panel. The hint of a smile briefly crossed his pale lips. The panel was ancient, as old as Zod, certainly, as old as the world. Agaran often thought of the men who had painted and constructed these panels; the men of higher learning who wanted to preserve their knowledge, to keep it for the survivors of the disaster. They knew how to translate these secrets perfectly into magnificent panels. Maybe the first inhabitants of Zod could still understand and read the secrets. Maybe. But the years had passed, the necessary years, and the hard, natural selection had operated, mutation after mutation. And men had gone a different way. And they were unable to decipher the panels. They only saw in them more or less artistic expressions. New religions had already arisen to fight man's fear and to simplify his purpose in life.

Agaran smiled again.

One day, he was born. He came out of the Birth Machine. He, too, in fact, had been a curious student, eager for immediate results. He had been one of those whom they kill today. He knew how to get by and hide his doubts and act at the right moment.

He was twelve years old when they crowned him First Master of Zod. And he had already spent half his life. So, he feverishly studied the secrets, the legends... And the Machine to count time.

He learned, through the legends, that men, before, when they were still living above Zod, lived a hundred years or more. He learned some of their terrible secrets. He learned about the cycle of life, the cycle of men. He believed he understood. Nowadays, sometimes, he had doubts again.

Agaran had deciphered the panels. They were not works of sterile art. They were graphics, the secrets of psychic transplants. The men before the disaster knew these things.

And Agaran, who learned the secrets—who was sure of it—could not let them fade away after his death without using them. He had a thirst for life, a thirst for that marvelous life that the men of old had known, that those of Zod would know again, at the end of the chain. He knew the secrets and wanted to use them... and he had the body of a good old, 25-year old man.

So, with the help of a couple of Senior Teachers, Agaran, who knew the secrets, built the body. The body of a perfect man. A marvelous vehicle. He had worked in the utmost excitement and anguish, following faithfully what the pictures told. At last the body was finished, then the transfer machine, and then the two Senior Teachers operated it.

The pictures spoke true. For 8,304 years, Agaran's mind had lived in the synthetic body of a perfect robot. The mind of Agaran the god led Zod and imposed his law, conveyed by a body that had no fear of death or hunger or pain or anything. Or joy or pleasure.

The mind of Agaran the man patiently kept track of the time that passed, waiting to be reborn into the real life of the Golden Age.

He was the only one who knew the secrets inscribed on the panels because he had to, because he had to remain the only one to know the secrets, at that time. Since then, the psychic transfer machine had been reused two or three times. But even the few robotized Senior Teachers who came after did not know all the secrets.

He was sitting and looking at the panels. In his mind he was remodeling the religious and social structures of Zod. He could not fight against this strange worry he had felt for sometime now. Zod had to hold on for 2,000 more years. And then Zod would die. And for the last link in the chain of survivors, the gates of paradise would open.

The walk down the dark corridors of Zod had already lasted long hours, very long hours. Time meant nothing to Horan. It was something completely hazy. He knew that he had to reach the heart of the Machine and its rapid breathing. The Machine was in the heart of Zod and the classrooms on the periphery.

He walked and did not talk. Sometimes he just whispered a word, a breath, to guide Lem or point out an obstacle. They had gone through hundreds of corridors, all pervaded by the same thick, unchanging darkness, the same silence. They had crossed dozens of empty rooms, deserted. They carefully avoided the noisy areas and the rooms where even the night—the time of night—did not keep some teams from their busy work. A ray of light, however weak, was enough to make them turn around fast.

Lem had followed without a problem, for hours. Now his hand was stiff and wet in Horan's. Stiffer and stiffer, wetter and wetter.

"Wait," Horan whispered. He released his numb, clenched fingers and slid open the round door at the end of the corridor. "Go on," he said. "There's a kind of step."

Lem felt his way up. Horan took his hand again to guide him forward. Then he closed the door behind them. For a few seconds he looked around, trying to figure out where they were.

"Where are we?" Lem whispered, his voice cracking strangely.

"A corridor," Horan told him in the same tone. "It looks like it goes around in circles. The walls in front of us have doors in them."

"Do you know where we are?"

A second of hesitation, barely. "Of course I know."

To admit the truth would have driven Lem crazy on the spot. For sure. It would have irreversibly ruined their chances. For maybe half an hour Horan had been lost. He had to avoid too many rooms because of some light peeking through; he had to make too many detours. Lost, yes, in the infernal tangle of blind corridors. Lost in the heart of Zod. And Lem's hand was so wet in his!

"Come on, let's go."

To cross the wide corridor and take the first door, open it. He did it.

"Oh," Lem uttered.

Both of them had the same instinctive recoil and Horan was already shutting the door, ready to run into the welcoming shadows, but... but he did not shut the door entirely. In the wild beating of his heart, rattling his chest, his instinct, or something else (simple and lively curiosity) was stronger than fear or caution. He did not close the metal door. Instead, he opened it enough to slip into the room. And it was Lem who shut the metal and plastic panel behind them.

For a time, they were unable to say a word or even look at each other. They could do nothing but let their eyes soak in this fantastic place they had chanced upon.

Apparently a sphere. They had entered the center of a sphere. It was made of transparent but apparently very hard material, behind which they could barely make out, very high up, the crushed, rocky layers of the sky of Zod. Everywhere in the thickness of the layer of weird matter that formed the sphere's covering, everywhere were thousands of little twinkling lights. Not much bigger than needle points, but sowed by the thousands. From these gold and silver tears came the soft light that bathed the place.

The floor they were standing on seemed to cut the sphere into two equal halves. It, too, was transparent and at a steep angle compared to the normal "equator" of the room. But this was not the most astonishing thing.

In the center of the circle of floor, another sphere looked stuck into the mass, also transparent and giving off a red light. This ball was the size of a big melon. On the same level, meaning also stuck in the sloping floor, not far from the central ball, was a second ball. Much smaller—a walnut—and giving off a bluish light.

Except for the central ball, the floor was evenly divided, split up, criss-crossed with lines. Each division was marked with incomprehensible signs.

The sphere continued under the floor, just like the "ceiling", like it was dotted with sparkles.

The room was totally silent.

After a long moment, Horan and Lem looked at each other. They were pale and speechless. In the murky light, Lem's face looked like a sick ghost. "We have to leave," Lem whispered, trembling.

And Horan was obviously of the same opinion. Nothing is easier to communicate than fear. He said, "The room with the Machine to count time."

Lem's arms and legs trembled twice as hard. He gulped several times before saying, "Quick! Let's get out of here…" (Then, more softly, surprised and scared by the sound of his voice in the ambient silence), "We came into the Machine to count time! It's… it's a gross sacrilege and we…"

"Be quiet!" Horan ordered curtly. No, really, he should never have burdened himself with this coward. Never!

The room with the Machine to count time... So, now they were not lost anymore: he knew where to find the first step of their escape. "Let's go," he urged.

He took one last look around the room, just before leaving. It was really very beautiful, very impressive, in this soft light. And especially in this fantastic, enormous silence.

Before closing the door behind him, a new detail in the strangeness of the room's structure caught Horan's attention. The floor, the sloping, transparent floor of the room, the floor was turning. A very slow, very regular rotation around an axis represented by the red ball in the center. The floor was turning and with it the little blue walnut around the melon.

He shuddered. First because he did not understand this fantastic machine; and also from what Lem said, speaking about sacrilege... he could rebel against their nonsense—since the awakening of his consciousness he had been guided, directed onto the narrow paths of fear. With the word "must" they inevitably magnetized the life of the Subjects of Zod... and it is always hard to fight against a real magnet.

He shuddered again when he saw how lucky they were to have opened this door just when the edge of the floor was at the level of the doorway. From the unusual slant of the floor and following the movement of rotation, they could just as easily have fallen to the bottom of the sphere and very likely been killed or maybe just tumbled onto the floor lower down, not so hard, but still fallen and remained prisoners of the sphere, since the door would be out of reach.

Lem's whining voice in the black corridor brought him back to the present. "Where do we go now?"

He grabbed the hand dangling at the redhead's side. "Follow me... and stop shaking." And he shot off down the round corridor.

Something cold and heavy fell slowly inside Horan. He stopped staring at the Machine, an incredible knot of huge tubes, a metal octopus throwing out its tentacles in every direction, everything drowning in the dull din of inhalations and exhalations, and he looked at the high, circular ramp. He saw right away that Lem was not joking. And Lem repeated, "I don't want to leave with you, Horan." His face was gray in the deceptive half-light. He knelt there doing nothing but shaking his head, back and forth, back and forth. His eyes were like still, troubled water.

Because he did not know what to say, Horan went back to looking at the room and the huge Machine sitting in the middle of it. From his vantage point, at one end of the semi-circular ramp, he could see the Worker-Subjects moving slowly around the controls and inspection units of the Machine. A dozen: pale, like ghosts in their long, white uniforms, most of them already at least 20 years old—almost old men. They stood calmly before the dials or else came and went, busy at different tasks, in the dim light that bathed the place. The sound of their footsteps on the metal floor, like their conversation, was muffled by the panting Machine.

"Why?" Horan finally asked without looking at Lem.

"It's... it's too much sacrilege," he let slip out. "And we'll never make it... I won't be able to make it."

Horan felt anger well up in him. In a certain way, he was happy about Lem's decision—to drag his dead weight all the way above the sky could only complicate the escape. In another way... he would have liked his escape plan to create a little more enthusiasm.

"It won't be hard," he said, for Lem, for himself. "Those big ducts there, above the Machine—the red tubes rising at an angle into the ceiling—they're the vents that bring the air in. That's the way that leads above the sky. We just have to get inside and climb."

"Climb how?"

Climb how? Horan had not thought of that. Not once. The tubes were probably very smooth inside. And then there would be the tremendous force of the air being sucked in, the force that would do its best to drag them back down into the huge fan blades of the Machine.

"There's got to be a way," Horan growled.

And he had not even finished speaking before he knew the way: he was sure of it, in a sudden, vivid illumination.

"Look! At the base of the tubes, just above the Machine, there are hatches, those little doors. That's where the men get in to clean the ducts, once a week. That's what they told us when we came with the class to study the machine. The Worker-Subjects get into the tubes, so there's a way."

Lem nodded. "We'll never get to the doors. The Workers will stop us first."

"And the ramp? This ramp crosses the room. It goes right over the Machine. It's not too high. We just have to drop down and..."

"I don't want to go," Lem said. "I'm going to stay... I'm scared, I can't, and... I'll only hold you back."

Horan lowered his eyes. "What are you going to do?"

For the first time in a long time, Lem smiled and slapped his hand on Horan's shoulder. He said, "I'm staying here... I'll ask the Workers if they'll hide me. It'll be fine. You, Horan, are the first. Good luck."

And Horan had no time to say anything, not even one word. Before he realized it, Lem had jumped up and was running down the ramp toward the ladder that led to the floor of the room. He was screaming and yelling his head off. He was scurrying down the ladder when the first Worker heard him and saw him. Then, most of them left their posts and rushed at him, screaming and yelling things that the pounding Machine drowned out.

With his eyes full of tears and his heart beating like crazy, Horan understood. He murmured the brand new name of Lem. It made him warm, but it also made him bitter because he had inwardly accused Lem of cowardice.

To wait any longer would be making Lem's sacrifice worthless, so Horan jumped up on his trembling legs and ran hunched over down the winding ramp. But long before reaching the ladder, he turned onto the bridge that crossed the room diagonally. His heart beating like crazy...

Down below, 10 or 15 Worker-Subjects were surrounding Lem at the bottom of the ladder.

Down below, there was the Machine, the huge, rumbling machine and its thick, hairy mass of red tubes. Slide down, hang on and then...

He landed, easily, in a relatively narrow space on the metal platform between two tubes. One last glance at the room… Lem was tiny, waving his arms amidst the men… *You're the first, Horan…*

He slid over one of the tubes and found the door. A handle to spin open. To spin quickly… quickly… He spun it all the way open and pulled with all his might. Nothing budged. And what if the tremendous suction force on the inside was blocking the door… When the Workers went into the ducts, they turned them off.

Finally the door unstuck and cracked opened. Horan leaned against the tube to open it more, still more… to open it until he could slip in.

A demonic roar exploded. A vortex of ice-cold air swept Horan up like a wisp of straw and the door slammed shut behind him.

The whole world turned to cold, noise, a dizzying fall, and fear. Colossal fear, extraordinary, while he fell, fell, smashed against the wall of the duct without even realizing it, sucked in irreversibly by the grumbling belly of the Machine. Sucked straight toward the fan blades.

CHAPTER IV

The abyss had a hole in it directly above, way high up, endless, among the noisy, crazy things. Living things that pulsed, howled, swelled and deflated spasmodically. And Horan was at the bottom of the black pit.

No light, nothing. He who could see in the dark, the friend of blackness and night, saw nothing. All he knew was that he was at the bottom of the pit, unmoving, unable to move, offering up body and soul to the icy pain that kept hacking away at him.

A clamp of fire squeezed his temples, drilled into his belly and chest. Thousands of razor-sharp blades butchered his breathing. And the noise! That infernal noise, all those mournful howls welling up, rolling around and pouring down on his wretched pain in sporadic waves.

Is this what death is like? Death and the land of monsters above the sky where the souls of those who could not become honest Subjects of Zod wandered endlessly, aimlessly, until the fulfillment of things? Is it like this?

He was scared. Really scared and in his fright he became aware of his body, of his vital force being abused by the atrocious suffering. No! This was not death. He still had a body, a mortal coil that could still feel the painful waves and was thinking this thought right now. But consciousness was another matter. There had been something... Something had happened...

Slowly, up above, the dull, deformed ceiling of the pit opened a little, a crack. A faint tear, almost nothing. A hint. A hope.

No, this was not death. It was…

All of a sudden, Horan got hold of himself. His surroundings finally stabilized, like they were instantly plastered to all the fibers of his being by a tremendous force. The howling became even more violent, more high-pitched, piercing, completely crazy and demonic… but it was only howling, sound waves, and not those living, yawing things of an instant before.

He opened his eyes and at first saw only a kind of hazy, substanceless whirlwind. Then he recognized the solid, cylindrical contours of the whirlwind. An explosion of light flashed across his mind. He wanted to move his arms and legs and stand up. He had the distinct impression that he had no arms or legs. There was another wave of fear, familiar now. Too familiar. Like a mysterious, invisible enemy bearing down with all its weight to cram into him.

He screamed, screamed again, without hearing himself. His eyes were freezing and he realized that his tears turned to ice as soon as they formed.

Then his entire being was seized by sheer panic. And the panic gave him the necessary strength. He could move his limbs and get on his hands and knees. He had to fight with all his might to remain in this position and not be dragged away by the incessant force of the howling whirlwind.

He dried his eyes and banged his frozen face against the floor. His nerves barely registered any pain.

Move… Move. Don't stay there, motionless, like a thing already dead. Don't give in to the crazy whirlwind… Do something!

Like an animal, he started ferreting around the floor. Just to move. The hardest thing was still to keep his eyes open, not to let this weird sleep overcome his senses. Not to give up… He found strange things on the floor: rocks and twigs. And then underneath… the thin, metal mesh of a grill.

He remembered everything. He had opened the hatch, slipped into the air vent, then… The fall had certainly not been long, but it had been hard. He had been sucked in and chucked against this grill. A new flash of inspiration crossed his mind, almost heating it up: the grill! By all means, this grill was protecting the fan blades against foreign matter! And these rocks strewn over it, and these twigs and branches…

These branches!

So, did the monsters really exist above the sky? In that region of space from where the people of Zod got their breathable air, there really were intelligent beings who cultivated plants and knew how to breed and grow trees. Come on, it was not the land of death, up above! A child could certainly survive there.

He stood up on his wobbly legs and fell back against the wall, which was no colder than the whirlwind of air that lashed his head, face, hands and shoulders. It was just hard and practically vertical.

He walked around, leaning against it as best he could, stumbling over the debris that covered the grill. A full circle. A full circle and his hands slid over the smooth surface without feeling the smallest bump. Nothing! Nothing except hard metal, glassy, polished over the centuries by the friction of air. So, he was going to die. It was absolutely impossible to attack the wall of the tube. No footholds or anything.

A little later, he opened his eyes again, purely by reflex. He noticed that he had slid back down upon the grill among the debris of vegetation and minerals that covered it. He was there being battered by the monstrous wind, with the howling belly of the Machine a few feet below. But he opened his eyes and he saw the notch, that line in the metal right in front of his face.

Falteringly, he lifted his numb fingers, touching and rubbing the narrow groove. Saliva and new tears froze on his face. He screamed again, but this time in joy.

It was really a bar, a kind of bar, locked in the wall. Looking up he saw a second one, then another and another. A ladder. There was a ladder here that climbed all the way up the duct! There had to be a ladder, for the Workers who had to clean the tubes sometimes. And during the normal periods of operation, the rungs of this ladder were pushed back into the wall so that the debris being sucked in from the space above the sky would not get stuck on them. Of course!

He could not feel his fingertips. His legs weighed a ton. With all his soul, he scratched the metal, chipping his nails in the thin groove. He tried to pull and push, he felt all around, hit and scraped... And suddenly, just as a new and terrible wave of desperation was welling up, the bar appeared, came slowly out of its housing in the metal. Not only *the* bar but all of them. The ladder sprang out of the wall.

Horan did not waste time wondering how he had miraculously tripped the mechanism, he put his foot on one rung, grabbed the other and with all his strength started pulling himself up. Blindly, all his weak muscles in knots, feverishly, he climbed. His body pressed against the metal outcrops, his hands like grappling hooks thrown up and clamping onto the rungs with precision, Horan climbed. Thus he passed over the hatch through which he had fallen and he kept climbing.

The pipe rose up at an angle now and that was when something strange happened: gradually, the howling grew softer and the air blew easier over the arched back of the fleeing child. At first he thought that it was only an illusion and he continued scaling the ladder. Then the feeling grew stronger until it was no longer a feeling but a real fact: down below, the intake machines had stopped working.

Did pulling out the ladder automatically cause this halt?

There was no more whirlwind, no more raging howls. Barely even a light breeze and the panting of the gigantic intake machines was out of breath.

Horan climbed.

With the heat and the blood that was freely circulating in his limbs, the pain came back. What did pain matter? He clambered up the rungs of this incredible ladder, fast, as fast as possible.

Sweat came. It made his hair sticky and after all the violent gusts of air plastered it over his head. It ran salty into his eyes.

He climbed and his fingers became iron, his limbs automatically knotted up under the effort. He had pulled out the ladder and indirectly turned off the blowers. How long would it take them to notice it in the control room? And get after him?

They did not notice it right away.

Horan felt like hours and hours had gone by. Crazy hours in the darkness and silence troubled only by the steady thud of his footsteps on the iron rungs. He had not stopped going up. Not for a minute, not for a single, paltry second. He had become an automaton, his movements dictated by some secret spring unwinding deep down inside him.

The angle of the tube had gradually diminished. He could walk now without the handholds. But Horan did not leave the ladder; by pure automatism he kept advancing, bent double, completely stiff, his lower back strained to the breaking point.

At one point the pipe turned abruptly to the left. Horan thought that this bend was not the work of men, but caused by some external phenomenon, most definitely. As if outside, the celestial magma had twisted the cylinder, dragging it along in a landslide. The walls were dented, even flattened over hundreds of yards. Farther down the body of the cylinder had been replaced with another, much newer portion. The sky of Zod had thunderous fury.

Horan was still moving forward...

Now he noticed that the pipe had changed again. It was old, very old. In very bad shape, dented like crazy and even... and even cracked open in places. Cracked open! The metal had burst, opening whiskered wounds onto the bowels of rock, earth and seeping water—where the rocks probably came from that he had found on the grill at the bottom.

All of a sudden he came across a second grill, also smeared with branches. But the space between the bars was wide enough for Horan to get through without taking the whole thing apart. He went through, continued his delirious progression in the crumbling tube, level flat now, chock full of holes. He kept on until a sudden narrowing forced him down on his belly. He crawled, his body twisted and bruised by the bars sticking out, praying to some unknown god for the bottleneck not to close off completely.

He got through. For the first time since the start of the climb, he let himself collapse, worn out, exhausted mentally and physically. Tears came freely and he did nothing to hold them back. It felt good, to cry.

That was when he heard the buzzing, far, far in the distance. Somewhere, through some crack in the metal duct, a pebble was falling and making this clear sound. The buzzing got louder, changed into a kind of unpleasant whistling. Under Horan's stretched out body, the ground moved. And he was terrified to realize that the machine had started working again, that the rungs were back in their housing... and that one of them had snagged the bottom of his coat and the end of his right sleeve. He realized that he was stuck there like a picture stuck to a wall.

He looked up and saw the monster.

It was there, two arm's lengths away, sitting curiously in the middle of the tube, and it was watching him. A ghastly monster, covered in spiky hair, and it did nothing but stare at Horan with its two little, yellow eyes, like two crevasses above the frightful, gaping jaw.

During the first hours of this new period of day, the light of the vibraphone on Agaran's metal desk flickered wildly. Agaran left his game tablet and pressed the button.

"Master!" the guard's voice boomed. "Senior Teacher Telzoat is here and wants to see you."

"Okay," Agaran said. And he took his place behind his desk.

A few seconds later Telzoat entered, pushing in front of him a pale, trembling child with tear-stained cheeks and red hair standing on end.

Agaran's face was marble as he stared long and hard at the child, whose chin was still shaking with sobs. Agaran did not like tears. He had made sure that the decadent sentiments at their source were banished from the inhabitants of Zod. He did not like to see failure.

He also stared at Telzoat for a long time without saying a word. Telzoat, huge in his flamboyant robe, his face like stone and impassive, said, "Student-Subject 23, from special class 45. At the end of the teaching cycle he had negative results and was to be led to the Death Chamber, as the law of Zod demands."

"Well?"

"He fled his classroom, broke into the room with the ventilation machines and stopped one of the blowers. The Worker-Subjects caught him and delivered him to supervisor 9876, who gave him to us. I bring him to you, Master."

"Is that all?"

"That's all."

"You can go."

Telzoat plunged forward in a little bow, turned around and left. And Lem was standing in the middle of that weird room, the walls covered with strange pictures, in front of the Master of Zod. He had not known that it was possible to see the Master in flesh and blood, the God whom they said was indestructible and who ruled over Zod.

He was there; he was looking at him. He did not even think of looking away. He was just a little ashamed of his tears and of that act he put on between Telzoat's legs a few minutes earlier.

Fear was gone. This was all too new for him, for a while... He remembered one thing, however: the strange attitude of the Worker-Subjects who listened to his story and his pleas, who had kept him with them for most of the night, without denouncing him. They had even let him wander around. That is how Lem had been able to turn off the pipe where Horan was. He had been able to close the pipe's hatch. The Workers did not seem to have noticed anything... and Lem wanted very much to make Horan's job easier.

Much later, just before the Guard arrived, someone had yelled out and pointed at the light board. Yes, they had seen it too late. They started it up again, but at low speed, it seemed. They had lied to the Guard, saying that Lem was alone and the system had stopped for only a few seconds. Could they have known?

"Why did you do that?" Agaran said suddenly.

The little redhead lowered his eyes but did not answer.

Agaran's eyes contracted slowly. Here was the danger... the approaching danger. An eight-year old Zodian child, sentenced to death by the law. The law created by Agaran. He had never seen the face of an eight-year old child, on the verge of adulthood, sentenced to death. Never. He had always known how to safeguard himself.

The danger, yes. They no longer accepted. They were escaping. They were trying to get around the law.

Keeping his eyes on the child, he got on the vibra-phone and in touch with the Center of Class Supervision. He demanded curtly, "Class 45. Pupils."

The child looked at him again. They were waiting together, without a sound, without a move. Then the answer came and Agaran, pale and cold, turned it off.

"Where's the other?" he asked. "Where's 47, your partner?"

The child's gaze was truly awful to suffer. No anger, no hate, no. Not even fear. Something else. The child said, "We didn't want to die."

"That's the law of Zod!" Agaran shouted, straight-away regretting having lost his temper in front of this kid. "That's the law and no one has ever dreamed of evading it."

"It's not a good law," the child said. "We didn't want to die, without knowing."

Agaran felt his body shiver, his plastic carcass full of electronic networks that so faithfully copied the life of human matter. He shuddered. The words had been pronounced; they clearly showed the face of the danger.

"Where is he?" he asked, quietly again. "Why did you stop that…" He broke off and his eyes turned an indefinable color. Then he spit out, "We have ways you never dreamed of, 23, to make your body suffer and make the suffering grow. Ways to keep death at bay when it's wanted most, when it's pleaded for with everything a being has. It's up to you to die quickly or to prolong your death over several days. He fled through a ventilation duct, didn't he? And you turned off the air to help him?"

Lem gritted his teeth to keep his stupid chin from trembling. He figured that the system had been off for more than four hours, at least. Horan should have been able to get a big head start. Maybe he was already above the sky… maybe he was saved, in that world he had chosen.

"Yes," Lem said. "He left… He didn't want to die either."

"Be quiet!"

"He's walking on the sky!" Lem yelled. "He'll be walking up above and you can't do anything about it!"

"Guard!" The guard, and then Telzoat entered, practically at the same time. "Give full power to the tube that this rebel stopped," Agaran shouted. "Quickly! There's another one inside it, another condemned kid trying to escape from Zod. Full power! To bring him back to the grill! He'll be sucked in like a feather! Then you'll open the tube and you'll take him out."

"And this one?" the guard asked.

Agaran turned his back nervously and said, "Take him away! Let him suffer the law, as is written!"

He did not see the child's eyes when they took him away, but the child's eyes were sparkling with a strange satisfaction.

A long time later, Agaran turned around again. Telzoat had not moved; he was waiting. Telzoat, first Senior Teacher, a thousand-year old mind in a fabricated carcass, him too.

"You went down there," Agaran said slowly.

Telzoat nodded.

"He wants to escape, the demon... Walk on the sky... If he succeeds, do you know what risk that will mean for Zod? For us?"

Again Telzoat nodded his head. After a while he asked, "Who do we send to look inside the pipe and get the prisoner? The cleaning robots are not programmed to pick up living bodies or fight with one, probably."

"You'll take care of it," Agaran said. "With some Subjects. We'll make sure they don't talk once the mission is accomplished."

Telzoat turned around.

"Telzoat!"

"Yes?"

"I think we can't take any chances in the next few thousand years we have left to live here. Not the slightest chance, to keep Zod from a second disaster."

"Maybe," Telzoat said. "But Zod belongs to you... and even if everything has to change, it'll be for the best for you. You'll know how to preserve life in our world until the Day of the Elect."

I admire your confidence, Telzoat, Agaran thought sincerely. But he did not say it.

CHAPTER V

So, the Teachers did not lie. They told the truth when they said that the land above the sky was peopled with monsters. The living proof of their words was there, in front of Horan's frightened eyes. Frozen, nailed to the ground, all he could do was suffer the sitting monster's gaze, without moving. His heart was beating like crazy—he felt it, heard it echoing in his hollow chest and against the metal pipe.

Around these two beings, watching each other, the whistling air got sucked in steadily stronger. However, it did not bother them, either of them. They were too far from the intake mouth. Much too far… and behind Horan, the abrupt narrowing of the metal passage was extra security. Only the sound was trying on the nerves and was bound to make the tension much more uncomfortable.

For a long time neither of them moved. Nothing happened, so that a hint of confidence, of self-confidence, grew again in Horan the fugitive. After all, this monster sitting there did not seem especially hostile, unless he had been caught off guard and was now waiting for the right time to pounce.

Horan moved, barely at first, and then he tried to get up on one elbow; he tried to free himself slowly, to wriggle out of the coat caught in the retracted bars. The monster simply moved its head in the child's direction while its dark, wet nostrils flared. Horan was pretty certain that this living thing did not see in the dark. He plucked up courage and finally, by means of careful, flowing motions, managed to slip out of his coat. The current of air immediately plastered his thin, Silohn tunic to his scrawny chest. He got on his hands and knees and dared to crawl toward the monster, dared to scrutinize it more closely.

A body entirely covered in coarse hair, a supple and long body, sitting down right now and shivering in the air currents. Four limbs with weird joints, also hairy, ending not in hands but in baffling, clawed fingers that were practically glued together. Its head was pointy with two triangular ears standing straight up on top. An oddly elongated nose under which a big mouth, stocked with frightening teeth, was open. Then the eyes… little yellow eyes that glistened in the dark. It was not humanoid, must have walked on its four limbs, which looked nothing like hands or feet. Standing straight up, it could not have been taller than Horan.

"I don't mean you any harm," Horan said cautiously.

At the sound of his voice, the hairy being stood up on its limbs—all four limbs—and swiftly recoiled. With one bite of its terrible jaws, it could have snapped the child's neck. But it recoiled. It looked scared and disheveled from all the air and trembling.

Now Horan was not scared at all. He remembered the books he had read, the stories told by the Teachers that spoke of ancient times, of the golden times that were to come back some day. In these times, the races of men lived with other sub-races whose main purpose was to keep man company, as well as to serve him. They called them animal races. Did these races really exist? Wasn't it just a mythological invention of the Teacher? Was this monster… an example of an animal race? An animal?

Horan had no desire to control it. Another feeling arose in him, confused and still hazy. He simply wanted to reassure this trembling being, to talk to it and touch its fur, to associate this being with the new, magic words, "father, mother, love, tenderness." No, he was not scared at all.

"I don't want to hurt you," he said. "Do you understand?"

But the animal obviously did not understand. It could only back up, press against the wall of broken metal and earth.

It's true, Horan told himself. How could it understand the language of men after so much time… "I'll teach you," he said. "I'll teach you and we can talk. But for now, we have to get out of here. Do you know the w…"

He stopped talking, remembered that noise that he had listened to at night, above the classroom. The inhalation and ventilation pipes were joined here. No, the animal could not know the way. For days, certainly, he had been wandering around in the maze of ducts.

"Don't worry," Horan spoke softly. "We'll get out of here."

Anguish had just exploded again in his belly, like a ball of fire, but he felt like the first thing he had to do was comfort this bristling thing that was sniffing the night in terror. He moved his hand forward, slowly, gently. He was alone and naked in the midst of the wild beating of his heart. Plastered against the wall, trembling, the animal waited, its eyes crazy. A feeble growl rolled out of its mouth when the child put his hand on its neck. On the soft, silky fur of its neck, like Agyrt cloth. A meager growl. And the child's hand ran through the fur, came back, slid down. The animal's nose pulsed rapidly. For a moment it accepted the caresses without saying a word. Then it gradually stopped trembling and pulled itself away from the wall. The strange, hairy appendage that stuck out of its read end was swaying, and the animal brought its face up to Horan's, raking its tongue across his cheeks. Horan was just about to jump back, to escape the gust of warm breath, but... he did not do it. It was not bad, this lick of the tongue. Maybe it was a rite, an obscure rite, the animal's greeting.

And the animal was now huddled against him, a ball of hair and muscles, getting to know him, with a great deal of strong sniffing. The cold nose against his skin, the wavy softness of the fur and all the little cries like panting words.

The "thing" happened just then, while he was petting the animal snuggled up to his side. "It" happened and "it" was in Horan, filling him up completely. He did not know how to define or name what he felt; it was just fiendishly warm and all over and inside him. It was like a really great happiness and more, though not exactly that. It put curious tears in his eyes.

And Horan knew that he was going to succeed in his escape, that nothing and no one could stop him now. He felt like he was two, four, a dozen.

He straightened up. "Wait, Animal," he said shakily. "We're going to get out of here, you'll see."

Animal let out a quick, loud shriek that rang out clearly in the tube. A shriek of joy, for sure.

It was the start of day in Zod the forgotten. At the same second, in all the dormitory rooms, the infrasound alarms buzzed in the unconsciousness of the sleeping men and women. They got up for another new day, for another portion of life, for Zod to last and live another day and then another day after that, like it had always been.

In the huge dining-tubes, they ate quickly, conversing about unimportant things or talking about Zod. Again and again about Zod. Then they hastened to their workstations. Men and women, all pale, with their colorless eyes, but not sad or forsaken: they went as always to take their places in front of the machines that created the nutritive chemical substances and the machines that took care of them. Or again they got busy in the workshops designed to take care of the machines themselves, or again they scattered among the laboratories of artificial cultivation, watching over the plants growing under the huge glass bell jars covered with plastic tubing. This was their work. They had nothing else to learn, except respect for Zod and the religion of faith, for the time of inexpressible riches that they would not know personally.

Some men, in the reproduction cycle, headed for the pre-natal rooms for the monthly drain of their seeds of life. Some women, in the reproduction cycle, waited in other pre-natal rooms where they were injected with a precise dose of these seeds of life. In the fifth month they took the fetus out of the bellies, so as not to bother the women for too long, and the Birth Machine continued the pregnancy for them, for a few weeks, speeding it up considerably.

This was life in Zod and nothing changed in the first hours of light on this new day.

Agaran was sitting in front of one of the recorder-pads in his residence. A kind of impetus had driven him there, almost unconsciously.

Telzoat entered, stood in the doorway for a minute, and then took a few steps toward the Master. He stopped again.

"Well?" Agaran asked.

"We gave full power to the tube," Telzoat said. "Then we turned it off and opened it."

"And you didn't find him!"

"That's right," Telzoat said rather pathetically. "I don't know how he did it. He must have climbed up very fast and is now out of range."

Without saying a word, Agaran stared at the microphone built into his recoding pad. For a moment. Then he looked up and said, "It's imperative that we find him. We can't let him escape. Take some Soldier-Subjects with you, right away, and go after him. Bring him back. Dead or alive, it doesn't matter."

"And if he's… if he's left?"

"He can't leave! But if, by chance, he has, you'll leave, too, Telzoat. You have to do whatever it takes to keep this rebel from having contact with…"

He stopped and Telzoat saw fit to reassure him. "He wouldn't dare. He's a child who's scared and who ran away from death. He'll also be sacred of taking on the monsters. Because he believes in them…"

"No! He doesn't believe in anything anymore. His crazy behavior proves it. And if he doesn't meet anyone, we can find him easily, and then…"

Telzoat nodded. After a pause he asked, "And the commando team, what am I going to tell them? They'll think I'm crazy when I talk about going above the sky."

"Time is running out, Telzoat. Tell them how desperately lucky they are, for Zod. It's an extraordinary mission and they should be proud. Promise them whatever you want: after a hypnotic injection, they'll follow you. But hurry. You can communicate with me here by radio. Bring weapons and lightweight gear."

"Okay!" Telzoat answered and he dashed out of the room.

For a long moment Agaran sat still, leaning over his steel table. Finally, with a weary hand, he pressed a button. A green light turned on in the control board. Then, in an instant, numbers and signs flashed ass it. Agaran raised the microphone a few inches and in his deep, hoarse voice he spoke:

"My name is Agaran, current Master of Zod. We've calculated time from the data of the eternal machine of the Ancient Masters who peopled the planet. According to these calculations, this is the year 21,975. It is also the year 8,304 of my reign in the Fish cycle, as the ancients called it.

"Times are perhaps going to change in the world of Zod and that's why I, Agaran, am speaking today of what my plan was and of what Zod was in the history of the universe. I don't do this out of hopelessness or fear, but simply because there's a risk now. I'll talk about this risk later. I've never neglected a single risk in eight thousand years of reign. And I won't start now.

"Therefore, I'm speaking because the risk is here and even if it's minor, it exists and it could, in some future unknown to me, wipe out Zod completely. In the event that this might actually happen, I am speaking. This history is meant for those who will find it in the ruins of Zod. For, by then, Zod will be in ruins."

He paused for a second and then resumed straightaway, "I don't know everything. I myself was born only in the year assumed to be 13,671 of the history of Zod. Such numbers are assumed because no one knows the real age of this world. So, I was born late, but I studied the documents, I learned certain things... I can't talk about today's unfortunate event without first putting it in a greater, global context. Because this might be the cause and the other the effect.

"Therefore, I have to tell the story of Zod. It is not to be taken literally or followed word for word. There are still many holes in this story that I never deciphered and that will probably always remain a mystery. Too much time has passed, certainly, without anyone before me bothering to translate the gradual changes in the ways of speaking, in the languages, the ancient texts and accounts of those who decided to build Zod.

"In the most ancient of my own translations, Zod was called back then "Zod the Survivor". These texts date back to between 3,000 and 11,000 years. Other texts, much older than the earliest of these, are, however, all dated back to the year 9,876, which tends to prove that they're older than the very birth of Zod. Those who added the nickname of Survivor to Zod advocate a hypothesis whereby, at an unspecified date, a massive disaster destroyed the world of humans. Zod was wisely created to escape this disaster and the project succeeded. This hypothesis is confirmed by events and by other translations.

"Zod is, indeed, the last surviving stronghold of the human race. And only those who took refuge here escaped the disaster almost 23,000 years ago. They're still here, still living in the heart of Zod. I am their Master.

"That's what I personally think of the period between year 1 of the world of Zod (and earlier) and the assumed year 3,000…"

He could not have said exactly if the suction had just stopped a few seconds ago or if it had been a long time. He straightened up and listened. If they had stopped the tube, *they* or some rare breakdown, it meant "danger". Or at least it meant (and he could confirm it) that the ladder was pulled out. There might be 20 or 100 of them about to set out after him. His escape must have been discovered now... And his trail as well.

"Come on!" he urged gently. He walked down the tube with Animal at his heels. He did not walk long. Barely a few minutes. And the tube turned, at a perfect 45-degree angle, straight up.

Horan stood in the dead-end for a minute, staring up and gaping at the crooked chimney. It was absolutely impossible to see the exit at the end of the vertical tunnel. There was only darkness and a few even darker spots bulging out of the walls.

Horan glanced quickly at Animal and murmured, "It's not possible. You didn't fall from up there, did you?"

Animal pricked up its ears. It looked scrawny but not injured and it walked normally. A fall from such a height would have killed it dead.

Horan stood frozen there for a while, pinching his lips between his fingers. Then he decided to grab one of the bars of the twisted ladder, but stopped. "You can't climb, can you?"

Animal seemed to understand, if not his words at least the worry in his voice. It stood up on its limbs and started fidgeting around and yelping loud and sharp. Its little game lasted a few long seconds and then it stopped, glaring at Horan, whom it could not see.

"I don't understand," Horan said, embarrassed. "No one taught us the language of monsters."

This time Animal took action, grabbed the bottom of Horan's tunic between its teeth and pulled.

"But what do you want? Where do you... you want me to follow you?" For an answer Animal pulled harder.

And the child followed Animal and they went back to where they had met, by the bottleneck of the tube and Animal sat on its read end. It sat down, looking terribly determined to stay there until the end of time. Intrigued now, Horan stood there thinking, tried to walk away but was stopped short by another yelp from Animal. It sat down and shook its head stubbornly.

Then he squatted and said, "But what do you want? We can't stay here, I…"

He stopped talking. Animal was starting to paw the dirt, then stopped and looked at the child again. Only then did he realize that the dirt, quite a lot of it, should not have been there. He realized that it had fallen from one of the cracks in the rotting wall of the duct. The crack was there like a gaping wound of jagged rust revealing a thick curtain of earth and rock. And Horan thought he finally understood Animal's behavior.

"That's it, isn't it? That's where you came from? And then the dirt must have caved in behind you and shut you in here."

He got on his knees and started digging into the debris with both his hands, with all his strength. Animal yelped in joy and quickly joined in the effort. That was certainly how the tragedy had occurred. Certainly… They rapidly cleared out the wounded metal until Horan's nails banged against a hard surface. "A rock fell into the hole," he told Animal. "That's why you couldn't get back out."

He was sweating profusely and every muscle of his body was a painful knot of fatigue, but he did not wait two seconds before starting to work. Of course, the animal could never, by itself, have cleared away the barrier of rock. A few minutes was all that was needed for Horan's hands and he rolled the block inside the duct.

Another load of dirt came raining down the hole and he had to sweep it away again. He did it fast. Then, before Horan, a kind of skinny tube opened up, dug into the earth and minerals that formed the sky of Zod. A very dark tube, seeping slimy grease out of its jagged walls, which were rough in some places but soft and muddy in others.

Animal let loose a real howl of joy, shoved past Horan and ran into the tunnel. It disappeared right away.

"Animal!" Horan yelled.

Animal was already long gone. Without a second thought, wildly, Horan also dove into the putrid tube. Dragging his skinny body on hands and knees, panting, stained with sweat, water and dirt, he pushed farther and farther into the chilling tunnel.

It took hours, maybe more or maybe less. Nothing mattered except moving forward. He had to keep digging with his hands to clear the dirt away; layers of earth kept falling on his back and in his hair. He was sure that he would die at any second. And he kept calling Animal, but got no answer.

And then…

Then there was that cool gust of air, that great wave of strange, intoxicating smells. And before he knew it, Horan fell out of the tunnel onto something soft and wet. A wave of terror mixed with joy washed over him. He struggled up to a sitting position.

It was black, pitch-black. But he saw it. He saw the unimaginable latticework of vegetation like some huge and ponderous screed above him. Unknown plants that had nothing in common with what grew in the laboratories of Zod. Giant, fantastic plants. Nothing else. A universe of plants, lianas, leaves, hard grass and roots.

The air was heavy, humid, almost tangible.

And then, like a shock, a whole concert of cries, screeches, shrieks, a whole explosion of cries and noises come from an invisible world.

He was sitting in the grass. A little white spot in the vegetal mass.

He was above the sky of Zod.

He had succeeded.

And then the grass moved, next to him, but he did not have time to be scared. Animal was there, communicating with its licking tongue, as usual. He did not know what else to do but put his arms around its warm, hairy body and squeeze. He must have fallen asleep like that, soon after, amidst the odors and sounds, at the foot of those gigantic plants that seemed to cover the whole world above the sky.

CHAPTER VI

The red light of the radio's intercom blinked and Agaran interrupted his narration, turning off the recorder. "Agaran. Go ahead."

"Telzoat," the distorted voice of the Senior Teacher came back. "I'm in the duct right now. Twelve Soldier-Subjects are with me. The conditioning went off fine and we made them believe that the purified air would protect them against the dangerous bad air floating in the canals—the gas, of course, which could put their minds to sleep. They obeyed and reacted, but asked no questions. And they'll accept leaving for the surface eventually… if we have to."

"What are the chances that you'll have to?"

The vibrating cover of the speakerphone stayed quiet for a moment, then, "In my opinion, we'll have to leave. Right now we're climbing up the duct. No trace of the rebel… And I honestly don't think that we'll find him in the pipe. He ran like the devil… or else the Worker-Subjects in the room and the other child we caught lied about how much time passed before the machine started working again."

"You have to bring him back to me at any cost," Agaran said. "And I repeat, dead or alive. Call me back when you have some news to give me."

"Okay," Telzoat said and the red light went out on the panel.

Elbows resting on the recording tablet, Agaran buried his face in his cupped hands, like a real human of flesh and blood would do. He had never been able to purge his psyche of these reflexes that were conditioned, acquired and stored during his human life when he was still a "mind" inhabiting a mountain of cells.

He sat like that for a good while and then straightened up, pushed the button of the recording machine again. The light came on and the numbers and signs restarted their interminable march. Alone in front of the machine, partly machine himself, Agaran began speaking again:

"I, Agaran, found out about all the nooks and crannies of Zod. I visited and searched the dead rooms. I gleaned all possible documents. That's how I spent my life. I made an inventory of these documents, sorted and classified them. There are hundreds of thousands of them and my work is not over after 8,000 years. I had to make a judicious selection in this treasure and reject what appeared to me to be faulty copies or translations of very old and genuine documents. The simple choice of determining between an original, an authentic translation and a mangled translation sometimes took me years of reflection.

"Today this work has finally born its first fruits. Today, after careful study of this fantastic body of documents, which has still not reached half of its total size, I can come up with a hypothesis that I believe is solid and tallies with the documentary evidence. It could be, of course, that this hypothesis, in spite of everything, is completely wrong and hundreds of miles from the truth. It could be that some of the first translators had deliberately strewn their work with false information in order to confuse the curious minds of the future. I have, indeed, avoided some of these traps.

"Who can claim to possess the absolute truth? That's why I feel compelled to express this reservation before speaking. With this said and despite the numerous lacunae that my hypothesis still contains, despite the total failure on certain points, despite everything that sometimes might look like unwarranted guesses, despite all these pitfalls, I believe it's very close to the truth. If not The Truth.

"Therefore, for methis hypothesis should be considered a theory. It tells the story of the people of men before the disaster—why and how this disaster came about. It tells of the birth of Zod, which was the final shore. Here I deliver the results of my studies:

"The very origin of the conscious animal "Man" is unknown. Time is too limited to measure the life of this being endowed with tremendous faculties. Maybe man has always been. No one knows and the Ancients who inhabited the planet surface (today the sky of Zod) knew no more. In sum: man *was*. In particular, he was on the ground of this planet and started living. This ascent into life probably took thousands of centuries because we can suppose that in this distant age man did not know, for example, the science of electricity or atomic fission or even, why not, the principle of the wheel, or even fire. The steady progression of humans in the scientific domain since harnessing electrical forces can, in fact, lead us to imagine an identical advance long before the electric age, starting from nothing to arrive there. I don't think this is senseless rambling.

"So, it appears that the human race was living on the surface of this ordinary planet in this ordinary solar system—this planet perhaps being the birthplace of the apparition of life, perhaps not. Man lived and reached the electric age, then the atomic age. It seems that at this period of life on the surface, some pretty dramatic and horrible disasters had already taken place. Man had discovered a certain kind of domestication of the atom,

76

which quickly proved to be an appalling defect, impossible to hide once brought to light. A persistent evil meant to kill.

"Then came the age of all-powerful biology. An indifferent science waiting in the shadows until then because they didn't recognize its dangerous "qualities": they really only took an interest in what was dangerous and could be used for power and destruction, for the benefit of an essentially dominating selectivity.

"The discoveries in the domain of bio-chemistry, neurobiology, etc. were able to offer fantastic possibilities to a certain category of the human species. Everything was set in motion to find the secrets. The great secrets of the species, which, without a doubt, once discovered, would be a mighty and terrible weapon in the hands of men.

"So, the time of profound study came, specializing in the biological domain. The time when man, who gradually deciphered the secrets of life itself, stopped being completely a man to become only life.

"The first positive results were bound to deal with grafting living matter, from one individual to another. Skin grafts and then organ transplants. Soon transplants of the main organs like kidneys, lungs, heart, liver, etc. Then limb transplants. The discovery of procedures of "pleasure free" fertilization, which allowed them to make up for the considerable loss of energy by subjects who mated in the bestial way. Men became masters of artificial insemination, starting with human or synthetic sperm, as well as the implantation of fertilized ova in the human body or in artificial matter. Men had total control over all domains of eugenics.

"There's no doubt that every way of living, every individual consciousness of life was swept away by this fantastic tidal wave of progress in the dark realm of genetics and the implementation of its secrets. The "ordinary" world, barely back on its feet after the cataclysmic contradictions of the atomic events, had to collapse again. What remained of the old family structures crumbled away pitifully and irreparably. The legal codes and moral codes joined in a colossal holocaust to be reborn anew, structured in a radically different way. (It's hard for me to imagine, for example, the application of a law of inheritance originally created for a society of family units but trying to be applied to the birth of quasi-artificial beings, created in test tubes and therefore having no father or mother or family).

"But the new society adapted, in spite of certain very substantial losses. It adapted, it was born of this new science, of this new wealth. It was composed of sensible, equal doses of hybrid, pure humans and humans "ransomed" from death by vital organ transplants (human, animal or purely mechanical). Then cervical transplants were possible and extended life even longer. DNA was harnessed, the cortex deciphered, mnemonic phenomena assimilated. This last giant step forward greatly facilitated the "memory transplants" when it was possible to capture the molecules of ribonucleic acid that carried and stored knowledge and memory. The ribonucleic acid extracted from the brain of a subject (dying or not) and injected into the brain of a second subject, gave the knowledge of the first to the second. Teaching under hypnosis became outmoded. A child whose brain was recognized (in the fetal stage) as particularly well formed in neurons and nerve cells—and it could automatically be a result of creating selected life and the use of certain pre-studied gametes or even pre-conditioned in their genetic message—this "child-king", in the warm unconsciousness of its life in the synthetic matrix, could soak up the learning of the greatest brains the world had ever known and in its infant birth cries be born richer than any human ever before.

"This technique was more than likely perfected until its methods were widely used, though still only affecting a certain class of humans. The intelligence for this class became a given fact, acquired at birth. The intelligence could even be transmitted by "levels" of intensity, according to the desired category of human and what these categories were destined to do with their life. A sub-class was indubitably formed comprising all kinds of hybrids and non-treated humans whom the rich normally considered inferior to themselves and whose anger they didn't understand when it exploded. But the rich had need of these slaves of common society—the need to rule, since the desire of eminence was still in them, inscribed in the structures of the spiral molecules of RNA. The gap between this intellectual nobility and the masses only got bigger and deeper. So deep and so big that the researchers who had discovered immortality and went back to explore the complex universes of death devised those drugs that alienated bad temper and that way of thinking. A very simple drug, in fact, that suppressed the excess secretion of uric acid in the subject by absorbing pills with a base of enzymes (Hypoxanthine, Guanine, Phosphoribosyl, Transferase) and thereby suppressing the latent aggressiveness in every man. The drug was distributed as pills and diffused as a gas. With this, humanity's rich tribe saved themselves from any possible rebellion by the non-rich.

"This state of affairs certainly lasted for a long time. Then, in spite of the HGPT drugs, the repressed, corrosive anger found its way into the unconsciousness of the masses until it finally exploded. It could be that the explosion broke out in certain types of hybrids who were less receptive to the drug and that these hybrids led the revolt—the biggest ever, much deadlier than the nuclear games. In no time at all, the population desirous of equality, desirous of powers that they'd never had—heightened intelligence, access to the ultimate knowledge, immortality, telepathic and extrasensory gifts, various paranormal faculties, etc.—this fantastic tide of the destitute, semi-humans, robots, hybrids, cyborgs, androids and all species, flooded the surface of the globe, freed of the effects of the drug. A massive tidal wave, a huge lava flow that carried away with it the structures of human civilization, that crushed all those rich who were so well-protected for so long that they had almost forgotten the basic means of defense.

"The war was certainly not long. The rich won a few victories using old atomic weapons, but to no avail—they were still overthrown, pitilessly knocked down, crushed, annihilated.

"You can easily imagine what followed the victory of the sub-class humans suddenly in possession of extraordinary biological weapons, drunk on power and liberated aggression. They forgot that their poor, conditioned intelligence could not measure up to such arms; they forgot that their only chance for salvation, their only chance to access the higher realms of knowledge someday, was patience and work and study. And also peace.

"We can only make guesses about the "first shot fired." Maybe it was started by the android class sensing that even in case of victory they might not reach the level of the new rich? Maybe the liberated aggression was the sole cause, bringing back a kind of competitive spirit between the victorious clans? Nobody will ever know, probably. But what is practically a fact is that they used the weapons taken from the enemy, and far too powerful for their understanding, against one another.

"Weapons like those light gases that spread like mad, utterly annihilating an individual's RNA molecules, wiping out his memory, *all* his memory. Throughout the world, enormous containers of this gas were blown up... resulting in the most astounding battlefield anyone could imagine: a world of silence and complete stupor. A dead planet, populated by dazed, human creatures without a past or future, without even a present. A world populated by idiots not even knowing where they were or if they were alive or dead. In a few hours it was a world stripped of all knowledge and all personality.

"A world populated by bewildered automatons with empty eyes, or crazed, frightened, maybe apathetic. A horror. An unbelievable horror.

"They straggled and shuffled into houses without knowing the names of things or what they were used for. They stood in the living rooms, in front of machines and did not understand—to touch one of these machines was enough to launch a new disaster.

"They became bodies. Wandering bodies, devoid of mind, not even remembering that they could "try to remember." Many of them were bound to die without knowing it, without expecting it, without understanding. The hybrids and cyborgs let their mechanical bodies run down.

"Very quickly, through natural selection, no one was left on earth but those who were fully human. Those whom technology had never helped to survive.

"We can imagine that space navigators, extra-planetary colonists, kept quiet and avoided coming back to the mother-planet after the first scouting teams, themselves victims of the gas, became like everyone else, complete idiots suddenly forgetting what they were doing in their spaceships and then letting them crash without a peep. We can imagine that they studied the phenomenon and decided to remain on their distant planets until the effects of the nuclear radiation and oblivion gas wore off.

"For those who were left on the cursed planet, life continued day after day in the deep dark that they dragged around with them. Hunger made them taste roots, without thinking, and some survived while others mutated under the effects of the radiation. They became like animals, minus the instinct, rediscovered the original procreation practices, and multiplied again... Monstrous pondering, which restarted the history of life...

"Of course, they were unaware that in these awful times, under their bare, savage feet, Zod had decided to survive. Maybe it was the year 3 or 10 or 20 of Zod the Survivor.

"Now it's the year 21,975...

"That's how I, Agaran, explain the disaster that destroyed the knowledge on this planet when men had conquered death and still lived under the sky—the other sky.

"Today there was an incident in the world of Zod. This incident will, perhaps, spell the destruction of this world. That's why I'm speaking, so that one day, if the day comes, for those who are listening to this, if ever anyone listens and understands, the knowledge will keep them from making the same mistakes as they did almost 25,000 years ago.

"Because of this incident, I am now going to talk about Zod and the life of the survivors under our sky of earth."

Agaran stopped talking. He watched the signs march over the lighted board for a while and then shut it off. The red light of the inter-radio was stubbornly blank.

With the tips of his fingers he pinched the bridge of his nose hard, closed his eyes tight. This was another typically human habit.

At the same time, Telzoat halted the march. In one second, the dull hammering of footsteps stopped behind him.

He took a quick glance at the Soldier-Subjects following him, and saw in the cold light of his helmet lamp a pale face, covered in sweat, tense and nervous behind the transparent visor of the protective helmet. He himself did not feel tired at all—he never felt tired anymore since the day when Agaran gave him the wondrous robot body. It was not so rosy for the Soldier-Subjects. They still experienced those muscle cramps and sweat, the salty moisture of sweat, its smell... They must have been swimming in it, in their hermetically sealed suits that were supposed to protect them from the insidious emanations that drifted around in the world above the sky.

Telzoat turned around again and said, "A few minutes rest."

They needed it after the staggering climb... and before what lied in store. With a dead eye, while the Soldier-Subjects behind him collapsed to the ground, Telzoat stared long into the abrupt narrowing of the tube.

They had to widen it if they wanted to get past. The space was big enough for a child, but not for an adult.

A vague worry slowly came over Telzoat. He was about to leave the world of Zod and also erupt into the surface... without having taken the tranquilizing drug. Of course, being a Senior Teacher, he did not believe in the nonsense they instilled in the Subjects, but there was still something to worry about... as is normal when you visit an unknown land for the first time.

He pressed the button on his ventral radio to contact Agaran. He had to inform him of this narrowing in the tube and the overall bad news. To admit the fact that the rebel was not in the duct. And to assert the hope of finding him outside...

CHAPTER VII

The golden drop was in no hurry. But stubborn, yes! Armed with a diabolical perseverance.

The golden drop was wonderful to see and even to breathe, in a certain way. Except, nobody was there to see or feel it... nobody but this multitude of strange cries that rolled through the tangled mess. And the cries were not like living things capable of perception.

It came from the sky, in freefall, straight down. And the fall was no different from hundreds of other similar falls. Like its billions of companions, the golden drop had been able to stop its fall, with the tips of its fingers touching the summit of this particular tree that rose up out of the green sea. But this drop was stubborn, curiously stubborn.

It started sliding. Just sliding along a leaf, like a yellow caress on a limb, to fall again at the end of its path, to flatten out on another leaf that a light gust of wind spirited away. And again the golden drop fell, always straight down, always stubborn, forging its graceful, steady way, maybe helped by the wind or some breeze that kindly opened a passage. It was a golden drop that came from far away—from the sun. It could have rested on a branch after such a long journey... but in its plumb fall it never found a leaf or branch solid and still enough to support it.

It sank like a rivet into metal. Clean. Raw. It fell into this glum, green atmosphere, into this compact jumble of ragged moss, "shredded" vegetation, bickering lichens, and lianas. It knew so well how to fall that it reached the bottom of the green chasm. And it fell not on the moss all around, not on the grass or the drooling, bearded roots, no, at the very end of its fall, there was a face.

There was a child sleeping in the grass and bearded roots, arms spread out in a cross like a felled tree. On the pale face of this child, the little drop of sun lay out flat. It was warm and quivered gently, rustled from on high by the countless claws of foliage.

The strange sensation of warmth woke him up and, at the gates of consciousness, his hand brushed out, sliding up to his face. The sensation of warmth spread to his hand. Then he remembered and opened his eyes. The brightness flashed between his fingers and burned his retina.

He was scared: a colossal and absolutely uncontrollable fear that made him bolt up and then threw him down. He was on his belly in the cold, slimy grass, stretched out, eyes closed, waiting petrified for some disaster to swoop down upon the place.

There was no disaster, nothing but the concert of cries and screeching on every side, surrounding him, blanketing him, penetrating his every pore.

Little by little he noticed that the earth, the grass on which he was lying had an odor. He noticed that the noises, the screeches and shrieking were not necessarily hostile. It even seemed that they were paying no attention to anybody, really. So, Horan sat up. And for the second time, very carefully, opened his eyes.

The light that had exploded into his eyes was still there, in the place where his head had been a few seconds earlier. A thin spot that turned a small patch of grass a different color. He looked up: it was coming from high up, higher than the infernal hullaballoo.

Horan's movements were like a robot when he stood up to look around, with a great deal of caution.

Yes, not everything was false, not everything was invented by the Teachers when they talked about the world above the sky. They spoke of the unimaginable and they were still far from the reality. Even he, even Horan, in his wildest flights of fancy, could not have imagined such a tangle, such a chaos of palms, lianas and bizarre plants. Spongy earth, slimy, hairy humus that his foot sunk into with a very unpleasant sucking sound. And on the earth, on the humus… the purest, most fantastic carnival. A universe of plants. A universe of green. Even the air looked the same color—the color of hot, heavy humidity, wet, that might, if absolutely necessary, pass for breathable air. A curtain, a blanket of green, of slime, of semi-liquid and semi-vegetal solidness. A thing full of faint or strong smells, mingled together, of persistent cries, of cries like resounding, repetitive waterfalls, constantly sucked into a mortal crescendo.

A world.

A world where Horan was at the center.

He dared to take a step, just like that, for nothing, just to move, and froze right away, his heart pounding, his eyes squinting and hurting in the green half-light. There, behind the thick, snarled curtain that surrounded the small, relatively clear space in the middle of which he was standing, something was moving, moving again, rustling the leaves and vines, still moving and more and more while Horan's heart raced faster and faster until it became a muffled bell, tolling dully at the bottom of his constricted throat… Until the green curtain finally parted to reveal a black, wet muzzle and two little, yellow, sparkling eyes.

"Animal!" Horan shouted.

Animal ran across the snarled grass and trotted up to him. The bunch of hair on its rear end was beating like crazy. In its mouth it held a kind of thick ball of very colorful rags. At the child's feet it loosened its vise-like teeth and the ball of rags fell to the ground. Apparently satisfied, Animal sat in the grass and waited.

"What did you…"

Horan straightened up, like an electric shock ran through him. He had barely touched the bundle of rags. They were not rags; the tips of his fingers were spotted with blood.

Not yet understanding, he looked at Animal and then at the unmoving "thing". Then in the low branches of the sweltering forest, a red arrow whistled through the small, open clearing. An arrow that was very similar to this other thing here, red, green and bloody, on the ground. A living thing, like the arrow was. A flying animal.

Did they speak of flying animals in the old books? Not in the ones that Horan had read. But the Teachers had talked about this kind of demon.

Horan squatted. With a wary hand he took out of his belt bag some of the dried food he ate. He offered it to Animal, who sniffed the crackers looking thoroughly disgusted.

"Is this world like this everywhere?" Horan asked.

Up above, among the cries and foliage, shadows sometimes passed over, like a dire threat. But Horan was not scared. Really, no more, not since Animal was here. He was no longer alone and that was enough.

"You came with me…"

Animal waited, sitting, happy. But it did not seem to understand a single word of what Horan said. Animal was superb in its coarse fleece of pure, shiny black, with that single pale spot, almost white, on its chest. Very clean. It was no longer the muddy, shaggy thing that had escaped from the tube.

The tube! He had got out! He had left Zod... He had evaded the ancient law of death... And now?

"Why did you come back? I helped you get out and now you can return to your people."

It sat and waited.

Did Animal have a people? Did it want to return? It would be normal and in the law of life, whoever goes off, returns to his people. And yet... yet, it was here and Horan felt particularly warmed by its presence. And still, he did not want Animal to go.

Lost in thought he caressed the dead, colored thing lying on the ground and then asked Animal several times why he had committed the crime. Animal did not answer. It simply wagged its rear end. The dead thing had a weird head with a big, horny, curved nose that ended in a hook and opened like a mouth. Its body was covered with strange hair, long and flat, like fibrous leaves. Under its hair, where the blood came from, Horan found a hard, very pointy thorn that had penetrated its flesh. He yanked out the thorn with his reddened fingers.

How could Animal have killed this flying thing with this thorn? Or was the thing already dead, already killed and...? Animal did not answer his questions. It never answered. It never asked either. It said nothing. The only language it used was the little yelps or hoarse growls. Nothing to do with articulate language.

"It doesn't matter," Horan sighed.

Even though a little disappointing, it was still true: what did it matter? And what was happening in him that he could find pleasure in the silent company of a being that was obviously feeble-minded and feeble-bodied compared to humans? Why this warmth?

He stood up and automatically nudged the dead thing back to Animal when something terrible happened. Animal turned its eyes on the child, eyes that were very clearly questioning and surprised. Then it lay down and using its teeth, its bloody mouth, *it started eating the dead thing!*

In the long run, the deep, burning sensation of terror faded away until it became only a kind of blind automatism. A phenomenon that was beyond, fallen from the enchanting atmosphere to tangle him up in its complex bonds.

He ran. He ran like a madman.

He rushed into the curtain of lianas, into the wet mass of leaves and grass, bursting through with all his weight. He ran. Billions of little flying things, in clouds, followed him on his flight like a second, noisy breathing.

Horan ran. Animal at his heels.

Fatigue was something weird, heavy and cumbersome, which he lugged behind him. For how long had he been running? For how long was he jumping from miry spots to spots a little more solid, from bunches of vines to tufts of grass a little bigger than his hands. How long in this hell since he had seen the shadow?

Time… time meant nothing anymore. Only his flight counted—because he had to run—and this hefty fatigue that he lugged behind him.

Several times, however, he stopped, listened to the cries of the living things up above and then to his own hurried breathing. To listen… to breathe this heavy atmosphere riddled with hostile noises and to detect, in this echoing mishmash, the sign, the faint sign …

Several times he thought he was out of danger. Escaped a second time from the horror and the fear. And then, there, close by, a rustling of leaves, a liana moved slowly to the side and the shadow. The shadow again. Always!

He had to get back on the run!

With all his strength, he forged on. But all his strength was not enough. The weight of the fatigue behind him was too close now. It was there in his leaden legs, in his knotted belly and his burning lungs.

Like something torn apart, Horan fell to the ground, into a soft peat bog overrun with slimy moss. All of a sudden. Something was detonating in his brain, veiling his eyes, scattering clouds of sparks in the dark night. The night... no, it was not night. It was just, still, this heavy half-light that persisted at the foot of the tall plants, in the layered roots of the rippled trees. This half-light streaked with bright flashes when Horan closed his eyes.

Animal joined him, its tongue hanging out, its sides rising and falling to a fast rhythm, but still not anywhere near exhaustion. Physically speaking, and compared to humans, he was maybe not so feeble-bodied after all.

Time stopped. His name was Horan, he was there, lying in the mud, fully possessed by a delirious heart. That was all. Nothing else. Time no longer existed.

Then, at some moment, time revived and with it this infernal terror in the eyes of the child. It was at this exact moment when the thick bushes parted above the peat bog. And the shadow came forward, cautiously, quietly. The thick, huge shadow.

And the child saw the monstrous face of the man between the parted grass.

The fear was too great in him and he passed out.

A man's face. A flat face, rough and wide, like it was crushed, with a prominent forehead, a hard, padded bar above dark eyes deeply sunken into the skull. A very flat nose and massive, jutting cheekbones. A wide-cut mouth with thick, bulbous lips. Barely a chin. But a man's face. And this face was two or three times bigger than a normal adult's face and it was topped by a cluster of something all tangled up in his long, oily hair.

The petrified child waited. Next to him Animal had stopped moving.

It was like this, without the slightest change, without any movement whatsoever, for a long time. For centuries or a few unusual seconds, time, again, stretched out, immobilized, slackened.

The monstrous man, hiding in the bushes, looked really just as astonished and petrified as the child and not much bolder. He was there and he was waiting, too, for a gesture, maybe hoping for a word, a sign. As if he was scared of the child: *scared of Horan*. In his cold, petrifying terror, this bizarre thought suddenly crossed Horan's mind. A flash. Scared of Horan, yes… Maybe. Horan had never, no one had ever before in the history of Zod, come face to face with one of these humanoid monsters from the land above the sky. Therefore, the monsters must never have met anyone from the land of Zod. And if it was true, in spite of everything, that these monsters were the deformed incarnation of the spirits of those who could not live, according to the law of Zod, once death came, if this was true, there was no proof that the spirit, on the other side of death, still remembered the time when it inhabited a normal human body. So, this monster could also be feeling fear and surprise.

A swarm of hypotheses crowded into Horan's head. He was still trembling, of course, but… it was already something different. And then, this flight, this fatigue… he was in the land above the sky. He had wanted it. Anyway, he could always run away.

He lifted himself feebly on one elbow and glanced at Animal. As if from it might come support, help, a sign, likewise. Of the three characters thrown unexpectedly into each other's presence, Animal seemed the most serene.

Then the man crouching in the grass moved. Rolled his shoulders. Crawled. While he moved forward, Horan got up on his feet, supporting his hands on the wall of the miry bog. And then after a loud noise of trampled leaves, the man was also in the bog with him. Huge. He was twice as tall as Agaran himself. A giant.

A great giant in a harmoniously proportioned body with long, supple muscles. Totally naked except for a cord of vine tied around his waist and knotted over his flat stomach, from which hung a small, leather bag. He held a long tube in his right hand.

"I don't want… to hurt you," Horan stammered, his nose pointing straight up, trying in to look into the man's eyes.

At these words the man stepped back. The edge of the bog reached halfway up his thighs. Slowly, he squatted. Animal yelped a little and shook its hairy appendage. The giant looked over it quickly and then brought his attention back to Horan. He seemed reassured, too, recovered from his initial, suspicious surprise. Something like a smile crossed his fat lips. Then, with difficulty, slowly, he lifted his left hand—enormous!— pointed to himself and spoke a word that sounded like "Roarg". After a moment he repeated the word several times until Horan followed his example, pointing to himself and saying, "Horan."

"Ho-rann," the giant said.

This time he smiled for real. He was practically not horrible. This time Horan lost his fear for good and knew that he had found his salvation, truly, in the land of monsters, above the sky of Zod. He felt very clearly about it.

CHAPTER VIII

The ability to adapt is really a marvelous gift given to the human being. If he had taken the time to analyze the phenomenon, Horan would have agreed wholeheartedly. But he did not take the time: he had too much to do, to look around in every direction, really drunk on the presence of the giant Roarg next to him.

A little earlier, he was just a little thing, barely alive, lost, running around in absolute terror. Now, his tiny, skinny legs were carrying him merrily in the stride of this gigantic man and fatigue was a pale thing that he knew existed but that he could not take the time to think about.

He did not let himself look at the naked man and his so thoroughly powerful body walking in the thick brush without paying attention to the child, often stopping to wait for him. In these instants, that strange smile, still fairly unsure, completely changed his rough face.

There was no doubt about it: Roarg (since that seemed to be his name) had also been scared when he found Horan. Scared. And utterly intrigued, so much so that his curiosity had annihilated the fear. He had followed the mad flight of this strange little man with white skin, wearing a second, stranger skin. And he, too, in his fear and doubt, was getting used to him. He probably felt that there was no danger here, that it could not exist in this trembling little wisp of a human.

They had taken a break, at a certain time. Without warning, probably just because he was tired of it, Roarg stopped walking and waited for Horan. Then, very slowly, meticulously, he leaned the long tube he was carrying against a rotting tree stump. Animal was hopping around like crazy and yelping. With one word Roarg quieted him down. Roarg seemed to know Animal's language. He motioned to Horan to sit down across from him, which the child did.

Roarg was "talkative". It took him only a few seconds to be understood by his gestures, precise gestures, that could capsulate his thought marvelously and leave no room for confusion in an attentive mind. In this way, in an extraordinary ballet of graceful movements, Horan listened to a long story that he mentally translated as follows:

Roarg lived in this land covered with gigantic plants. He did not live here alone. Animal had been at Roarg's side for a long time. They were together. Animal usually followed Roarg. One day Animal disappeared into a tunnel dug in the earth. (It seemed that something might be living in this tunnel—another variety of sub-race like those flying things that Animal ate—and Animal was running after it to catch it). It entered the tunnel and did not come back out.

(Horan believed, then, that he knew why Animal was in the air duct: he had followed the tunnel dug in the earth and then due to a cave in, maybe, had landed in the eroded tube, then the rocks and dirt fell in after him and blocked the passage, imprisoning him for good in the metal duct).

Today Animal came back. Roarg found Animal again and he was happy. He figured Horan was responsible for its return and he seemed even happier. He also explained that the living thing that Animal ate had been killed by him, Roarg. Just as he was about to pick it up, Animal swiped it first... and he, Roarg, had followed Animal to Horan.

One thing was hard for Horan to understand: the fact that this gigantic man had killed the little flying thing. He coul not translate "kill" by "death"; his mind could not put a picture to the gesture. He shrugged, touched his head and lips and shook his head no. Then Roarg gestured to him to be quiet and not move. The faint smile that played across his lips faded away and his whole face became hard and attentive. He listened to the sounds of the forest and scrutinized its tight weave. All of a sudden, Horan saw him grab the long, hollow tube, bring it to his mouth and point it up toward the sky. An instant later, to the sound of trampled leaves, a flying thing fell straight down at Horan's feet. Roarg and Animal fought and growled until Roarg finally picked up the flying thing and offered it to Horan.

That was what it meant, to kill.

It meant lifting a tube over your head and a flying thing fell. Dead. Maybe it also meant pointing the tube in every direction. The tube was the killing machine. The machine that turned a living thing into something dead.

"Sabie," Roarg said, pointing to the tube.

"Yes," Horan said.

The name of the tube was "sabie". Inquiringly, Horan shrugged his shoulders. "Why?" Why the killing machine, why kill the flying thing?

Roarg touched the dead thing, then his lips, while his jaws chewed nothing.

"Arg," he said.

"To eat", of course! Just like Animal, he ate the dead thing! He must have noticed and, in some way, feared Horan's disgusted grimace because he quickly let him know that he knew all about his tastes. There was no question of Horan eating the dead things, right? Horan had what he needed in his bag... The giant had certainly been spying on him already when he fed himself.

"Yes," Horan nodded. Horan no arg. No. He would not eat the dead thing... And Roarg stood up, very satisfied.

After this long chat, they got moving again. The giant led the way, heading flawlessly into the green, murky jumble. He knew exactly which branch to lift, instead of another, and exactly where to go in the putrid pond. He knew the way and followed it unerringly. Animal frolicked around him, bouncing all over the place. The child followed.

During the entire march through the heart of hell, the only signs made by Roarg to the child were to hurry up. And the child hurried. He would have followed the giant to the end of the inhabited world and even into other worlds. With him he no longer feared the forest and the tangled maze of plants; he was no longer something tiny and lost. The goal where Roarg was heading was his own. Sometimes it is enough just to have a goal... a meek, invisible goal. The feeling was new in him. It was the opposite of the pallid terror that had been knotting his stomach and chilling his blood. It was... something new, indefinable in the heart of consciousness, and soon it was going to explode into a thousand fires.

He was walking behind the naked giant and countless species of flying sub-races whirled around them. Living beings, tiny but living. By the thousands. Sometimes they landed on Horan's hands or on his face. They stung a little and he had to brush them away.

Up above, in the roof of leaves, among the cries and chatter, other forms were dancing, sometimes soaring off, vague forms, often colorful, many which had the fleeting appearance of a human.

It was not dangerous or troubling, for Roarg was there, smiling.

All of a sudden, the vegetal magma tore apart.

And for a few seconds, Horan forgot to breathe. He was suddenly frozen, and would have stayed there, not moving, if Roarg had not gently tugged his arm. Then, like an unconscious robot, he followed Roarg. He was not completely Horan anymore. He was something that had not enough eyes to see or enough ears to hear.

A bright, warm, full light flooded the noisy hole in the jungle. And as far as the eye could see above, there were no more trees, really not a single tree. And the sky had changed again: the sky was big, blue smoke, as high as could be, certainly, no one in the world could ever have touched it. Incredibly high! In the center of this smoke, the light was hanging, like a flash or a frozen explosion.

It was, of course, absolutely fantastic, unimaginable and of matchless beauty. But it was real and Horan was not dreaming. He was really and truly in the middle of the hole in the jungle with Roarg and Animal. He was here! He could see a group of shelters in the center of this clearing, very big shelters, like bells with a door cut out at ground level, built with branches and leaves. Roarg's people lived here.

He saw a dense crowd of naked men and women, children too, gathering around, babbling at Roarg and at him. Dozens of beings like Animal were running every which way, barking.

All giants. Tall, rough, supple. Some had the bottom of their face decorated with tangled hair; some had incredibly wrinkled faces. In the world of Zod, the first wrinkle on the forehead of an old 30-year old was the mark of death and the old people carried out the law themselves. Here the old giants looked thousands and thousands of years old.

The women, for the most part, were smaller than the men and their long, long hair often fell in shiny waves all the way down to their butts. On the top of their chest they had a pair of weird glands… and Horan did not understand right away that they were breasts that were abnormally overdeveloped compared to the women of Zod. Many carried children in their arms; others seemed to be suffering from some unknown illness—their bellies were distended, huge.

He felt like the ground was spinning amongst the noise and whirlwind of movements and the light glittering on the naked skin, and he had to force himself not to give in to the fatigue.

Roarg was talking. He kept talking and talking and the others listened, or talked too. It sounded like strange, pleasant music.

And all of them were watching Horan, coming up to him, curious, their eyes a little frightened though, but unable to resist their curiosity. Hands reaching out in timid attempts to touch, pulled back right away as if shocked by some electrical charge when Horan made the slightest move. A compact circle was soon formed, balmy, full of color and sound. Many of the children whom the women were carrying in their arms were taller than Horan.

Then the chatter gradually died down. The curious circle opened onto a man who came straight up to Roarg. He was old, but pretty much the same height. Knotty muscles, wiry, and wrinkled skin. On his head he wore bunches of that weird skin from the flying thing killed by Roarg. Between his skinny thighs, his penis hung like some dead thing.

The old man listened patiently to Roarg, but his eyes did not leave the child for a second. Then, when Roarg stopped talking, the old man took two steps back and everyone around the circle did the same. In a magnificent gesture he raised his arms toward the light-filled sky and let loose a great, endless cry in which words rolled out like the sound of a marvelous machine. Then the old man—who must have been a kind of master—was quiet. His eyes were warm, good. In the silence, he brought Horan into a shelter.

In front of the door, there was a big pile of furs. Like a kind of primitive throne. The old master invited the child to sit.

Then the light from the sky went out. Here, too, just like in Zod, there were times of day and times of night. On this night, Horan the fugitive knew that these giants were doing nothing but welcoming him as a friend; they were doing nothing but accepting him as an equal.

They welcomed him as a master, as well. They offered him the group of shelters and begged him to stay forever. They had been waiting for him. And Roarg, who had brought him, seemed to be held in very high esteem.

They welcomed him like something or someone extraordinary and incomprehensible is welcomed into the ordinary sphere of existence. Something or someone who inspires respect, admiration and... fear, all at once. Secular fear of the supranormal...

They welcomed him like a... deity, an incarnate force.

They danced, on this night, before Horan's shelter. An interminable dance of glistening, smeared bodies around a huge fire, strange, too—a very unusual fire, made of colorful billows that consumed no compressed gas and was not produced by the heating of electrical elements; a fire that fed on pieces of dry wood and armfuls of crackling grass. For a long time Horan admired the fire of these giants whom he could not understand, but whose magical beauty he drank in with all his being.

Another strange phenomenon aroused his admiration... at the same time as a vague anxiety. The phenomenon of this world's sky at night. Up above, the blue smoke turned dark and dense as the light disappeared. Then, in this velour, a multitude of small, bright dots appeared, motionless in the space, but blinking softly. Like the vault of that room that he and Lem had wandered into by mistake in their flight from Zod. That spherical room that held the machine to count time.

In this world, at night, the entire sky looked like that room. As if this world were in the center of a gigantic time-counting machine.

This mystery stunned the stray child. Enveloped in the sweet chant, in the folds of the night, he fell asleep. Animal was at his side.

There was a new day and then another night. Then other days and still other nights.

It was a strange world. But the strange never lasts forever. It just takes time and the strange fades away little by little, soon to become almost the usual. In the center of this world, dug out of the thick blanket of crazy plants that covered the ground, Horan watched and listened to time pass by.

He learned simple things and other things that took him a long time to get used to, to believe, to kill the strange.

He learned the name of the old master and this name was "Logh". He learned that of Roarg's companion, which was "Irn." In this world of giants, the women and men lived together in the shelters. The children with them! All the men and women worked in the same way, taking care of simple tasks such as decorating sticks with the help of bones or making containers out of dirt. The main occupation of the men was to kill. To kill things that flew or other beings that lived in the trees—some almost human, very agile, others with long, scaly, crawling bodies. To kill to eat. The also gathered fruits, plants, but above all they cut up the dead things and gave them to the fire to purify them. Then they ate them. As hard as he tried, Horan could not, in all good sense, understand this curious practice.

One day he left the compound of shelters, Animal at his heels, to take a little stroll on the edge of the forest. He felt happy, strong, and stuffed with fruit. It was then that he found—purely by chance—the most marvelous secret of these people.

He heard the noise and at first paid no attention to it. But Animal stopped short and pricked up its ears. Horan heard the noise again and easily identified it as a human groan. More groans followed. Intrigued, he dove into the high grass, cautiously, and then stopped short himself. His eyes bulged at what he saw before him, there, just a few feet away. Lying in the grass was a woman. And Horan watched.

…He had seen the woman with the huge belly writhing in pain on the rumpled carpet, her skin streaming sweat, her face taut. Then he had seen her get up on her knees, at one point, grab the lower branch of a tree with all her might. He had seen the water and blood, the weird liquid, run down the woman's thighs. He had seen her bend down and receive that living form in her hands, that child form which had come out of her body. He had seen the woman cut the link with her teeth and lick the little, bawling man!

In this world there were no birth machines! Men fell out between the thighs of women! The birth machines were the women!

He had seen this mystery with his own eyes. He was not frightened or disgusted, but utterly amazed... then after thinking about it, as time passed, rather proud. Rather proud, yes, without knowing exactly why.

He learned words, too. But few. The giants' language was complicated and, apparently, in some circumstances, they used different sounds to designate the same thing. It took him a long time to learn and really assimilate the giant's language.

With Roarg he learned river. The river was made of water, a lot of water, running freely under the trees. They could go on the water by climbing into a kind of hollow tree trunk. What he felt then could not have been more enchanting. In the river were living beings covered with silver and Roarg killed them with a long stick. To eat them afterward...

To go on the water was really very good.

It was a strange, hot world, a huge world. Horan wondered if the giants, like men, sometimes died.

He lived in a shelter with Roarg and Irn. They were the only ones to touch him, sometimes, with the tips of their fingers. The rest of the people never really came close to him. They brought him fruits, but it was Roarg who gave them to him. The day of the river, Roarg killed many, many fish… but it was Horan who was celebrated by the crowd, as if the fact of his being in the trunk with Roarg…

He was in a strange world. And he was happy when he watched Irn. She was beautiful. Her face and body were something beautiful. She gave off a kind of odor that was not an odor. Something that made Horan, on seeing her, wish he already knew the language of this people.

Several times, often in the evening, he had the strange feeling that a secret force was pressing him. Pressing him to go to Irn and… snuggle up to her, against her bronze skin. In the sweetness of her skin, snuggled up, without moving, without speaking. To be there like the other giant children sometimes held tightly against the bellies of the women.

It seemed to him that nothing in the world could bring him more peace or calm; that nothing could be greater… not even going on the water in the hollow trunk. He never did it, however. Another force was there, holding him back. And Irn watched him and smiled and made a little gesture and the warm lights shimmered alive down her hair so black!

He tried to remember the magic words, the works like treasures deciphered in the forbidden books… and he could not. Zod was so long ago, before he had met Roarg! But he believed that the meaning of the forgotten words was there, very close, within arm's reach…

One day, once again, something strange happened. He was running and jumping with Animal when Roarg called his name. Logh the master was with Roarg and behind them the entire people. Roarg tried to explain something but could not; he motioned to Horan to follow him and led him straightway into the thick jungle. They walked for half a day before arriving in the middle of a hole on the edge a small river. There, on the shore, was a pile. A pile of things.

The things were: rolls of old cloth, a handful of ugly jewelry and a bunch of small plastic bags. Things that had nothing to do with the world of giants, but, on the contrary, stank badly of Zod. The giants did not use plastic bags; nor did they wear hideous jewelry and they were ignorant of cloth.

Obviously, they were very surprised at finding these objects, but they made a possible connection between this mystery and Horan. They had come here for him to judge, for him to guide.

Horan opened the bags. They contained weird, colored pills, rather like the regenerative pills eaten in the universe of Zod to fight off the effects of fatigue. An unpleasant shiver shook through Horan. This place could bring nothing but bad. It was lying completely under the shadow of Zod. However, the pills could come in handy. With his hands he told the silent men that they could bring the bags, but that they had to get back to the shelters fast.

That evening, he arranged the little bags in his hut and then lay down, resting his head on Animal's side. For a long time he watch Irn oiling her hair. There was a small fist of embers between them and a long thread of silent smoke.

CHAPTER IX

Times of day and night had passed by. How many exactly, Agaran could not say. He only had to think about it but he had no desire to make the effort, as small as it might be.

He lumbered across the room to the recorder and stood there, for a long while. A radio update from Telzoat had made him leave his post, interrupting his tale. There had been a certain number of times of day since then. He was coming back to the Machine for the first time since the alert.

An alert! Not even an alert. Telzoat had announced that his commando team had spotted the fugitive. He had been picked up by a clan of giants, somewhere in the crowded mess of the up above. The team was lying in wait, being very cautious. It was just a matter of choosing the right time... Agaran had hoped. But "the right time" Telzoat was waiting for might be a long time coming. The fugitive was literally smothered by the clan and to get near him without setting off a general alarm, and then risking a bunch of snags and setbacks, was impossible. They had to wait.

Agaran had waited. Forcing himself to hold his anxiety in check, to convince himself that the risk was not really great. These giants who had "adopted" the rebel were not dangerous, due to their very low I.Q. To discover an inhabitant of Zod, totally different from themselves must have unleashed some strange emotions among these monsters, but they did not have the necessary malice to examine it in depth. They had judged and explained it in their way and their way was not dangerous, to Zod.

But up above, there were other monsters. If they showed up and entered the game, they would likely be as disastrous as a bomb.

During all this time, Agaran strolled around Zod. He had walked through the rooms, searching for some mysterious clue to justify his anxiety. No clues. The general atmosphere was the same as always. No trace of revolt among the Subjects... The teaching classes were calm, too. They did not know. They were ignorant of the revolt of two students destined for death.

But if they did find out?

They could not find out. The Worker-Subjects in the room of "breathing machines" and their guard had been led to death and replaced right away.

Nobody could know...

However...

However, there was a rebel up above who had escaped from Zod and this had not happened even once in 22,000 years.

However, he had to remodel all the moral and religious structures of Zod, forestall the collapse that he felt coming... What methods should be used? You cannot overturn the ethic of a civilization overnight, even though this civilization, as a whole, is not destined for progress and evolution, but instead for the preservation and perpetuity of a certain sphere of knowledge.

Of course, it was necessary to resort to the soulless machines that synthesize and settle. The machines that work out solutions to the problems fed into them. But the machines only give the solution and they are useless for implementing the proposed results. To transform a coded formula into a concrete situation would be the job of Agaran and the Senior Teachers. Time would still be necessary, both their ally and enemy. Yes, it would take a lot of time to change the world of Zod and give it the possibility of holding on for 2,000 more years. To hold on until the Day of Light...

Agaran had never felt alone or weak. Right now, he felt alone and weak. Because a condemned child had not accepted the sentence, his mind all muddled by that poison—the instinct to live. And for a long time Agaran had believed he was master of that poison.

When he sat again before the recorder, his movements and attitude looked a little like someone going to bed. He sat like that for a little while, his hands flat in front of him, and then he nervously started the recording. The lights went on and Agaran spoke:

"Time has passed. A lot of time, during which I, Agaran, who is speaking, had hoped I wouldn't have to continue the story of Zod for those who, one day maybe, will find this document in the sterile ruins. During this lost time I hoped that those who are working for me and for Zod would have managed to destroy the risk. But the risk is still there and, in a way, even greater. It can still cause the fall of Zod. That's why I have to sit down again before this mechanical memory to record myself. I have to continue the story.

"Agar was the name of the man who created Zod. I'm pretty sure of this fact. And even if "Agar" represents a group, a particular knot of survivors, it's a term that we often find in different translations of the documents. Agar might represent a sum total of intelligence, of knowledge. That's why I'll speak of it as if it were the name of a man. For convenience.

"It's certain that before the cycle of biological disasters, before the war that pitted the rich against the wronged of the land, a portion of the elite safeguarding the treasures of intelligence and some of the quasi-immortals were able to predict the aforesaid events. This group, this fraction of the rich people figured it preferable to protect themselves against the effects of the disasters and catastrophes rather than sit idly by, enjoying the numerous benefits of their caste until the last minute.

"For this reason Agar built Zod. At a precise point on the planet, Zod was built. A world in miniature for the wise; a world that contained all the secrets, or at least all the means to produce these secrets. A world that would save them from the cataclysm.

"In Zod, a number of men and women shut themselves in, determined to wait.

"They waited. They were in the shelter when the cycle of disasters roared across the surface of the globe. They were there, in Zod on the mountain, after the great disaster I spoke of earlier. While the inhabitants on the surface of the planet lost their memory, their consciousness and turned into pitiful, wandering things, those in Zod became the sole survivors. I think they had to isolate themselves even more to fight against the effects of the annihilating gas.

"The entire surface of the planet and its atmosphere was biochemically contaminated for a long period of time. Zod had to wait.

"Zod is waiting.

"I can guarantee, on the strength of the documents I translated, that at some undefined epoch, the planet's crust must have suffered important geological modifications, for unknown reasons. It's probable that entire continents were sunk, that others were born, that mountains collapsed. The mountain on which Zod was built was one of these and once standing on top of the world, Zod

110

found itself buried under tons of earth and rock. This was probably *the* disaster. They had to get around the damage done quickly, dig tunnels connecting the world of safety to open air, implement air conditioning systems, ventilate and disinfect the air, create from scratch a "breathing machine". Create lungs for Zod. Consolidate the structures of rooms to withstand the enormous pressure from above, etc.

"All this was done. Zod, at present, right now as I speak, still has scars from this time.

"And the wait went on, for centuries. They just had to live and wait. They had overcome death. They could wait. Up above, the human waste from the disaster barely dragged on, through mutations, toward a new consciousness.

"But the waiting time was getting long for those in Zod. They were prepared for everything except this life they had received as a "gift", this perpetual life. There were a hundred of them, maybe, hardly more. A hundred, eternally, forever, in the same, relatively restricted space. Condemned to life in Zod, unable to go back to the surface. (They had predicted the disaster, but not the means of causing it, or the flood, the deluge of annihilating gas: what they had in the way of "vaccines" and "serums" for this infirmity of consciousness was definitely not enough to protect them during a normal lifetime on the surface. And what could they do faced with the human animals that were repopulating the planet?)

"Some resumed the abandoned research on the possibilities of "life in death". Boredom came.

"After a number of undetermined centuries, some of them asked to die. They'd had enough of waiting. They couldn't wait any longer.

"Agar gave in to their demand. But with their deaths, they couldn't abandon the experiment and let everything fall into oblivion. He had to go back and reconsider the biological problem of the transmission of life. For a long time sexual pleasures hadn't, in any way, had anything to do with procreation, but were experienced through the normal absorption of drugs. For a long time, the implantation of sperm and the culture of fertilized ova had stopped being put in artificial placentas. Why would they have kept these outmoded methods, they who had life for all eternity? And Zod was not equipped with the old machines that created life. They didn't want to go back to the processes of mechanical preservation—lack of equipment, impossible to create from scratch, impossible to get it from the surface. Life didn't interest them anymore.

"Agar managed to perfect a machine that could accept new life, but as a fetus. So, it was necessary to use women again. This was the only condition laid down before his final approval for their deaths. The women accepted. They were inoculated and progenitor cells were transplanted in them. Then the five-month old fetuses were taken and poured into the artificial matrices of the "Birth Machine". And those who wanted to die did so.

"The new roots of a new generation were planted in Zod. Who could have predicted the reactions of this generation once the members became adults? Nobody, not even Agar. So, he had to take basic precautions to preserve the scientific legacy of the survivors and save it from a possible uprising of those born without knowing, but destined to eternal life. Agar found the solution by another limited return to the past and an essential modification of the deoxyribonucleic acids, the carriers of heredity: those who came into the world, out of the in-cubators, were new mortals, genetically programmed for a life comprised of two thirds training period and only one third "adult" period. As a result, the modifications of DNA gave more or less open personalities to the cervical cortex that was more or less stocked in neuroneurolgic structuring.

"The time came when Zod was occupied only by these new subjects of the "old way". Males and females endowed with the power of death and thereby even that of evolution. Males and females who lived, died and reproduced through artificial insemination because Agar had had the foresight to keep the source of pleasure through the sexual act bottled up in them: although they had to go back to archaisms, there was no need to adopt all of them.

"Agar was alone and he watched his world live.

"He watched for a long time, for centuries. He watched the natural mutations evolve under their particu-lar living conditions. He noticed that the lifetimes were getting gradually shorter for all of his subjects. Natural selection played a big part and at first Agar thought it was a good thing; he made a kind of religion out of the natural phenomenon. It was necessary to give a goal, a reason for living to these subjects. A reason that they would accept and preserve after Agar was gone.

"For, Agar, too, was tired, after countless years of patience in Zod. And at this time, the possibilities of leaving Zod were zilch. He couldn't let his subjects out of the world of Zod, the only world they knew. And their atrophied intelligence wouldn't allow them to recon-struct the world lost before the disaster on the surface—they would've had to reconquer the planet for this, which was still in the hands of the old mutants who continued their slow, unseen evolution.

"Agar decided to die. He, the last expert of the great secrets. So, he prepared down to the last detail for the time after his death, giving some instructions to certain chief-subjects of the race. The chain of life had to go on—through it the message would perpetuate until it was time.

"Firstly, Agar transcribed some of the principle secrets (or judged as such) in the pictures and panels that decorate this room and that are the blueprints for psychic transfer. He left a pile of documents, some of which have been translated by me and in particular contain the story I've been telling. Many still remain hermetic. Many were badly translated before me and because of their distortion are almost lost to human comprehension.

"Then Agar gave his orders to those who would lead the race and who would know certain things. And that's how, after his death, all of Agar's memory was transferred into a few embryos so that the descendants of these fetuses would hold within them, progressively, the possibility of the intelligence needed to save Zod.

"Among the subjects of Zod, then, an unborn class was arising, able to learn, little by little, as time passed—not to learn everything, or too early, but progressively. Remember, over the course of time...

"They would be able to understand, in their time, the messages left by Agar. They and their sons. And no one but them, destined to lead the chain of life unto the final goal of new beginnings. They would no longer hold the dangerous secrets inherently: they would have to earn them, to discover them.

"That's how it was.

"And those who were let in on the secret, being mortal, died. And the chain of life rolled on in Zod.

"I, Agaran, come directly from the fetuses selected by Agar, my ancient father, I was born in Zod. I had the power to learn and to escape from the social system then in force in this world. I could read the pictures, certain pictures that are very complicated calculations. In time, I could read them and raise myself to the top of the hierarchy of Zod. Thanks to the graphics I avoided death by transplanting my psychic energy into an eternal body, totally synthetic and manufactured. I'm not human. I'm better: I'm post-human. I'm the knowledge that will save Zod and avoid a new disaster in the world above.

"But I have not yet discovered the principles of spontaneous regeneration that will immunize the human body against the effects of aging and death. I have not discovered the secrets of memory transplants. I don't know many things. If I have the time, I will find them. If, up above, the risk is not a real danger…

"I have 2,000 years left, roughly. I know this thanks to the Machine to count time, the machine created by Agar, my ancient and first father. I also know this from everything Zod has picked up about the life and evolution of the monsters up there, above our sky of Earth.

CHAPTER X

The members of the "Surface" commando team were not talkative, which was just as well. They were not surprised at the orders they received either, or at the environment (extraordinary to say the least) surrounding them for the last few days. They had been conditioned to obey and act, nothing more.

If Telzoat had given them the order, they would have attacked, without the slightest hesitation, the whole clan of savage mutants, without even realizing that, in spite of their "perfected" weapons, the outcome of the battle would certainly not have been favorable to them.

Telzoat was there. He was the mind and soul of the team.

But the envoys from Zod did not make a frontal assault on the clan of savage men. In no way did they try to take the rebel child by force from the "protective surveillance" of the naked giants. This method was unquestionably doomed to failure.

They just observed. Observed attentively, without missing a second, marvelously hidden in the vines and leaves of this strange world. Simply observed... impatiently waiting for the right moment, the opportunity... It was like this, for days and nights, without an opportunity presenting itself once.

The calls from Agaran the Master in buried Zod became more and more urgent. But action was not possible. Telzoat was watching the child live, observing his acclimation with growing curiosity. That animal with powerful fangs almost never left his side—or when it was not the animal, it was the giant couple in the shelter where he lived—either the man or the woman. Sometimes the child took a little walk by himself, but it was in the heart of the "village" and he was surrounded then, at a respectable distance, by a watchful, mindful crowd. He, too, was naked now, or practically naked, wearing nothing but a strip of animal skin tied around his waist. Tiny and naked and white in the midst of these gigantic people.

One day a group of men from this tribe left the clan's confines to go into the forest. They brought the child with them. A sudden anxiety shook Telzoat's entire being. The danger for Zod was not great, not really a danger, as long as the child stayed in the confined sphere of the clan, as long as no foreign presence wormed its way into this sphere. But, now... a hole was being dug in the sphere—a hole to elsewhere!

The "Surface" commando team from Zod, Telzoat at their head, took great pains to follow the group of savages and the child. All the way to the pile of anachronistic objects in a small sylvan clearing on the edge of a water channel. These objects represented the danger. They were out of place here. They were the voice of other monsters, certainly more worrisome than the giants who had welcomed the child.

They had taken some of these objects and returned to their clan, Telzoat and his team in their wake.

And Telzoat had revealed nothing of this discovery to Agaran the Master. But he had decided to act. His orders were precise and the members appointed to the commando team had executed them like the perfect human robots that they were.

Every day, alone or in groups, men from the clan went into the forest, armed with those strange, long tubes with which they killed animals. To spot one of these giants by himself was easy; to knock him out with a shot from the annihilating pistol was easier still. Then they only had to steal his "weapon" and ammunition. As it turned out, it was not a tube but a rope of unknown substance stretched between two ends of a curved branch. The arched tension, pulled tight and released, propelled the straight, sharp shafts across a rather long distance.

The next step of the "program" required several days of effort from this faction of the team in charge of the mission. Four times of day and three of night, to be exact. At the end of this period, the five men came back and found Telzoat and the rest of the group still on the lookout around the giants' camp. They were bringing good news and Telzoat was delighted to learn that another clan of giants had been spotted two days away and two members of this clan were killed with shots from the annihilator. The flying wooden shafts had been stuck into their dead bodies.

Now they just had to wait.

This time, Telzoat got in touch with Agaran to inform him of the situation.

Something was different from before.

This something was not visible, but it wafted through the atmosphere with the air they breathed. It was in the gestures and eyes of the people of Roarg. And it was not something good.

Of course, Horan noticed it. When he became aware of it, he could not say exactly how long this state of affairs had lasted; at what precise moment the routine had changed its tone. He asked Roarg some awkward questions using the words he knew and the gestures that seemed best to him. Whether he understood or not,

Roarg did not give a satisfactory answer. He stopped at saying that a man of his people had fallen asleep unnaturally in the middle of the jungle. When he woke up, his weapons had been stolen.

There seemed to be a mystery in this that far surpassed the giants' understanding. A mystery on top of the "things found in the forest". And mystery was synonymous with fear.

They were scared. That was it.

These gigantic beings were scared, in this incredible world that they seemed, however, to have tamed.

That was the change. It was the fear that loomed over the group of shelters. The fear in the eyes of the men and women when they met Horan's.

Days went by like this. Horan still played with Animal and slept on its side watching Irn's tall, smooth body and dreaming that he could make up his mind to cuddle against her belly. Irn, too, was scared, that was obvious. Her eyes were no longer the same as "before". He wanted to know the words to comfort her. And this was as irrational as could be, this desire to comfort her, because he, too, was slowly being pervaded by fear.

A viscous breath was floating over everything, everywhere. A breath that stained his face, that crept into him...

When he woke up that morning, he knew that the fear had taken on a new air. He felt it without really knowing why or how. Then he noticed the silence. A total, absolute silence. Nothing but the roving cries of the green world. Nothing else.

Then, swiftly, he left the hut but stood stock still on the threshold. The group of shelters was not abandoned, as he believed at first. Quite the contrary. Everyone was there, gathered before his shelter. Unmoving. Silent. Everyone, men and women, were there, waiting. At the front of them were Roarg, Irn and old Logh.

"What's wrong with you?" Horan asked.

Roarg had one of his twisted smiles and signed to him not to be scared. Roarg had never deceived him, never even tried. Horan felt better, instinctively.

Then, in a series of gestures accentuated with one or two words, the giant told him that he had to follow Logh the elder. Horan nodded and through the middle of the parting crowd, feeling a little nauseous, he followed the old man. They crossed the entire empty space in the middle of the huts and entered Logh's shelter.

The silence was still as thick and monolithic.

The darkness was heavy inside the hut and only a fist of smoldering embers diffused a meager light. Horan felt like his stomach was crawling up his throat. Everywhere in this half-light, on the walls of the shelter, were masks with gaping eyes and strange ornaments. And the smell, some kind of smoke...

Logh sat near the embers before inviting Horan to sit across from him. Horan was in no condition to refuse. After he had squatted down, the old man launched into a long, chaotic speech. The words came out of his mouth without his lips moving, like a stream of water running down a rock. He made a lot of gestures too, struggling so hard and so well that Horan thought he finally understood that they were going to try to "talk" together. They were going to understand each other. The elder had the means.

The old man waited a few seconds and then took from the fire a kind of firebrand with a burning tip and he put it between his lips. He sucked on it a few times and his wrinkled mask grew frightfully darker, deformed in the red glow creating the most hideous effect. Then he exhaled big clouds of pungent smoke. For Horan it was absolutely impossible to look anywhere else. Only that grimacing, swollen, deflated face…

And soon… soon he was unable to see anything but that burning tip of the firebrand. Nothing else. But the point grew bigger and bigger, became a red sun, huge, fantastic! A ball of fire that was sucking in old Logh, deforming him horribly until he was entirely swallowed up. Afterward, the ball of fire pushed back the walls of the hut, split them apart, blew them up.

There was no ball of fire, no hut, no old man. There was nothing but a great, flat expanse, completely flat and red. A smooth ground without the smallest cleft, without the tiniest crack or the puniest bump. Above the ground, a sky. A sky that was not smoke nor earth. A great, red expanse, like the ground. But it was the sky. He needed to know and Horan knew it.

Horan was there, on the ground, or maybe on the sky. It was impossible to tell. But he was there.

He was not scared or thirsty or anything, or hot. He did not feel like he had a body. And yet, he had one and could move it. He could sit at will, get up, walk. He just had to want to. So, he started walking, all the while remaining seated. It was easy to do.

To say how long the walk lasted is impossible. There was no time or any system to measure duration. Duration must not have existed.

All of a sudden, at the exact spot where the sky was spinning around to become the earth and the ground, at this exact spot—which was not exact—of a curved universe—which was not a universe and not curved—the thing materialized.

It was very far away, but suddenly very close. It looked like the flying animals that the giants killed, except it walked like a man and was definitely alive.

It stopped in front of Horan, who was walking, and Horan stopped, too. The living thing was very small, much smaller than normal. Horan could have crushed it with one stomp of his foot. He did not do that because he felt no need or desire to...

"My name is Tôo," the thing said.

"Mine's Horan," Horan said.

"I know," Tôo said.

Horan said something that he forgot immediately after the words were out of his mouth.

"I am the people of Roarg," Tôo said.

"No," Horan said, "because the people of Roarg are very big."

"That's true," Tôo said. "These people are very big, but you are still bigger than all the people."

Harmful beings showed up on the edge of the horizon that did not exist. Horan knew right away that these beings were harmful because they looked like things that existed in Zod. They did not have clear-cut forms, but it did not matter: what mattered above all was the impression they engraved in Horan's mind.

"Don't fear anything," Tôo said calmly. "It's not necessary. Here, you don't have to be scared."

"I know you are the people of Roarg," Horan said. And it was true. Roarg's people were something living that was called Tôo.

"Come," Tôo said.

Horan followed Tôo.

Together, without a word, they walked for a long time. Once in a while, on the flat ground, rocky blades stuck out, shaped like arms stretched out toward the disguised sky. Tôo was not watching out for them. He was walking like a beautiful round rock.

Then the sharp blades duplicated and started screaming. A force pushed Horan past Tôo and he led the march from now on. There were many screams and many sharp blades, but it was Horan who said, "Come, follow me, Tôo."

It was like that without changing. Without changing. Without changing.

And like that until the blades disappeared to give way to a multitude of living things like Tôo. A sea of Tôos. Colored and noisy. Infinite.

Horan did not slow his pace and he crossed the colored sea without a problem, Tôo the only one behind him. Then the cries and the colors vanished. And Horan turned around, alone in the middle of the void, facing Tôo.

They remained the two of them. All around there was nothing but sky and ground. Nothing more. Nothing around. Simply Horan and Tôo.

"That's good," Tôo said.

And then, again, Horan spoke for a long time. The words barely out of his mouth, he forgot them. They were precise words, well used. But he did not know them.

It was Logh's shelter again and the half-light and smoke. But the red dot in the middle of the old man's face had disappeared.

Now there were a few short flames racing over the fire between the stones, enough to light up the scene. Horan was in a corner of the hut, lying on his back. The masks and ornaments hanging on the wall were scattered over the ground now, in a terrible mess, everywhere.

And Logh the elder had collapsed in the middle of these objects, his body covered in blood, his skin ripped apart.

But the fear had left Horan. Just a kind of dazed worry...

Outside, like a breath of wind, the syncopated, monotone chant was rumbling softly. Endless. Eternally repeated.

Then, panting again, old Logh spoke to Horan. He spoke and Horan understood!

He spoke without opening his mouth, without looking at him, without moving. He remained prostrate, breathing hard, haggard... And the words entered Horan like translated images.

"You are with us, thank you," Logh was saying. "You are the strength and you come from the Earth. With you, we will be strong and the bad luck looming over us will end. I know where the bad luck comes from and I know how to fight against it and free him among us from whom fate stole his hunting weapons. I know. You will be with us and you will give us the strength."

He became quiet. At the same time, his body sat up slowly; his smiling eyes fell upon Horan. With surprising agility, the old giant jumped to his feet and approached the child. His huge, wrinkled hands were very soft and he helped the child stand up. He led him outside.

Outside, there was the crowd, there was the blinding light of day, on the bare skin of this crowd. The crowd stopped chanting.

Then, at the top of his lungs, Logh screamed out some things. Things that Horan did not understand. But he understood the joy, the relief of the crowd! He was with them in their cry of happiness. He was with them, with Roarg, with Irn who was smiling again, with everyone. The people parted to let Animal through. Animal was jumping around like a mad dog.

In this brand new joy, incomprehensible and yet… normal. In this joy, at one point, Horan tried to remember what had happened in Logh's hut. But he could not. Probably nothing had happened in Logh's hut.

CHAPTER XI

Then they started dancing, for Horan and for Logh, both sitting before the entrance of the hut. Maybe, too, it was a dance for themselves…

An unreal dance.

They had lit a big fire with branches in the empty space in the middle of the group of huts. And the dance was there, like the flames, a second flame. The dance was human fire.

For hours, without stopping once, the people spun around tirelessly. The women were together apart, in a long, double line. They were swaying back and forth on their heels. Always this same movement while out of their tightly closed lips arose a deep chant with little modulation.

A chant like the tide, like an ocean swell, that rises, crescendo, to reach its peak for a long moment, in a single, shrill note, before dropping straight down, heavy, to resume its climb again right away.

Facing the women on the other side of the dance, were three groups of men beating in rhythm on weird containers with a membrane stretched over the mouth. They beat with their palms or used little, wooden hammers. And the music mingled with the women's chanting, with the shuffling feet of the dancers.

Horan did not understand. But he was very excited and, justifiably, wanted to understand. In him, all the strange events he had participated in or had been witness to in this astonishing world, all the warmly tinged memories resurfaced and jostled around anarchically. Here, men and plants were gigantic. They had welcomed him among them, had fed him with fruits and vegetables, without even asking him to work in exchange. Without asking anything of him.

Strange men commensurate with the strange world they lived in.

Here, there were rivers. The women made bloody, bawling babies in their own bodies. Here, there were many different races of living beings, sub-races, some of which were killed and others not. Here, the night sky was like a gigantic copy of the room to count time.

Here, in Logh's hut, one could sometimes understand the language of the naked men, without even trying and without anyone talking. Time, all of life could sometimes explode all of a sudden, in Logh's hut.

There were still other mysteries in this world. Other terrible mysteries that brought fear into the eyes of men. Like a parallel life, an addition, an invisible, impalpable life, made from the tightly woven network that seemed to cover the entire world.

There were dances and chants and music...

When evening came, the dancers were still spinning and the women still swaying. An infernal round, slow and stubborn, that seemed like it would never stop, never, despite the sweat on the naked bodies smeared with colored earth, despite the wincing faces, twisted in pain, the eyes rolled upward and empty.

A mechanism. A law.

The sight took on a new dimension of troubling surrealism in the night swept by the crazy bursts of flame.

It's a celebration, Horan thought. A grand, terrible celebration.

But he repeated this too often to be really and truly convinced. He was there, next to Logh. Somewhere in the round. Roarg was spinning. Somewhere in the chant Irn's lips were closed like the dozens of others over the low note of the song. But the chant was becoming dance and vice versa. With the chant and the dance it was as if the giants knew the secrets to bring out of the shadows something of this other parallel and invisible life that hung over the jungle.

The music and the forms were in Horan; they took possession of his entire being. He could not help thinking of the red dot in Logh's hut; and he was waiting for the explosion.

It did not come. Instead, some dancers suddenly started leaping high over the fire, then rolling on the ground, groaning, drooling, eyes rolled up white. They were "exploding", each for himself, and no one worried about them. It was the same for some of the women who abruptly dropped to their knees, rigid, their faces stiffer than a stone mask.

And then all of a sudden, it was over.

No more dance, no more crazy round. No more chant or music. Just like that, all at once. No more anything.

But the fire still up and the dazed bodies of the dancers motionless, panting, like broken down inside for a moment, disoriented.

The silence and the distant sounds of the night.

Then, finally, after a long while, the men got the use of their legs back. They dispersed slowly, left the circle of the round. Those who had fallen on the ground got up. The double line of women also scattered.

On Horan and on Logh—still frozen and apparently lost—the night weighed down like terrible steel.

Then the men were there again. No longer dazed or dumbfounded, but perfectly conscious, perfectly awake... and in their hands they held those weird weapons that hurled the murderous shafts or the small thorns that could kill with a scratch. They were also carrying long, pointed sticks beautifully decorated with skin-of-beings-that-fly. They gathered before the old master in silence. Roarg was at the front of the line. With his eyes and hands he asked Horan to stand up and Horan stood up. He asked him to follow them and Horan joined them and entered their silence and smell.

Then, with the child among them, tiny, the troop left the huts and disappeared into the humid thickness of the monstrous, green carnival.

At one point Roarg came next to Horan. He bent down, grabbed him around the waist and lifted him onto his shoulders, without a word.

The march continued. It was absolutely impossible to see more than a few feet ahead in the wild, hazy tangle of the night. However, Horan felt all the members of the troop, there, around Roarg, scattered in the high leaves. They were there and they were moving forward like shadows in the shadow, just as silently, without the tiniest twig cracking to betray their presence.

Roarg's march rocked Horan gently; so gently, so regularly that his eyes got heavy and heavier until they finally closed all together.

A violent jolt. A jolt inside. How long had he slept?

The sudden light was in him and all around. While Roarg was putting him down on a high tree stump, Horan had time to see the cleft in the bushes. For a second he thought the troop had returned to the shelters after a mysterious trek around the jungle. Then he corrected himself.

It was not the group of huts of Roarg's people. It was another. Very little difference between the two places: same huts made of branches, same arrangement. There were simply a few more of them and a little less jungle. For the rest, hazy outlines busy at various tasks among the shelters; some living beings pretty much identical to Animal ferreting around here and there.

Dead calm in the first lights of day and the croaking, chirping blanket stretched evenly over the gaping jungle.

A calm that suddenly burst, gutted by a thousand howls that ripped through the child's chest at the same time. Stunned, jaw dropped, he saw the nearby thickets spit out a multitude of men running full speed, shaking their wooden weapons. He did not understand right away that they were the same men who had danced all day, the men with whom he had crossed part of the forest perched on Roarg's shoulders. The men who knew how to walk silently in the night...

They were pouring out now like a storm wind, naked, howling, into the cool morning steam. They were running toward the peaceful group of shelters!

At that moment Horan had still not understood. He screamed, "Why are you doing this?"

Without knowing. Without hearing his yell among the cries. His belly knotted by a strange fear. Bad...

Nor did he understand when he saw the first silhouette collapse to the ground over there, at the entrance to a hut, its chest pierced by three thorns. Then Roarg's painted devils were in the circle of the shelters. And there was another dance. A terrible dance.

Then, Horan understood that Roarg and his giants had come there to kill. To kill like they killed the things that fly. But this time the targets were men, women and children. Naked giants like themselves, but whose brown bodies had no paint on them.

A hideous sight.

He was standing up on the tree stump at the edge of the jungle, his legs trembling and his heart beating wildly. Petrified in horror and incomprehension, and despite his disgust he was unable to take his eyes off the hideous sight.

Everywhere screaming, howling, running like mad.

He saw women running frantically to break through the circle of attackers; he saw these women skewered alive on the stakes, splattering blood every which way; and screaming that froze his blood. He saw Roarg's killers stab away at these victims, digging into the steaming guts of their falling bodies with their spears. Red blood spurting, spurting so strong and so high! Flooding the grass, which was still wet with the night's remains.

The children who were running around aimlessly, too scared to scream, who were just running in the carnage and the deadly dance; and at the last second, a devil jumped up and grabbed their leg, hoisted them in the air to smash them as hard as they could on the ground, again and again, like hammering a stake into the dirt; and finally throwing the broken little body away. Throwing it and beating on it to crack open the chest with two blows from a stone sword and plunge their hands into the warm, slimy, fuming of what was, maybe, not yet totally dead, though still not totally alive.

He saw Roarg, yes, Roarg, go at a child like this! And with his lips he tasted red magma dripping grotesquely between his fingers and down his arms that were still bristling with soft arteries and drooping stuff.

"Roarg!"

A scream. A tiny scream, lost in the tumult. A scream that not one of these giant madmen heard. Over there, big puddles of blood were spreading through the walls of mud and branches. Huge bodies, mountains of muscles crumbled, hacked up, ripped apart, burst open, bespattered.

Then the first of Roarg's men fell, too, likewise mowed down.

Horan realized that he was running, that he was not frozen on the tree stump anymore. He was running amidst the screams without knowing why, possessed by an unnamable horror. He cried out Roarg's name. The entire earth toppled over and Horan's feet got bogged down in the chaos, fell into a warm, red chasm. He threw himself back with all his might; his hands and face were slimy. The dead woman's eyes, hollow and blind, stared at him. Next to her, a small, red, mutilated pile that used to be her son.

"Roarg!" Horan roared, petrified.

He had the feeling that the dance was stopping, that the screams were fading into another world, that the movements were slowing down, were heavier. Weightier. A nasty, warm rush surged into his throat, drowned his eyes and burned his scalp.

Then he heard cries of joy from Roarg and his men. And cries of horror from the others.

He saw them flee as fast as they could in all directions into the jungle. He saw an old man who was nothing but a carcass of wrinkles, totally petrified, unable to move at all. And he, Horan, was the cause of his stupor.

The old man fell, without a scream, without looking away, pierced all over by a handful of shafts.

"Roarg!" Horan called desperately.

He was there, amidst the corpses and the victory shouts. He was covered in blood and in all this blood a perfectly white smile cut across his face.

"Why did you do this?" Horan mumbled.

Roarg did not hear him. He lifted the child onto his shoulders again and started dancing.

Telzoat's white face was rather tense. After hesitating for a long time, he slipped the cover off his chest mic, which stuck out of his right breast, and contacted Zod. He reached Senior Teacher Raruth and said:

"Nothing's gone as planned. It seems that the rational acts of these monsters are totally unpredictable. Their common sense, if they have any, certainly does not obey the same criteria as ours.

"As a result of our previous action, it would seem logical that the neighboring tribe we discovered would accuse our tribe and decide to take vengeance. Through this act of war, letting the work be done for us, we'd have the opportunity to get the rebel back.

"Nothing of the sort happened. On the contrary, for some unknown reason, our clan took it upon themselves to start the war—I think, perhaps, the decision had something to do with our attack on one of the giants of their clan—and it brought the battle to the neighboring tribe. Why exactly this one? I'm not able to say: maybe it's the only one in the area or maybe the two clans have been at war for a long time, I don't know.

"The rebel child participated in the combat by his presence. It appears that just his being there decided the outcome. Once the surprise of the attack wore off, it didn't look so good for his friends and they were about to be outnumbered when the rebel arrived in the middle of the carnage. He surprised and terrified his friends' enemies—they had never seen a Subject of Zod... They probably believed it some ineffable mystery and so ran away.

"It's obvious that the rebel's tribe, now more than ever, considers him a god, a representative of a benign force. Obvious that they attribute their unthinkable victory to some action of the rebel—maybe just his aura.

"Now they've left the site of the massacre to return to their camp. We're following them.

"Things are getting out of hand and I can't say whether the rebel realizes the influence he has over these savages. If yes, with the help of his twisted mind, which he already turned against Zod, he'll use this influence, his superiority, to his utmost. No matter what the cost, we have to act now."

Without waiting for an answer, cutting short any comment he might dislike, Telzoat broke off the transmission.

He could have felt really happy, filled with joy, flooded with an inexpressible amount of love and respect. This time, he was sure, the songs and dances were for him. Only for him.

It was like that day on the river when he had accompanied Roarg and he had killed a lot of living things under the water. It was just like that, but multiplied by a hundred, a thousand. In the middle of this riot of shouting, of laughing, in the fantastic carnival of smiles and stretched out arms, in the circle of women dancing for him, he was not happy. There was a huge hole. A huge emptiness. There was burning and a noxious odor.

Roarg, Logh, Irn… Everyone. Everyone there… Yes, they had welcomed him and had not done him any harm. But it was not free. It was not riches discovered in a magnificent illumination. For all the fruits and smiles and energy they spent to make him happy, for all their efforts they asked for his presence, Horan's presence among them.

For, he was the other. He was a mystery that sprang out of the forest one day, next to Animal, whom they thought had disappeared into the belly of the Earth. He was a total mystery, an unknown force that was good luck for the slaughter.

And they were scared of the mystery; they were scared of him; they had never stopped being scared of him. And this fear would grow over time, with the constant "exploits"… until the day when a wooden shaft would be stuck in his heart, too. He was a danger. So, they had to keep him. Acting like they did toward him they were earning his good graces. They would keep him with them, forbid him to go and spread the effects of his force anywhere else.

Fear…

No, it was not free. It was simple and fair and good and normal.

For the first time in a long time, in this disgust, in this emptiness flooding him, tears came and ran down the cheeks of the child, who was watching, without seeing, the dance of giants consumed by fear.

That night, the dances were long again before dying out. The women were still rolling around before his eyes and the chanting was still echoing in his ears when he went to the hut to lie down on his bed of furs.

Roarg! Roarg who knew so well how to smash up children and eat their steaming entrails... Roarg, worn out, had fallen to the ground.

Irn... There was still Irn. Only Irn. She was sleeping, too, in this soft half-light that was only pierced by the usual pile of burning embers. Irn and her supple movements, her skin with copper glints, her long hair striking her face, her chest firm, straight, round.

Only Irn.

But he did not take two steps in her direction and this desperate surge of emotion lasted only a few seconds, cut short by Irn's panicky eyes that, like all the rest, were scared, now more than ever, and did not know how to hide it.

So, he went back to bed. And he knew that he would never be like a giant's child, balled up against the warm belly of a woman.

That night, the skinny child, the hollow child from Zod stood up on his bed, without a sound, really without making a sound. He tightened the loincloth around his waist and through the cord slipped a pack of the regenerating pills that they had found in the forest. He would need them in the course of his journey.

He had never felt the world as vast around him... He had never seen himself so small...

He left. He could not stay there.

He left and did not know where he was going. But he went.

He knew nothing (or very little) of the fantastic world in which he had landed. Nothing except that the forgotten magic words were probably not actually represented in this world; that they were simply impressions of nonexistent riches. Dreams of children.

The words did not exist.

He left the circle of huts without looking back, not for Irn or for anything.

Then he went straight into the forest, straight ahead and fast to get as far as possible from this place before the light came.

At one point he stopped, all his senses alert, concentrating on the rustling of leaves behind him, ready to run, to flee anywhere, as quickly as possible, as wildly as possible. And Animal poured out of a bunch of tall grass, paused, as if it was trying to understand, then came up to him, to the hollow child, its glistening eye, wagging its rear end.

CHAPTER XII

When Telzoat's commando team got back to the world of Zod, Agaran was there in person to welcome his First Senior Teacher.

Agaran looked happy.

In a few words, he congratulated Telzoat who, it seemed, was trying hard to look polite and thankful. And Agaran did not notice his stiffness, or, if he did, he did not say anything.

Telzoat said, "I don't deserve any credit for what happened. It had to happen like that..."

"Of course," Agaran admitted lightheartedly. Under other circumstances he would probably have detected the strange bitterness tainting Telzoat's words.

In very strict secret, the surface commando team was brought to one of the Death Chambers and reduced to definitive silence. No trace of the abnormal events could remain. No trace would remain.

After this, Telzoat requested a long period of rest. And it was granted. Before heading for the Sleep Chamber, he said, "I think we should fix those worn out ventilation ducts as soon as possible."

"It'll be done," Agaran agreed. He watched Telzoat until the door of the Sleep Chamber closed behind him. Then he let out a heavy sigh and went slowly back to his private den.

How long had he been sitting there, anxiously brooding in front of the recording panel? How long had he been waiting in frustration?

Today, Agaran the Master had taken his sweet time, giving himself the pleasure of savoring the moment. Then, finally, he made up his mind and sat in the padded, steel chair, hands flat on the table. He hesitated a long time, then a short time, and suddenly nodded his head, before turning on the device.

But this time, the fluttering microphone was bound to remain unused. Agaran had sat there not to speak, but to listen. To listen and maybe relive the hours of recent anguish and, who knows, to tremble one last time in hindsight.

His voice exploded out of the mesh and lights of the speaker. Agaran swiftly adjusted the controls and sat back to listen to a specific entry: the last. He was comfortable in his chair; his unblinking eyes stared at the speaker. He listened:

"If by chance the world of Zod collapses one day, the present risk—the risk that made me speak—will not be the cause. This message might just fall into the hands of the monsters who live above the sky of Zod and who will bring about its destruction. There might also be some survivors in Zod who will resist and cleverly escape the wrath. They might be the ones who preserve this message.

"That's why it is addressed to both the monsters on the surface and to the subjects of Zod.

"Men of Zod, as you listen, you will understand certain secrets and you will know the reason for such strict laws in Zod.

"Men up above, as you listen to this language of mine, that you will certainly translate, you will understand not only my secrets and those of Zod, but also the danger that lies in wait if you continue in your errors.

"That's why this message is addressed to two distinct kinds of understanding, two totally different societies. Whether it fall into the hands of the one or the other whoever is lucky enough to hear and understand, they will tell the difference and take from it what they need.

(A short silence, then, again, more firmly, Agaran's voice):

"After the biological disaster and its nuclear aftershocks had swept all of conscious life off the surface of the planet, after this world had become the cursed territory of the solar system, life, however, continued in Zod, as I said before. Life continued likewise on the surface of the planet, down through the centuries, as I also said. At first, those who had not died were really no longer human but total, brainless idiots, without the slightest trace of memory—empty bodies.

"The hybrids were the first to go, but we can still imagine that some crossbreeding took place, through the instinct of racial preservation, if we can say that, between hybrids of all kinds and the humans.

"The race became a hodgepodge, the result of the explosive combination of multiple genes, certain of which had been modified by the radiation. But the race survived. And at the same time as the hidden evolution in Zod, another, slower, time-hungry evolution was unfolding on the surface. A people of subjects not much richer than the mutating animals that they lived among! Caricatures of men.

"They had no more conscious memory, but there was still this deeply-buried mechanism of fabrication that was bound to enrich them again. They were bound to rebuild their lost consciousness that could sort the sum total of lived experiences in the memory to make knowledge of it.

"That's how it was and time passed. That's how it was according to the immutable law of eternal rebirth. Men were naked, mentally, but little by little some of them discovered the first "clothes" of an evolution toward knowledge. Groups were formed, peoples were born and with them, to guard them from the fear that every force causes, social structures to protect the clan, then the people. Laws to make them not just a formless mishmash of more or less conscious beings, but a real force able to live and survive in the heart of the chaotic dance.

"Among these peoples, some structures held out well through the centuries while the individual human, over generations, gathered the fruits of knowledge.

"Today, you monsters living on the surface are all the descendants of these first mutations that survived the disaster. And you know nothing about it, except for a few subjects, maybe, who sometimes formulate arcane hypotheses that are immediately judged absurd by the societies.

"You believe you are the more beautiful "machine" created by natural law or by the gods whom you invented at one time or another solely to preserve those social structures that are the basis of evolution. You are neither of these, but simply beings endowed with a certain form of reason on the road of lost consciousness. You have discovered nothing—just rediscovered.

"Maybe it was the same for those who gave birth to the people I came from some 50,000 years ago. And those who awoke to consciousness on the threshold of those far-off 50,000 years were maybe picking themselves up after a terrible disaster that had just swallowed up an even greater season of man. And on and on. Maybe we're God, its remote descendants, season after season, sliding through natural evolutions toward irremediable decline. Maybe we're God in a state of death, dying. Maybe that's our life, we humans below, and also mine. Yes, God who was the time to launch the process; God who was. And straightaway died... God has been dead for a long time—thanks to that we're alive.

"Maybe it's like that. Nobody can categorically affirm or deny it. Mystery is the very essence of the phenomenon life.

"I'm speaking like this because I know the cycle of seasons of man. It is inscribed in your sky and some of you know it as well, even though you pay no attention to it.

"Agar, my ancient father, knew the law of the cycle as well."

"In your most evolved societies you call this law the "Precession of the equinoxes". I, like Agar, call it the "Law of Zod". For my people, it's a matter for the Machine to count time. You, too, have divided the sky into a dozen parts of 30° angles and in each part, in each slice, is a particular constellation. The names you use are: Capricorn, Sagittarius, Scorpio, Libra, etc. You have, moreover, sometimes made strange use of them for predictions... You know the sun's role as calculator, which tells you, depending on its location determined by the equinox in such or such constellation, such or such slice of 30° of the sky, the period in which you're living in the course of the cycle.

"It has been established and some of you know it, some of you make it the first law of life, that the location of the vernal point in some such celestial sign measures the evolution of human knowledge in the cycle of seasons of man. Your Capricorn sign equals the period of disasters that swept life away. The next, the sign of Sagittarius, marks the new beginning. And so on goes evolution, little by little, because it requires a lot of time to accumulate experiences and this time is calculated, naturally, on the vernal progression of the sun in your sky.

"Right now, the sun in the equinox has just left the celestial "slice" of Pisces. And you are entering Aquarius. This slice of the cycle, like the others, will last approximately 2,000 years. Then the age of Capricorn will come, which will end the cycle and for 2,000 years continue to destroy the ascent of man toward the light.

"You are not unaware of this law. For all time, in every cycle, it's a known law that comes in its time, like a terrible sign given to human destiny for its protection. Like a terrible threat that should redirect the efforts of intelligence to avoid the final disaster.

"As if God did not want to die too quickly.

"And this law given to man can save him, save God from total destruction, for a few hundred thousand cycles. But man does not understand. He has never known anything but to have hope in God or deny it, while maybe it's God who has hope in him.

"I, Agaran, also know this law and its meaning. For, I was given the power to understand the Machine to count time, built in Zod by Agar. This machine is just a huge, very precise planetarium representing the strip of sky seen from the Earth down to the smallest details. This strip of sky moves and the Earth with it and the elliptic traced is so perfectly inscribed that it becomes the "floor" of that spherical room on which man is sustained.

"Agar built this room, this veritable machine with the complicated mechanism copied on the mechanism of the sky and even made the translucent vault display the new astral bodies over the slow course of time. The entire universe is enclosed, or *almost*, in this room.

(Another pause, very long, with Agaran's breathing in the background). Then:

"Such is the law. It has always been such, but those who understand it usually don't have the strength or power to get it accepted by the entire human race. The fragmentation of the race into distinct peoples is certainly the reason for its incommunicability. However, thanks to those who created Zod, this law has been preserved until today. It was the strength of the people and the treasure to preserve down through the descendants of the mind of Agar. This law has skipped a cycle.

"Now the time of Aquarius has come, which is the time of man almost at the peak of knowledge. And like every time, society has been reformed, restructured among peoples, breaking up its initial force. Like every time, the structures of these societies are such that they create demographic, economic and political problems that normally lead to a total power and the supremacy of one of these fragments of the race over the other systems. Like every time, on the threshold of knowledge, the danger is there.

"For you who might find this story and understand it, the current age of Aquarius is the age of awakening. I know your research, your discoveries in the nuclear field as well as in that of biology. I, Agaran, know all this because Zod's radio network is always listening to your world and the information is selected by computers— they are nothing like yours. There are spies from Zod living in your world. You know nothing about them. They are not human. Some are completely invisible and live like "waves".

"I know your erratic behavior; your gross errors that are already likely to repeat those made by my people 22,000 years ago now. You and your governments will never be persuaded, I know. Because I also know how to fix these mistakes in good time.

"I, Agaran, will be the savior of the law. I know the secret that will allow me to save the present world from a new cycle of disasters. I possess the means to transform this age of coming destruction into an everlasting Golden Age. For this I have lived for 8,304 years. For this I have guided the people of Zod, I have given it a religion, as obscurantist as all religions, but necessary, vital. Thus I had to imprison my people and continue the chain of life whose first link was Agar. I had to condition my people like this to keep them alive, generation after generation, until the day of awakening.

"The time has not yet come. For this, two fundamental reasons must join together.

"The first of these reasons comes from the fact that going back to the world on the surface is impossible now. Your minds are too turbulent, too prone to work individually or for the benefit of some megalomaniacal nation rather than for the whole human race. The time has not yet come to give you the secrets and entrust you with using them prudently.

"The second reason is exactly because the time for such a revelation will never be possible, will never come. Cooperation is henceforth impossible.

"So, I, Agaran, will have to act alone. And against you. On the chosen day, I'll leave Zod with my people. I have the necessary means to convince you… in spite of yourselves. And they are destructive means, but they are the only one available for a chance to save the human race. My conscience, obviously, is clear when I say this.

And it could be that if my plan fails, so if you don't listen to me, you will consider me a dangerous lunatic.

"However, I am the only chance for the human race and for the God force that is dying.

"I will leave. You won't realize it. My weapons make no noise and spill no blood. I will leave and you will be billions without reflexes, frozen, not yet completely dead. But on the point of being so. Some of you will be spared. On their awakening they won't remember because they will already be their own sons and daughters. On these foundations will begin the eternal Golden Age.

"And the mistake, the great, unpardonable mistake that you are making—for the first time the disaster will not happen.

"This world cannot last overnight. Nor any time. I am Agaran, post-human, a mind in a manufactured body. I, too, need you and my people with me. We'll need some of your scientific and especially biological knowledge. This science is developing in your world, fumbling around in fits and starts because you're scared. But one day, you won't be scared of the consequences of its implementation. One day you'll take the leap… And you'll discover the means to transplant organs and minds. You'll discover the possibilities of psychic grafts, the science of longevity and a practically eternal life.

"On that day, thanks to you, Agaran will become a man of flesh and blood again. That's why I'm waiting. When you're ready to receive me, I'll act. The moment must come.

"You'll be ready, you'll have the means and I'll know how to keep you from using them to destroy the human race. These means that I am unable to perfect myself, in my own society of survival, you'll have them and I'll use them for my people. And the Subjects of Zod will become great again and will wipe out the various waste brought about by the mutations. And those of you who will be saved will be able unite with mine for complete and eternal happiness... Freed from death, all identical in consciousness and beauty... All...

(Again a pause, a very long silence. Then, calmer, almost whispering, Agaran's voice):

"Such is my task. I have to live and hold out for 2,000 years yet, until that day when you will be able to biologically serve the grand designs of Agar.

"In Zod today, the minds are awakening. The seeds sown by Agar's mnemonic transplants into preselected fetuses are bearing fruit. More and more of the children born from the chains of artificial placentas become rebel subjects who smash against the barriers that I had to build to preserve Zod. This time, curiosity is rising up and the danger is in the heart of my people. The structure can no longer deal with these new minds coming from the "Agarean insemination".

"Today the risk of death is here. When I started narrating this message, I thought it would be eliminated before I had to explain it. That didn't happen.

"The law of Zod is hard but necessary for the very preservation of Zod. I had to banish emotional thought from the consciousness and forge from scratch a "goal of life" for the subjects. A false goal, of course. It offers the first step of knowledge to an intelligent being and it doesn't stop until he reaches the second step and so on. For Zod, the next ascent has not come. The people have to maintain life, fabricate subjects more and more resistant and fit to jump up the ladder leading to the Golden Age, when the time comes.

"I had to fight against these awakenings of rebel minds. And for this the children exhibiting tendencies to unhealthy curiosity and to questioning received principles were put in classes of psychic remodeling. To kill the harmful instincts is the goal of these classes. After eight years, the subject under treatment is supposed to be on the right track. If not, it's eliminated.

"It's a part of Agar's mind that is eliminated. I am the mind of Agar. I am enough.

"When I sat down for the first time before this table, having decided to speak to perpetuate the secret, a rebel child of Zod... a child destined for deletion refused death. He escaped, outside of Zod. There's the risk. Fortunately, Zod is located in a place on the planet where the mutant races have not evolved much since the disaster, where the most horrible monsters live, direct descendants of the worst harmed, original mutants. But if the rebel child were found by others... and the revealed mystery be the cause of a rush to Zod... a bunch of researchers and more or less honest intellectuals would be trying to understand. A bunch of fearful people would be afraid. They would discover Zod, which has to stay hidden until Aquarius is complete. And everything would be destroyed.

"The risk is just a tiny child who is walking on the sky of Zod." The voice went silent.

For a long moment Agaran sat still, staring at the light blinking in the void. Then, with a heavy hand, slowly, he turned off the light and pressed the button to eject the recording from the belly of the Machine. For another long while he stared at it in his hands. Then he got up to turn on a small waste disposal unit and threw the recording into its gaping hole. Three seconds later, there was nothing left but a great, heavy, interminable silence, and something like a strange hint of a smile in Agaran's riveted eyes.

Afterward he went back to the device, started a new recording, sat in front of the microphone and spoke clearly, precisely, calmly, dictating:

"General conditions to respect for a new socio-religious structure of Zod the Survivor. First condition affecting the open-mindedness of a certain category of subjects and the conditioning from the fetal stage."

He spoke for a long time, alone in the heart of Zod, in the total silence that filled the room walled with strange, decorative panels.

CHAPTER XIII

One of the men asked, "How many days are we going to wait like this?"

His name was Ferez. A tall guy, unbelievably thin, a real skeleton swimming in his filthy, drooping clothes. A bony head with a shaggy beard and bleached hair, with huge, deep-set, fiery eyes.

Carlos kept looking at the fire, as if he had not heard anything. The fire was nothing but a twisted knot of smoke over a few handfuls of wet leaves.

"How long is this going to last?" Ferez repeated. He came up and planted himself in the smoke. The others did not move, but their razor-thin eyes edged over to Ferez. They had discussed it and Ferez had been chosen to talk.

Finally, Carlos decided to look up and for a second caught the eye of the other big guy. He took a fat cigar out of the torn pocket of his jacket and stuck it between his rotten teeth without lighting it. In a slow, deep voice he said, "I'm as fed up as you."

One by one, Ferez' feet peeled out of the mud, but he stayed in place and said, "That's not exactly what I meant. But it's been long, that's all."

"I know it's been long," Carlos spoke again. "We're waiting for Ben, that's all. He'll be here soon."

"Unless…"

"Unless what?"

Ferez shrugged his shoulders, lingered a minute, then finally turned around and joined the others.

In the smoke a purple spark burst out then died. Carlos lay flat on his stomach on the spongy ground and started whispering, "Unless…"

Unless he is never coming back, that's what Ferez wanted to say. Of course. They were all thinking that and they had the right. Nothing is ever certain in the forest. He, Carlos, had seen how many during his bitch of a life, tough guys like Ben, suddenly disappear, for some crazy idea, in the unknown country? How many never came back… That's the forest, the jungle. Anything can happen. You're here and a second later you're dead. Anything can happen. But on the other hand, hope springs eternal.

Hope… That is not exactly the right word. "Habit" fits better. Or even "apathy".

Carlos knew this. He had his life behind him in the forest. His whole life. An incalculable number. After four or five years in the forest, if the sicknesses and the fevers have not completely burned you out, or you have not died of hunger, if a knife thrust or bullet has not gutted you, if you have not dropped dead some fine day under the lashes of the seringalista's henchmen, if the wild animals have not devoured you, if the snakes have not put you down or the wandering savages with their arrows, then after so much luck, time does not matter anymore. There is nothing left for you but the habit of living in totally insane circumstances that you find normal and ordinary, out of habit.

Carlos was as old as the forests. He was born… he must have been born in 1940 or something like that. Approximately. Somewhere, in Setao.

He had been a seringuero, too, a rubber gatherer, like everyone. Counting the years meant nothing. Hundreds of years, probably. Always in the forest, always alone, with a gun and a knife. Alone, in a palm hut perched on the fork of a tree. Alone… and day after day, for hundreds of years, always the same walk, always the same path in the same forest. The same slashes with the knife to gash the trees and gather their blood. The same movements to tilt the *borracha*.

Always.

He had not died and after some time the seringalista boss had said, "Carlos is strong. We can use him differently, he's got guts." So, he became *capata*. Bodyguard, henchman, jack-of-all-trades. Especially killing. But killing is the law of the forest. Killing to survive. The job of *capata* meant Carlos' survival. He had to do it and do it well.

He did it.

He did missions like this. He had many behind him already, with Ben. Ben was the oldest of the *capatas* of Don Olfo's seringal.

Fear did not exist for Carlos. It was like life. A habit anchored inside him that he no longer paid attention to. Habits have no color. However, for this mission, Carlos had found his old friend again, the one that grabs hold of your belly and does not let go for a long time. His old friend fear.

He could say he had had his fill of missions in the forest. Never any fear. Habit. But this one… This one was something else.

Here, the maps of the forest were blank. Virgin space, approximately bordered by the Xingu, the Tapajos and the Amazon. *La tierra prohibida*. Unknown land. Nothing. Nothing that they knew. A garbage dump where a whole bunch of Indian tribes were moved as a last refuge. The most fearsome, the bloodiest. Those who refused all contact and who shot arrows... Those whom they had burned too much...

Terra incognita. A small space, nothing, compared to the huge extent of the Amazon forest. And on this space, legends. Crazy legends that spoke of unknown tribes, of white and ferocious Indians. Other legends about the names of Fawcett and Verrill.

No one who entered *tierra prohibida* ever came out again. Never. Not even certain Nazi war criminals, though their families received letters from the captives in which they admitted they were being held captive without saying anything more[3].

Unbelievable legends, flying from seringal to seringal, spread by the caboclos and garimpeiros. Legends that the whole forest knows.

And Carlos like everyone. Like Ben.

Like Don Olfo who had not hesitated for a second, in spite of everything, to send out the expedition inside this cursed region. There was a mystery at the heart of it. Don Olfo dealt with Heveas and rubber. Even incredible fields of Heveas would not have justified this scouting in *tierra prohibida*. Anyway, Don Olfo was not the master. There was someone bigger behind him, in the shadows, in Brazilia or in Europe or in the States. The seringalistas are never masters.

What were the powerful looking for in *tierra prohibida*? Not rubber, Carlos would have bet his life on it. Minerals, maybe. Diamonds? No, probably minerals.

They would have to clear the land before exploiting it. Clear it, clean it, and crush whoever was on the land, which they only had to develop in order to own it. Clear it, that is make the troublemakers disappear. And the

---

[3] True.

troublemakers in this case were totally unproductive, naked Indians. Clear the land of Indians. The eternal law.

And this was Ben's mission, and Carlos'.

Ben went to have a look inside where they were launching their campaign of disindianization. Carlos was waiting, on the edge, with four men and when his old friend came back...

With twilight falling, the forest turned dark, black, swarming with bad shadows and flooded with shrieking. The fire lit by Carlos had finally decided to produce a flame.

This evening, after five days of waiting, the green curtain suddenly split open and four men came through, dressed in rags, leaning on the butt of their rifles like canes. Carlos unwound like a spring. He did not say anything, but his eyes burned with a fire that was not fever. Ben smiled.

They gathered around the fire, ate what was left of the cassava and dried meat, as well as the crackers. They gulped down the rum-spiced coffee. Then the men lay down for the night, off to the side; two of them a few feet from each other, their backs against a tree, rifles between their knees. Carlos and Ben were alone around the fire.

It was like that for a long time, amidst the birdcalls of the night, the glow from the fire and the clouds of mosquitoes. Then, when he could stand it no longer, Carlos asked, "Well?"

Ben's face looked like a tree trunk, a rough trunk, split open, on which foul lichen had started to grow by mistake. He looked at Carlos, then again at his cup full of rum, shrugged and said, "I think it'll work."

Carlos jutted his chin toward the left sleeve of the jacket, in rags and scabbed with blood. "Trouble?"

Ben's eyes changed. They became dull, vague, odd. For a long moment, he sat thoughtful and then shrugged again. In his hoarse voice he said, "It'll happen... but God knows what they'll find when they try to dig up their minerals."

"Minerals?"

"It has to be that. It's certainly that... They wouldn't be in such a hurry to get rid of the Indians."

"Why do you say that? You said you didn't know what they were looking for?"

And here again Ben's eyelids drooped more. He leaned forward, his face right over the glow of the fire, and said, "In two places, the packages disappeared. In another they just stole the candy. In two other places, nothing was touched. With everything they did take, it'll do pretty good work. But that's not what's bothering me."

Carlos waited. It was irritating, this heart he had forgotten about and that was suddenly starting to beat like crazy.

"We found something funny," Ben said, "after a while. Something funny..."

"What?"

"A kid," Ben was staring straight into Carlos' eyes. "A kid, just like that, in the middle of the forest."

"Good God! The buggers also have ki..."

"A dead kid. He must have come from one of the tribes that found the packages: he had a little bag of candy tied to his loincloth. I guess he was taking a walk and he ate one of them—there was everything in that candy: plague, coryza, cyanide, everything in those pills. Can't say which one he ate."

"If you already found a kid," Carlos said, "then a bunch of others will follow. It'll go fast. Not counting the contaminated blankets and all that."

"That's not what's eating me," Ben was getting worked up. "The kid wasn't Indian. He was white."

Carlos' eyeballs almost popped out of his head. He suddenly felt like he was suffocating under the weight of the legends.

"And not only white," Ben said again. "Tiny. Not at all deformed, but this tall. Two feet at most. All white and this tall. A miniature."

"Holy crap," Carlos whispered. "No one will believe you. Why didn't you bring him back? That would've blown their minds, all those people who talk about *tierra prohibida* but know nothing."

"If I speak, they'll believe me," Ben said. "It'll get around… I wasn't the only one who saw it. But to bring him back… no way. He wasn't alone… and, well, he was already in damn bad shape. Not much left for me to lug around in this hellhole."

"He wasn't alone?"

Ben's eyes became even cloudier. Without looking at anything in particular, he said, "A dog. One of those Indian mutts, half wild and never totally tame, see. One of these dirty, mangy things with a mouthful of fangs this long. The little beast was there, as skinny as anything, barely standing up. A miracle. But a goddamn rabid miracle. No way to get close: it was howling like mad. And no way to shoot in that place without stirring up god knows what. Hack it up with a machete—nada. Rabid."

He paused for a moment before continuing. "Not really a dog you could eat, a hair's breadth from dying. But it had enough strength to stand up rabid. To defend

156

that weird kid there, who the ants were eating. To defend him to the death... Dogs are like that, see. Able to do things you can't explain. You'd take your chances alone and too bad for the other who's left behind. Everyone would do that. Not a fucking dog... he stays there. He's probably still there. Go and explain that."

Carlos did not try. He was thinking of the unknown Indians—and now tiny, white Indians—who would soon be dying like flies, wiped out by all kinds of viruses and microbes. The germ trap had worked. A lot less dangerous than armed expeditions, less noisy and reckless than bombing with napalm. He was thinking of this *tierra prohibida* of legend that the señores were going to exploit some day. And he was thinking of what they were going to find in the heart of this forest. But that... that was impossible to imagine.

It was just a bitter taste in the back of his throat and the feeling of stepping into something both mysterious and terribly dangerous at the same time. A feeling of blasphemy, like when you see someone spitting on the cross, for example.

Ben nodded once or twice. Then he lit a cigar, looked at his torn coat for a long time, then again at his cigar. After another nod, he said, "Go and explain that, that dog and everything..." Whispered.

But the forest was screaming so loud, all around, that no one heard him.

Anticipation
FN
FICTION

Pierre SURAGNE

MAIS SI LES PAPILLONS TRICHENT

fleuve noir

BUT WHAT IF BUTTERFLIES CHEAT?

If this story has to be written, it must use words.
But words are nothing, to "Them".
Trying to describe "Them" necessarily amounts to conjuring up some kind of image in the imagination of a reader. "They" are not images. "They" are nothing that you can imagine. To describe "Them" would be a mistake, madness, and incommensurably presumptuous.

However, in spite of everything, one must use words. Letters strung together to form images. One must dive into the impossible, knowing that the attempt will be a lie.

One must.

There are two of them.
With no body and yet lying down.
Lying down, asleep, even though their sleep is nothing like the sleep that we know.
There are two of them, lying down, asleep.
They have no names, but we will call them Creator-Candidates. There is Creator-Candidate One and Creator-Candidate Two.
They are, inevitably, in a place. And they are not alone. There are other Creator-Candidates. But these two are the only ones who interest us.
They also interest the two Supervisors who are in this Place. The two Supervisors do not have names ei-

ther. But we will call one of them Elio and the other Alam.

Without cheating like this, nothing would be possible.

CHAPTER I

Price woke up but stayed in bed, lying down, eyes closed. For a long time he listened to the fatigue rolling through his body, gliding in soft waves along the muscles. This new brand of sleeping pill that he had been using for a while really worked well... maybe too well. He told himself, for the hundredth time, that it would be wise to change it again and go visit a psycho-counselor. Among the whole range of sleeping pills, there certainly had to be an ideal brand. A brand for him, Price.

Eyes closed, he listened to the outside, letting his ideas wander at random. On the shores of sleep he slowly dragged himself out of the heavy waves. Everything around him was dead calm.

As far back as he could remember it had always been hard for him to resurface after sleeping, after resting, after unconsciousness. It had always been hard to start the day. A marked tendency to asthenia, he knew it. All the psycho-counselors in the city had told him so. But it was not very serious. According to the last official statistics, 57% of the global population was living in asylums. A few billion mentally ill of all kinds, millions of dreadful psychoses. Of course, among the 43% of normal individuals there were a good number of various neurotics. Anyway, in the middle of all this mess, a "simple tendency to asthenia" was not such a big deal.

Gently, slowly, the memories of consciousness came back to Price's mind. It was really nice when he could allow himself this peaceful refresher. Nothing was worse than snapping back into the real; nothing was more trying than a sudden awakening without the slightest phase of acclimation.

He was Price Mallworth and he was 30 years old. He had lost his mother at the age of nine; his father was still "living" in a retirement home on the east coast, lost in the invisible maze of schizophrenia.

He was a priest of the New Enlightened Catholic Religion, appointed to parish 16 in Tucumcari, Fascist Union of the States of America. The parish church was run by 22 priests and it controlled 3000 regular worshippers.

Price had problems with the Faith, but he was hoping to get over it. He lived in a nice mobile bungalow, all in bay windows on a meplast frame, which belonged to the Church, parish 16. He was one of the Normals and by this fact alone could say he was relatively happy.

A faint sound made him jump. He thought "Natcha" and was just about to open his eyes. He held himself *in extremis* to hang onto the final moments of this atmosphere of inner peace in which he was immersed. To think about, to imagine Natcha, in this wave of delights, could only be an extra pleasure.

Natcha was pretty. She was 25 years old, tall and graceful, with long, black, shiny hair. She did her four hours of mandatory weekly work at the Tucumcari's

Abnormal Penitentiary, paranoiac wing. The rest of the time she spent painting and sculpting; she also studied unified theology in order to assist Price in the future. When they would be united by law. Because they would be united by law, as well as by the Church.

Price loved Natcha and Natcha loved Price. They were going to live together, to support each other, forever. Then the Church would make them a gift of the bungalow in parish 16. They would have a home. They would…

His brow furrowed a little and hollowed out three deep lines across his forehead.

He would marry Natcha *if all went well*. And the more he thought about it, the less certain he was that all would go well. It was like a nagging arrow stuck in his skin. A poisoned arrow. Day after day the venom spread in him, ran in his veins, burned. That was the end of the peace and quiet. Price opened his eyes.

Dark curtains covered the bay window that took up the south wall of the room. It was not enough to block out the bright light from outside, but the golden half-light barely deserved its name.

Price stared at the ceiling for a long time. The white ceiling, smooth, cast from a single sheet of flawless plastic. He knew this room imprinted on his eye: the walls were also white, livened up by three vividly colored works signed by Natcha; the bed on the floor he was lying on; the low tables and cushions; the built-in amps of the stereo system whose music, sometimes, gladly replaced the sleeping pills; the oval screen of the 3D.

What insurmountable difficulties might their plans for a union face? Stupid question. He could ask himself this question with a kind of raging belligerence as if to defend himself against the inevitable answer! It was still just a stupid question.

Natcha did not know her parents. Her father was a Black, which had automatically caused her mother to be thrown into a State Prison where she died a few years later—suicide. Of course, they did not hold the mother's faults against Natcha. They simply hid her origins, for a long time, and she only discovered them when she had to get a genetic card for her future union with Price.

This, certainly, was the first shock for him.

She hated the mother whom she had never known. She hated all Blacks because her father was one.

But that was not the problem. And Price knew it. He, too, hated Blacks, Indians, Yellows and everyone who was not American. All normal Americans hated whoever was not American, just like the Chinese must have hated the non-Chinese. That was the law. That was the order of things, as they taught children since time immemorial, as they kept repeating to normal adults. Nationalist sectarianism, maniacal patriotism, pure fascism—those were the weapons, the last weapons with any effect against the proliferation of mental illnesses. The last defense of the Normals. Selection at the root, selection forever... Americans! Your race is the least affected! Your race is the healthiest because it has only 33% Abnormals! Be proud to be Americans and still able to read these lines and understand them! Be proud to be able to still be proud! The usual propaganda, slogans in the newspapers, on the 3D programs, slogans everywhere... Like so much dope to deal with the major illnesses...

Where does the Faith come into all this, Price? The Faith is to believe in a god who chooses, who protects. It is, above all, to fear. Are you afraid, Price? Have you always been so afraid? Have you always wanted to be saved, to be chosen? Or now, are you realizing that, like everyone, like all men and women, Normals and Abnormals, you the priest, you the automatically saved, you're just another dumbass, conned by everyone and by God first and foremost…

What does this have to do with anything? You were thinking about Natcha…

Yes… Natcha…

Of course, their genetic cards were unfavorable to their union. There was his father, schizophrenic and lost. There were her parents, especially her mother… They would have no children and that was that. The risk was too great. The risk of adding a few more moronic children to the population. No children. And after?

How many other couples were in this situation? Thousands, probably. And yet they were couples. And happy couples. One simple surgery reduced the risk factor to nil.

If you wanted a child, there was always the possibility of adoption. To adopt, you simply needed to be a normal couple, a solid, stable couple. Would they be a stable couple?

Price had said nothing. He had never dared to let one word slip out. But he was scared. Scared about this future stability. And he was scared because of Natcha. He had noticed the symptoms on several occasions. Little things that at first he had taken for simple signs of depression. And not only "tendencies" like he himself showed. Sometimes Natcha was cheerful, excited, bouncy and vivacious; sometimes she was apathetic, gloomy and withdrawn. There were also those incredible periods of aggression that ended in tears and the deepest despondency.

She had holes in her memory; she spied on him and watched him like he was a danger to her mind. And then she started to get confused about time. Sometimes she imagined that they had already been married for years and years...

It was mental confusion and he knew it. And she knew it, too, probably, and she must have been fighting with all her might not to let it show. She must have been living in hell.

He had never said anything, always hoping... But he knew that the day would come when he would have to talk to her. And on that day, everything would be finished. On that day, walking through the door of a psycho-counselor to denounce her, he would forever crush the plans for a union between him and Natcha. But if he had to do it, he would do it. For the good of the race, for... for all those things that they taught him when he was a child. For those things that the posters and newspapers, his superiors and the 3D kept repeating to him all day long.

He turned his head and his eyes met Natcha's. She was there in the doorway, gorgeous, wearing only a flimsy, see-through negligee that hid nothing of her body. She had heavy but firm breasts with brown nipples, a cute little bulging belly above her pubic triangle, long silky legs; her hair fell in thick, black waves over her golden shoulders.

She was carrying a glass platter with a steaming teapot, two cups and an impressive pile of toast. She came smiling into the room. He smiled, too, leaning on his elbow. And he was happy to be living this moment. He told himself, Today it's okay.

Natcha knelt down, put the platter on one of the low tables and rolled it all over to the bed. She felt happy to be living this moment and told herself, Today it's okay.

Price looked relaxed; his big, green eyes were perfectly calm. She loved to surprise him like this when he woke up, *when everything was all right*. She loved to be here with the breakfast platter; she loved to nibble the toast next to him and watch him drink his steaming hot lemon tea, in little sips, carefully.

He was handsome. The most seductive priest in the parish. Who knows, maybe in the whole city. His body was graceful, muscular, hard and hot. So many men at 38 years old were becoming bald, pot-bellied, soft... Price would never be bald or pot-bellied or soft. He would always be 38 years old; he would always be just like he was right now.

She did not say anything so as not to break the fragile, precious silence. She poured the tea into the cups. The smell of it mingled with the toast was marvelous.

She felt Price's eyes on her skin, on her breasts, her thighs, on the bushy nest of her sex... And it was good; it was like a languorous caress. Her eyes plunged into Price's. They were burning. His hair was disheveled and pink spots colored his cheeks. Just looking at his cheeks and his unshaven chin, she quivered.

They would make love, she knew it and wanted it. And she knew that he knew it, without saying a single word, just with a look. After eight years of marriage and union it was still like the first day, in those first moments. After eight years...

It was even better and better.

Of course there had been stormy times. Couples without storms are not couples, just one individual existing at the expense of another. They had seen many storms, for different reasons that she no longer remembered, which had been important at the time. Like a storm that breaks out and passes, the cause of the storm had broken out and passed.

Eight years… Yes, it was beautiful. It was good.

There was, indeed, this issue of not being able to have children… They would never have children. Without this voluntarily accepted condition, they would not have been able to marry or to unite on the altar of the church in parish 16 in front of everyone. Eight out of ten chances to give birth to a moron—it was too risky.

Maybe one day they would go to the State Center for Adoptions. Maybe… If they felt the need. Personally Natcha had no desire. A child would be a restriction and a responsibility. A real responsibility. As for Price… Did Price want to adopt a child? He had never mentioned it. And then…

And then in his condition.

No! Don't think of that! Not now… Don't ruin everything. It was okay. *It's okay!*

"What's wrong with you?" Price asked softly. He was carefully buttering a piece of toast.

She felt herself turn pale. "I'm just watching you," she said.

He smiled. "Are you okay?"

"I'm all right." Sometimes she felt like he suspected something, that he knew and he was spying on her slightest reactions. Poor Price! It must have been hell…

She repeated cheerfully, "I'm perfectly all right. The sun is hot, hot! Did you sleep well?"

He bit into the toast. It made an adorable crunching sound. "Slept marvelously," he said. "But I'll have to change sleeping pills again."

"It's really hard to find the right one the first time," she said.

"Not only the first time. I've tried I don't know how many brands. This one is good but too strong. I had a hell of a time waking up." His eyes changed suddenly like they were flash frozen. "Have you been up for long?" he asked.

"An hour or two. It's gorgeous outside."

Price lowered his eyes. He grabbed his cup and brought it to his lips. Took a sip. His lips were trembling. To avoid what she felt coming, in a really unpleasant hot flash she said, "You have to go to the church today. It's a pity, we could have taken a walk to the desert… I love being in the desert with you…"

"I love it too," he said and added, "When we're married, you won't be getting up first anymore. You won't be getting up…" He stopped.

For a second their eyes met.

Here we go, Natcha thought with horror, it's finished. It's finished…

Every day it was the same anguish. Every day… and every day the symptoms were more and more blatant, more and more atrocious. Every day Price's neurosis took deeper and deeper root.

A quick smile and he tried to put on a normal face before saying, "I'm joking, Natcha."

And this was even worse: the fact that he imagined that she was the one who was crazy. Moreover, she felt like she was slipping into a bottomless pit. It wasn't possible!

She knew! They really had been married for eight years! This was not the first time that she dove deep down in her memory to try to clutch a different past. No, she was not crazy. She was the one who was right... It was not possible otherwise. Not possible!

"I know you're joking," she said. "Anyway, it's true. It'll be much easier when we're married. Really married. I hope we won't have any problems..."

He let a few seconds pass before responding in what he hoped was a gentle voice, "No problems, you'll see."

He took another sip of tea. It was bitter.

This was the worst. The fact that she imagined that he was the one who was crazy, that he was the one confused about time. It was... There was no name for it. It was awful.

This game she was playing where she admitted her doubts and at the same time tried to hide them... My God, make this stop! Make her get better!

He leaned over on his elbow, being careful not to wake her. They had made love, abandoned themselves to each other, both of them, furiously. Now she was sleeping. Her mussed-up hair hid half her face and her parted lips were red.

He got up.

Let it go on like this, in the same way. And too bad if it was hell sometimes. Let it go on for as long as possible. And then, one day, at the end of his rope, he would go see a psycho-counselor.

He got dressed and then sat in the living room and drank two more cups of cold tea while listening to the news drone softly out of one of the 3Ds. It was always the same news. The mental cases registered in the poor districts of the city, the hunt for blacks in the slums, the subversive campaigns for "free neurosis" and the right to uncontrolled unions, the reports from psycho-counselors. Then the Enlightened Church put on a variety show.

Price turned off the set and left the room. He did not feel good. Maybe it was just a dizzy spell, but maybe it was a prelude to this incomprehensible situation in which he was about to be immersed. A situation that had nothing to do with the worst psychoses or the blackest of insanities—it was beyond all this.

CHAPTER II

The sunshine fell straight down on the white streets, the small yards and courtyards, in front of the bungalows. Children were playing outside and a few adults (especially the elderly) were sitting on stone benches in the shade of their front porches. But most people who were not working stayed indoors, in the coolness of their houses. The sunshades were drawn over the bay windows. The bungalows looked like boxes of white stone... empty boxes.

In the yards there were a few trees that once bore fruit and a few dreary conifers that were supposed to act as thick hedges. The lawns were brown, badly scabby.

While wiping the drops of sweat off his forehead with the tips of his fingers, Price told himself that this summer would be another scorcher. As always. Moreover, the summer now covered most of the old seasons, like spring and fall. These seasons still existed, of course—like the cycle of life still existed—but they were reduced to their most rudimentary form. In the winter it rained.

On his way, he watched the pale lawns with a critical eye. The law forbade the use of water for plants or dishes or laundry—this law dated back now a good 30 years. For the dishes and laundry there was the detergent that was pressure-sprayed by the appropriate machines. For the plants... oh well! They had to count on the rain. Where would the race and country be if just anybody were allowed to use water for such nutty reasons?

There were still people, however, who insisted on planting lawns in front of their houses, in the naïve hope that the sky would come to their aide. Price had not planted even a blade of grass or the puniest flower. The courtyard in front of his bungalow was as dry as the heart of the Mohave and the slightest movement kicked up a whole bunch of little dust clouds. Being a priest of the N.E.C.R. Price had to set an example.

The street was empty, naked, sparkling. Glued to his steps, Price's short, black shadow crawled along the asphalt.

There were a few private cars along the sidewalk, but very few. This type of vehicle had been forbidden by the State for a long time. They were no longer of any use, being generously replaced by a wonderful State Transport System, both underground and aerial, which comprised not only the municipal lines, but also linked up with all the important cities in the country. Moreover, wherever the hovercraft ramps had not yet popped up, the flying machines of the American Air Transport Company were hard at work. Private cars really had no reason to exist; they cluttered the roads and no longer did what they were supposed to do; they used and wasted too many energy batteries that could be put to better use elsewhere, for example in the neurosurgery centers. They had not, however, completely stopped manufacturing them. In some cases, the private car could still be useful for certain sicknesses as a proven therapeutic tool—it provided an ideal outlet for all kinds of aggression, for neurotics with psychotic tendencies, for example. They said that some people in Europe and Asia still used private cars a lot. This was not so surprising because those people also had a high percentage of mental illness and they were definitely lost. Of course, these were only rumors and you could never really know with rumors...

Price had never felt the need to have a private car. He was normal and his minor tendencies to asthenia triggered no such need. When he got to the parked cars, he made a little detour. He did not like these machines.

The church was 15 minutes away from his bungalow on foot. When he had moved there, he could have chosen a house closer to his work, but the government said that convenience is neither rewarding nor, especially, patriotic. Convenience breeds laziness and all kinds of defects that if you don't watch out will carry you straight to the most twisted neuroses. Seek out difficulties in order to overcome them, that is the honorable way, worthy of an American; that is how you get feelings of immaculate pride. That is what the government said. The Church used the same language.

Price did not choose convenience. Plus, this 15-minute walk was good physical exercise.

He passed by an exhibitionist walking down the middle of the street, dressed only in a shirt that stopped at his belly button. The man took long strides, showing his wares, his long, hairy, skinny legs like dry, spindly bird legs. He greeted Price politely and Price waved back. The law of the Medical Association for the Protection of Mental Equilibrium (M.A.P.M.E.) concerning exhibitionists was barely two years old. It stipulated that any form of exhibitionism is not a sickness. Since then, the number of these pseudo-sick had been considerably reduced. On the other hand, a rash of rapes and murders had followed the promulgation of the law. The government immediately created squads of Protectors who patrolled the seamiest streets 24/7.

After 200 uninterrupted yards, the street ran into a perpendicular crossroad. You had to follow this road after turning left. Another 500 yards or so and there was the church, although you could still not see the building because the road curved slightly to the right. All you could see was, again, a double row of white bungalows with their little courtyards, bunches of children playing quietly, filmy outlines of old folks in the gritty shadows of their shaded porches covered with dry creeping vines.

The man was standing at least 100 feet away, casually leaning against the cement block of a streetlight. It was almost impossible not to notice him. At first he was alone in the street, alone with Price who was walking toward him. And he was wearing a blinding bright scarlet tunic, electric blue shorts and a fur cap dug up God knows where. His bare feet were stuck in worn leather boots whose uppers were cut off at mid-calf.

At first sight Price judged him as was fitting: a repressed exhibitionist with masochistic tendencies, that was for sure. Someone who walked around dressed like that in 2534 could be nothing else!

When he got near the individual, the man stood up straight and took a step in his direction. Price stopped. "Well now!" he said.

The man's face was bearded and dirty. His greasy hair spilled out from under his preposterous cap. But his eyes, especially, made Price stop. Scorching, penetrating eyes. Eyes that stabbed like a knife. The left eye was black, shiny, and too full compared to the small iris. The right eye must have been gouged out and the half-closed eyelid revealed only a thin line of murky gray.

"You're the priest, aren't you?" the one-eyed man said.

He reeked. It was hard to classify the odors that gusted off his body at the slightest movement. But Price identified old urine, sweat and the smell of that tobacco they grow in the State of Annexed Mexico. Before he could answer the question, the one-eyed man added, "You're Price, one of the priests of parish 16." It was not a question.

"That's right," Price said. He had always hated people who talked to him in the middle of the street, just like that, of their own free will, without receiving any kind of invitation. It was physical: he felt like he was being attacked.

It dawned on him that this individual might not be normal. They were talking a lot about a new psychosis, growing fast, that had taken root in an old political ideology. The government's psycho-counselors spoke of anarchopsychosis or of "warped-mania". The affected subjects could be classed among the megalomaniacs, with a few subtle differences. Their mania was particularly obsessed with considering the individual in itself as the most important manifestation of life, at the expense of established society. They advocated the equality of individuals and attacked all forms of self-sufficiency with respect to society but, oddly enough, to hear them talk, they were almost ready to admit this self-sufficiency with respect to the individual! They advocated the opening of borders along with all the risks this would entail of war and the cross contamination between foreign peoples! They advocated the equality of sexes and races; they said "brother" when they were talking to blacks... In sum, the theories they tossed about were made up of nothing but paradox and nonsense. They had been around forever, among the neurotics, but they were becoming more and more of a clear threat to society. And that is why the government, through the services of the M.A.P.M.E., declared them Abnormals, dangerous psychopaths.

This Cyclops here looked like one of them, totally.

Price made a move as if to start walking again. The individual sidestepped and stood squarely in front of him. A very unpleasant shiver ran down Price's spine. The rays of the sun fell straight down on his head and shoulders. "I don't have the time," he said. "Excuse me... I have to get to the church... It's one of my work days and I..."

For a quarter of a second the gleam in his one eye softened. And in the tousled undergrowth of his beard there was even something like a fleeting smile. "Don't be scared, Speaker. I don't mean you any harm. I'm in sound mental health... I can even show you my card..."

If there was one thing that Price hated it was being called "Speaker". The nickname, which was given to all priests, had become almost common usage. But personally, whenever he heard the word, he could not help feeling a certain pejorative nuance that rubbed him the wrong way. Did a Protector really like to be called "cudgelman"?

He tried again to escape from this individual's claws, but the guy planted himself in his way again, this time searching frantically in his pockets. He pulled out a plastic card that would have been torn to pieces long ago if it weren't for the protective coating. He stuck it in Price's face and said, "Read, Speaker! Read this..."

Price read. What else could he do? He read that the man's name was Devedias S. Muks and he was in sound mental health. He also saw the photo that did not really match with the person, but it could have been taken a while back when he was still presentable, without his beard and wild hair.

Muks promptly pocketed the card. "I wanted you to see, Speaker. I've seen a bunch like you. I've seen a bunch, you can be sure of that. Not a one to help me, to give me advice. They told me you weren't a bastard like the others, that you listen to people."

"I listen to people... in the church," Price said. "Not in the street. I have nine hours of work per week, spread out over three days, and it's work that I do in the church."

"Hey!" Muks said. "Don't be a bastard! How do you expect me to find you in the church, huh? How do you expect me to get in, into this damn church, without the 15-dollar entrance fee? I don't have 15 dollars. And I don't have work anymore to earn it. But before, I belonged to the church! Before, I'm telling you, I was going there regularly! I'm telling you, Speaker, and I memorized all the sermons you can imagine..."

He really stank badly and his one eye had a right nasty sparkle in it.

"What do you want me to do about it?" Price groaned. "It's not my fault if you lost your job..."

"So maybe it's mine?" the other screeched. "I was a packer over there at the other end of the city. A damn good packer, one of the most productive. 16 machines under my management, you think it's bad maybe? Like it's my fault that I started getting claustrophobic maybe? I was a good American! When I felt it was going bad, I got myself cured, yes! It took three years. That's not a drop in the bucket, three years. And then, in the end, I was healed. I showed up at the packers and they wanted no more of me. I wasn't capable is what they said. I would relapse, they said, because I had tendencies... No, they didn't want me. Had to go work outside somewhere. But where, huh? In what branch? I'm 37 years old and I don't know how to do anything but pack those frozen goods. What the hell do you think I can do outside, Speaker, without even the most basic training for it!"

"There are apprenticeships..."

"Apprenticeships, yeah! But in the apprenticeships they take the young ones first and then it has to be paid for. And me, after three years of cure at the expense of the State, maybe you think I can pay for an apprenticeship? Maybe you think that with my unemployment benefits I can pay the entrance fee for the church?"

Price swallowed hard and said, "Nothing is easy and that's a good thing, Muks. Every joy has to be earned, every satisfaction won." He was a Speaker; he was speaking. He reeled off big talk, slogans, words. Hollow words, horribly hollow, more and more hollow. It was awful. He struggled to get a hold of himself. It was true that nothing was simple. And it was true for him, too... maybe. He went on, "Everything has to be earned, Muks! For peace on earth like for peace in heaven."

For a few seconds Muks shifted from one foot to the other and each shift made a soft, dull sound from his leather boots. This time his one eye staring at Price was downright evil. He said, "Peace in heaven, my ass!"

Price jumped. "I forbid you..."

"My ass, Speaker! You forbid me nothing at all! And you're just like the others, like all the other Speakers of your damn shitty religion! I see clear! I see everything! There's no doubt I was a good citizen before, a patriot, religious and all that. I had to fall, I had to get sick because of that goddamned shit packing factory. Because, yes, it was the factory that made me sick! And it's the government that created the factory that made me sick!" He put his heavy paw on Price's shoulder. "You're like the others, Speaker! Like all the other bas-

179

tards of your religion. You speak. You don't stop speaking at your appointed hours. You take turns reeling off the same hollow words, the same scams! You make us believe that this enlightened religion cares about man, watches over his salvation! You say you're here for the love of man, to help him… My ass! I'm telling you, you're here to get money by talking bullshit! You're here to hold the people…"

"That's enough!" Price barked, red with anger.

The other stopped talking right away. Drool had squirted into his beard. He was breathing hard and a dull mist veiled his only eye. He slowly took his hand off Price's shoulder.

"I hope," Price said, "you realize what you just told me. I hope that you know how serious your words can be if they are held against you."

The dull veil tore. Again, a steely flame crossed Muks' eye. He sported a mocking smile and started rocking from side to side again. Again, Price felt a shiver of fear run through him.

"Are you going to hold them against me, Speaker?"

Price balked. The man was huge and could certainly kill him with a well-thrown punch. He saw that all the time in the news. He hoped his voice would sound firm, "I will do nothing of the kind. But I will give you some advice: get yourself to a psycho-counselor as soon as possible. You'll be cared for and fed and you can consult the priests of the institution without spending a cent."

"But I don't want to be taken care of and fed again without giving something in exchange," Muks said calmly. "I have my damn dignity that they taught me to cultivate all my life… I was simply a little confused, Speaker. I wanted to ask you stuff about God and the idea they make of him. I wanted to know what you think of it, without the ready-made slogans that you recite between such and such hour on such and such day of the week. It was important, Speaker."

"Take my advice," Price said. Dryly. He started walking again and the other made no move to stop him.

"Watch out!" Muks yelled. "You're married and your wife is charming... Wait until you hit a snag like mine, either one of you..."

Price stopped in his tracks and turned around. He was pale, riddled with nervous tics. "You're crazy," he roared. "Who told you I was married?" It was a stupid question.

Leaning against the cement pillar, Muks shrugged his shoulders. "I learned about you. They told me you weren't as much of a bastard as the others..."

He learned... From whom? It could only be from one person! Only one person who imagined that she was *already* married to him.

He closed his eyes for one second. The ground shook under his feet.

New God! It was awful! He had done all he could to push farther and farther back the day when he would have to denounce Natcha to the M.A.P.M.E. All he could... He had prayed with words that were not just ready-made slogans... He had hoped like crazy. But if Natcha was behaving like this now! If she was confessing her madness to just anyone... *Everyone* knew that they were not married, not yet.

And inevitably a kind soul would show up who would understand, who would listen to Natcha ramble on and then who would denounce her...

"New God," Price mumbled.

In the midday heat he felt a chill.

He opened his eyes. Muks had disappeared. The street was empty.

And then Price realized that the street was not the one he knew. It was a street that he had never seen.

Moreover, it was raining.

Natcha woke up. Stretched. A cooing of satisfied joy purred in her throat. She opened her eyes. Blinked in the sun. The house, which was spinning, was not actually spinning and the harsh light from outdoors had breached the barrier of the protective curtains over one of the bay windows. The sun was hot and turned Natcha's ample body a wondrous gold.

All of a sudden she sat up in the bed and her hand instinctively patted the rumpled sheets where Price slept at her side. Price was not there.

She shouted, "Price!" The only answer she got was a calmer, heavier silence from the empty house.

The clock inlayed in the headboard showed the hour: 11:40 a.m. She sighed. Price had left for the noon service at the church. He had got up quietly, being careful not to wake her. He had dressed and left. It was Monday. Monday was a day of service for Price.

Kneeling on the bed, Natcha noticed that her breasts were covered in a thin film of sweat and her hands were trembling. Yes, she was scared.

Scared, instinctively.

For sometime now she was always scared… for Price whose neurosis was taking more and more control of his mind every day. Price who no longer knew and whose memory was ripping apart in a horrible way, playing with time, with real and unreal life. Price who imagined and firmly believed that he remembered…

How long could he hide this condition from every-one? Over the last few days it had become increasingly worse. How long before another priest noticed that he had lost his sense of reality… before they accused him of losing the Faith?

She got out of bed, crossed the room and shut her-self inside the air shower for a few minutes. She came out fresh and rosy and picked out some underwear and a lightweight tunic, very low-cut, from the wardrobe.

This wardrobe, for example. Why did Price refuse to see proof of their marriage in this piece of furniture? A wardrobe full of clothes for her, many of which Price had bought… Wasn't this, among so many other things, proof of their cohabitation?

But Price said, "This wardrobe is all ready for you. It's waiting for you."

She did her hair.

And if Price was telling the truth? If he was right? No! More than once she had asked herself these kinds of questions. It was awful. Impossible.

Yes, it was impossible! In such a situation she would at least have a few scraps of memory… Every-thing would not be so clear, so certain…

But for Price, isn't it clear and certain?

She shook her head furiously, forced herself to think about something else. Letting herself get carried away by all these mind games was really the surest way of going crazy fast.

What she had to do was to follow Price, to be with him. Leave him alone as little as possible, keep him from betraying himself in front of a third person. Since he himself imagined that the neurosis had affected her and since he did not want to lose her, he would let her do it. He would do whatever she wanted.

She was about to leave when, through the glass door, she saw a weird-looking individual standing in the street beyond the courtyard and shaking his fist at the house. He was tall and bearded, hairy and wearing a preposterous blood-red tunic and menacing blue shorts.

She stayed in the shadows.

This law allowing exhibitionism was maybe not the best. How much liberty could an exhibitionist take knowing that he no longer shocked the people around him—seeing that he was accepted by them—how far could such an individual try to push his offense?

The man dressed in red shouted for a moment, alone in the harsh sun. Then he dragged himself away after casting a few more murderous looks at the house.

Natcha left. The heat fell on her shoulders like a panting breath. She looked at the dry, vibrant courtyard, the street, the bungalows. Then she started walking. 15 minutes later, or thereabouts, she was in front of Price's church. She had met nobody on the street. It was really too hot.

CHAPTER III

God is by your sides!
New God, for a new people!
Read the Enlightened Bible of Stan Laurdy ($300).
For the guiding light of clear explanations,
the word of the prophets—
You will see that the chosen people are
The People of America!
God is by your side!
God is American!

The street was wide and gray and Price was standing in the middle of it.

"New God!" he mumbled, aghast. "What happened to me?"

"It" had happened in a fraction of a second, totally incomprehensible. The instant before he was in the street of parish 16 in Tucumcari, heading for the church, and now...

An instinctive surge of revolt flooded his mind. He said out loud, "This isn't possible. I'm dreaming." But he knew already, deep down inside, that he was not dreaming, that something really astonishing had just taken place. Before fear became too overwhelming, he took a look around. Greedily.

The longer he looked, visually recording the alarming details of the landscape, the more absurdly certain he felt that he was no longer in Tucumcari. Or maybe not even in the F.U.S.A.

The street looked like nothing he knew. Never, in all his travels, was he in such a place. Nor had any documentary films left anything in his memory that could answer to this reality.

Reality?

New God! Yes, it was surely and truly a reality. Even just this rain, this spluttering drizzle and cold...

The street was very wide and gray, metallic. It led straight ahead, perfectly straight, to disappear a long way off in the blur of a hazy horizon behind the garlands of tangled rain.

On the right as well as the left, it was bordered by very thick, very green, very imposing hedges. Price had never seen so many green leaves, with the rain above powdering them with silver. The hedges were relatively deep, or so it seemed, and so tall that a few men standing on each other's shoulders could not have seen over them. Behind them he could make out buildings. They were most likely houses. Of stone or metal, it was hard to say. Everything was gray under the persistent rain. The houses were square or rectangular and their angles were all atangle in the jolly chaos beyond the fleecy green hedges.

The sky, which was also huge, was gray and full of bloated clouds, more or less dark, painting a shifting monochrome on the huge celestial canvas, breathlessly admirable.

Price's heart started beating faster. Fear had sunk its claws into his belly and it was climbing. "What did I do?" he mumbled. He remembered that guy... that Muks who had accosted him in the middle of the street to tell him his troubles. He remembered how annoyed he got and the feeling of guilt that came over him as he listened to the one-eyed man's jeremiads. He had finally managed to escape. The guy had mentioned Natcha and then...

And then he was scared for Natcha.

And then... there was this street, this strange landscape.

There was a noise. Faint, purring, faraway.

Price jumped and without thinking, impelled by an inexplicable reflex, he ran to the shrubbery on the side of the road. He dove in and landed flat on his stomach on the sweet smelling, warm earth. His slightest movement provoked a waterfall of droplets from the heavy leaves.

The noise got suddenly louder and a weird machine passed by on the road. Then the noise faded until it melted away and disappeared. The rain's melody on the leaves remained. Alone. And the beating of Price's heart.

He had only caught a glimpse of the machine that had passed by on the road. A red body topped by a kind of transparent cockpit. Inside the cockpit the vague shadow of a human form. Nothing more. Impossible to say if the vehicle had wheels or not or if it was flying low. It went by too fast.

I'm not in Tucumcari, Price told himself, horrified. Something happened and I came here. A time shift or maybe... I don't know. A hole in space-time, the resurgence of another dimension? Good New God! How is this possible?

He was utterly incapable of explaining it or finding an appropriate response to the question. But that was probably it. A violent passage from one universe to another... At one time, the government Researchers had devoted a lot of time to these theories of a parallel universe.

But why me? Or well, no! The whole universe didn't turn upside down. That's impossible!

Behind him the leaves rustled and Price felt a chill run through him. For one or two seconds he could not budge an inch, could not make the slightest movement.

"Hey ho!" a voice said.

It's really not a dream, Price told himself. I knew it. It's really real.

"Hey, friend," the voice again behind him.

Price turned around. He saw a man. A man crouching in the leaves on his hands and knees. A man who was watching him, smiling.

"Don't stay here," the man said. "It's always dangerous to stay on the side of the road." He backed up under the low branches of the hedge motioning to Price to follow him.

Price followed him. The man was pretty skinny, dressed in blue cloth pants and shirt that were faded and ripped. He went barefoot. His face was bony, his eyes (the same color as his clothes) sparkled. He did not look abnormal. On the contrary, he gave the impression of being friendly and kind.

They crawled a few dozen yards before the individual stopped by a hole in the foliage. He sat down, crossed his legs, smiled and said, "You're new? My name's Sher."

"My name... My name's Price," Price said.

The other nodded, as if the fact of knowing Price's name pleased him a lot. He spread his fingers and ran his dry hand through his yellow hair saying, "I don't like to be too close to the road anymore. And this is why: I almost got caught twice by their Guards."

"*Whose* guards? Where am I?" Price asked.

Sher knitted his brow. For a few seconds his eyes narrowed. He murmured, "Ah, so that's it..."

"That's what, New God!" Price raged. "By all the Weight of the Sky, can you explain to me…"

"Don't shout," Sher interjected. "Don't shout, friend. That'll only bring them back. They leave us alone, for the most part, in the hedges. But it only takes one patrol to pass by when you're yelling and it'll be finished…"

Price watched him for a few moments without saying a word, dazed, and then he put his head in his hands.

"Come on," Sher said, "I know what it's like *when you first get here*. It's baffling. I'll try to explain."

"When you first get here?" Price said. "So, I'm not the only one? What happened? What is happening?"

Sher shook his head, smiling amiably, "What's happening? We have a vague idea, but opinions vary. Me, I believe we've been *cured*. I'm the only one who thinks this."

Cured… Cured of what?

"Cured of what?" Sher said before Price could even ask the question. "Cured of the other world. That's what I think."

Price felt like the ground beneath him was starting to roll. He put his hands on the lawn and asked in a croaking voice, "And… where is here? Is it the future? Is it…"

"It's the real," Sher said. "That's all I can say."

Price shook his head slowly from side to side. An unpleasant hum was droning inside his skull, beating against his temples and his forehead. Weighing his words carefully, articulating with mechanical precision, he said, "The real is Tucumcari. It's my parish 16 in Tucumcari. It's the Fascist Union of the States of America. It's the year 2534 of the New God Era."

Sher smiled again. He put a soothing hand on Price's knee. He was obviously trying hard to comfort him. He said, "At first, I, too, fully remembered my universe of sickness. I wasn't cured all at once. I had a few relapses. Yes, that's a memory I bear. But now... now, it's over. I've gotten rid of that obsession forever. I'm really cured. It's possible that you, too, will relapse. It's your first clear vision, isn't it?"

"I don't know what that means," Price admitted. "I don't know what's happening. You're... Good New God! I'm Price Mallworth and I'm a priest of the New Enlightened Catholic Religion, the only religion recognized by the government of the F.U.S.A. It's not madness! I'm not abnormal. It's Natcha who..."

"Don't get upset," Sher soothed. "It's the best way to bear the shock: don't get upset. You'll see, little by little, you'll understand, you'll accept. Here, in the real, you'll see how wonderful it is to live. There are I don't know how many pleasures. Everyone finds what they're looking for, at least that's what the others say."

"The others?"

"Sure. The other cured, like you and me. There are quite a few. Some relapse, but some of them are completely healed."

"Those who relapse," Price said eagerly, "do they remember the F.U.S.A.? Is there anyone who talks about Tucumcari?"

Sher smiled again and calmly shrugged his shoulders. "They remember their universe of sickness, yes... Sometimes. But what they say is so mixed up..."

"Still!" Price urged. "Whether it's incoherent or not, do they talk about our world? The other world, I mean."

"Don't shout. They talk about *their sickness*, so, yes, if you want, of the unconscious world they created, where they were shut up. No one pays attention to what they say. Don't worry, it'll pass. You shouldn't get upset."

Don't get upset!

Around him the entire universe was doing it's utmost to prove that he was totally deranged and he shouldn't get upset! Real, unreal, dreams and conscious perceptions were all ajumble in a frightening mess. The smallest solid point that he tried to cling onto soared up and flew off instantly, at staggering speed, dizzying… And he shouldn't get upset!

"Why can't I shout?" Price asked. "What's the danger with the Guards you were just talking about?"

Sher grimaced. "*They* don't like us much. I think they don't trust us and they're trying to *control* us. That's what I think."

"But who are *they*?"

"Well, the others. Those who weren't sick. The men and women from here. From the real. Truthfully…"

"Yes?"

Sher made a vague, almost desolate gesture with his hands. "Truthfully I believe we're still a little bit sick. I mean I think we're not yet totally reintegrated into normal life. There you are. There's still a giant step to take on the road to total recovery. There you are… Well, they hunt us down, search us out to save us for good…"

"And what are you scared of?"

"I don't know. It's stupid. It's what's left in us of our old sickness that makes us act like this, I think. We're conscious, but in spite of everything, it's hard, or even impossible, to get rid of all the remnants of phobia… Some of us let ourselves be caught, just to know.

To tell the others about it afterward. But we never see them again. Maybe they keep them from coming back once they're cured... Maybe they don't remember us at all once they're 100% cured... I don't know. No one knows. And not knowing is another reason for us to be wary."

He paused, looked very serious. Then another smiled crossed his lips and he continued, "But we're not complaining. It's really marvelous to feel cured already, freed of the phantasms and delusions... You have no idea of the pleasures, the sensations... I can't tell you, words aren't enough..."

Price closed his eyes. "I don't want it!" he groaned. "I don't want... I don't want to be cured of the year 2534! That's where reality is. I'm living a nightmare. I'm going to wake up. I'm going to open my eyes and wake up."

He opened his eyes. Sher was watching him, looking sorry for him.

And after a moment, Sher spoke softly, "Follow me, friend. There are a few of us in the forest. Relatively safe since the Guard patrols are spaced out. And they never venture too deep inside. Come."

He started crawling again. Price followed him. What else could he do? He told himself, I can't give up. I can't. Resist, resist with all my might...

After ten or twelve minutes of crawling, the shape of the shrubs changed. Not only their shape but also the way they were planted. They were less dense, less thick. And then, more and more, there were tall, very tall trees whose vast roof of branches and leaves hid the sun.

They were able to stand and walk. The ground was less humid, covered with a thick carpet of dry leaves and needles. Walking on this thick natural rug was very nice.

And there were smells, too. All the smells of rain, leaves… Perfectly silent. Not a single insect chirping or the faintest birdsong.

There has to be birds, Price told himself. With all these trees, how can there not be… Such perfect silence is not natural. The vehicle a little while ago on that endless road… None of this is natural. Quite the opposite, they're all typical manifestations of a dream. It's a dream world. I'm dreaming. It happened to me somehow and well… Maybe it was Muks, back in the street in Tucumcari… maybe he was part of the dream, too. I'm going to wake up.

After walking for a little while (ten minutes, fifteen, maybe more), Sher got back down on all fours and urged Price to do the same. After another 100 yards they suddenly crawled through a fairly wide gap in the foliage. Around a dozen men and women were on the other side. They welcomed Sher with friendly faces and smiles.

"Here's a new one," Sher pointed out Price to the gathering. "A *convalescent*."

Some of them nodded to greet Price. Others smiled bigger. Most of the men wore shabby pants and no shirt. The women wore skirts or ragged dresses. One of them, with two naked children clasped to her belly, was sleeping on a carpet of moss, away from the group.

"Take a rest," a redheaded woman said. "How are you?"

He did not answer. He could not answer.

He watched one of the men sitting in the gap of foliage. A man in his forties with a rough face deeply hollowed by wrinkles. A man with white hair, sloping shoulders under a wool coat that was too big for him and that was missing one sleeve.

Something white, something terribly bright ripped apart in his head. Sher came up to him, said something that he did not understand and then shook him gently by the shoulder. Price kept staring at the man with white hair. Finally, without meaning to, he let the word slip out of his mouth. "Father."

The man was astounded and raised his eyebrows.

"It's not true," Price said. "It's not possible... I recognize you. You're my father... and that's impossible because my father is abnormal. My father is schizophrenic, in a State Center on the east coast..."

The old man very slowly nodded his head and said, "Stay calm, my boy. It's over. Don't worry. I can't be your father, but stay calm. The first moments are the most painful."

"No!" Price howled. "Stop! You're my father! Your name is Anton Vallmach Mallworth and I pay for your life in the Center of..." He stopped talking. His hands were trembling.

The white-haired man cast a quick glance at his companions and then brought his attention back to Price. He spoke softly, "My name is Lice. I have a boy, that's true, but he isn't cured yet and he's only three years old."

"What's his name?" Price flung back. "Your little boy, what's his name?"

"What does it matter? A name is nothing. You said yourself that my name was Anton... Anton something... but my name is Lice."

"What's the boy's name? What is it!"

After another glance at his companions, the white-haired man said, "His name is Price, I think."

"My name is Price!" Price roared. "Price Mallworth! I'm Price Mallworth..."

The white-haired man nodded sadly. A very nice but contrite smile was born and died on his lips. He said, "How can you be sure, friend?"

The white rip swept all of Price away. He knew that he was going to scream, scream with all his might…

He opened his eyes and had to close them again right away in the blinding sunlight. Then he heard voices. He was startled and sat up. There were five or six of them around him, including a young boy watching him with an absent stare while sucking on his right fist.

"How do you feel, Speaker?" asked the man kneeling at his side. He was a middle-aged man, balding, and his nose was peeling from the sun. His armpits had two big sweat stains.

"New God…" Price mumbled.

"You're feeling better, aren't you?" the sweating man said. "It's this sun, I'm sure."

"What the hell am I doing here?" Price asked instinctively.

The man smiled and looked at the others. He said, "My faith, we'd love to know. We saw you walking across the bungalow courtyards like this, with no hat on, and then you collapsed in front of my house…"

"We're in Tucumcari, aren't we?" Price asked. "Parish 16 in Tucumcari… Isn't it?"

The man's eyes turned suspicious. After a moment he said, "In Tucumcari, yes. Parish 16, exactly. But do you mean…"

"No… no… excuse me. You're right, it's the sun." Price stood up and brushed the dry dirt off his clothes. The heat was awful. He did indeed recognize the bungalows of parish 16, but he must have been at the other end of the parish now. Not at all where he had "left"…

"Thank you. No, I'm okay. I'm okay. Don't you worry. Thanks." The somewhat confused eyes of the group of men watched him leave the courtyard. The child sucking his fist was drooling. In the street Price started running. To anywhere.

CHAPTER IV

The Tommy Spunk gun is your guardian angel;
The guardian angel that costs only $1,045.
The Tommy Spunk gun cannot only relieve your re-
pressed aggression, but it can also guarantee
your protection.
The most effective weapon against the
warped maniacs and anarchopsychopaths!
Good people own a Tommy Spunk.
The Tommy Spunk is an American weapon,
therefore perfect.
(Two models sold over-the-counter when you show
your health card: the 38 Special and the 50.
Helix bullets, jacketed or lead shot. Nice choice!)

Natcha had gone to the church only once before: for
her union with Price. She had a very clear memory of it,
hideous but very clear, and it was, deep down inside,
another proof that she was not crazy—she really had
been married to Price for eight years.

Before the ceremony she did not go to church. Nevertheless, she was in perfect religious health. She had
tried sincerely, but she just could not do it.

Since the union, she had not returned to the holy
place. There were two main reasons for this marginal
attitude. The first dated back to before her union with
Price. All normal people were more or less phobic, a fact
recognized by the government and the M.A.P.M.E.
Natcha suffered from claustrophobia. She never traveled
on the airtrains except on the private platforms and she

only rode in outside elevators. The churches—which are basically enclosed places without windows for the sake of the ceremonies that take place there—were not made for Natcha's mental stability.

Plus, Natcha was united to a Speaker—the social status was supposed to protect her from the mandatory churchgoing. That was the second reason.

There was maybe a third, less important certainly, but that still existed. Apart from her phobia of enclosed spaces, Natcha's psychic balance was perfect. Her sexual relations with Price caused no kind of release through transference. She did not feel like a sinner and, quite the contrary, the Confessions of the Flesh made her uncomfortable. It had nothing to do with her.

Maybe it was pride or pretentiousness or God knows what. She often drilled herself on the matter. But Price assured her that she did not have to, that if she kept on, she would give herself a nice perfection complex and that everything was going well as it was. She always listened to Price... At least, she used to listen to him before he started getting confused about time, before this neurosis that was eating into him, deeper and deeper.

For a long time (several minutes) she hesitated at the door of the church. A somber door, horridly dark, cut from hard, venous wood—real wood. The flat, concrete forecourt reflected the heat and light in an infernal way. Natcha felt this grim heat sliding over her skin and legs.

She had to make an effort, an enormous effort. And who knows, maybe her phobia had passed. Disappeared, extinguished. Whatever the case, she had to enter and make sure that Price was really there. And maybe also... maybe also make sure that she was not the crazy one. Talk to people. Try to find out. Deep down inside her, there was—awful—this doubt.

She could not leave Price alone. For his own good. At any given time he could betray himself, confess his mental confusion... New God! Price locked up... Price separated from her, isolated... Price rejected by the society of Normals. No, she did not want that! At any price!

She pushed the door, entered and closed the heavy panel of real wood behind her. The coolness grabbed her shoulders while the soft smell of mingled fragrances went to her head. She closed her eyes for a second, took a deep breath, opened her eyes again. It was still the same room. Although she had seen it only once, she had retained a precise image of it, incrusted like an open wound in her memory.

It was a long room flanked by two straight walls with a metal ceiling from which hung a riot of colored globes. The walls were bare except for a few decorative panels that turned slowly on their axes. Yes, it was still the same room in the center of which were three round altars at varying heights, with their three spiral staircases.

A gust of heat rushed into her forehead. She closed her eyes again and waited a few seconds until the dizziness passed. A confused din arose from the audience. The room was almost full and in the enclosure bordered by ironwork that had only one narrow entrance all along its perimeter, hundreds of men and women were standing around, shifting impatiently, waiting for the priests to arrive. It was a few minutes past noon and the ceremony was about to start. Natcha was aware of this and shivered. She was only worried for Price... and for his phobia. She had entered in order to make sure that Price was really there.

All of a sudden cymbals crashed and Natcha jumped; she could not hold back a little, startled cry. A satisfied groan ran through the crowd while the cymbals continued clanging to a faster and faster rhythm.

The entrance guard at the gate of the ironwork barrier pointed to Natcha and said, "Enter, ma'am. 15 dollars and you enter. The ceremony will begin in a few seconds." She opened her mouth to respond, but no sound came out. She shook her head.

At first the guard was surprised and then he changed, became immediately suspicious. "Hey, ma'am!" he called out. "You can't…"

"I'm not participating in the ceremony," Natcha managed to say.

The guard screwed up his thin lips. His eyes narrowed. His yellow, bushy hair was sticking out in all directions and it made him look oddly like Millie Wooks, that crumpled puppet whom all the kids loved on the 3D children's show. "In that case," Millie Wooks said, "you can't…"

A deafening music exploded. Natcha had the impression that the notes were actually material things and that someone had taken a whole bunch of them and dropped them haphazardly on the floor. The main lights went out. Only the globes hanging from the ceiling diffused their rays of every shade of red and yellow. The globes started turning slowly just like the decorative wall panels. A throng of shadows and distorted lights started crawling along the walls and ceiling and over the audience.

"Ma'am," Millie Wooks repeated, "you can't stay. You have to…"

"I'm the wife of one of the priests," Natcha said.

The guard opened his mouth, but said nothing. He just stared lustily at Natcha. She felt his eyes crawling over her skin like a real, slimy caress.

"I'm the wife of Price Mallworth," she said. "He's one of the priests of this parish."

"Price Mallworth…" the guard pronounced slowly. "Could be. I don't pay much attention to the priests. They come and go…"

"But Price has been in this parish for a long time," Natcha was forced to shout because the noise from the crowd and the cacophonous music were too loud.

"Very well could be," the guard said. "You know, ma'am, entrance guards like me don't have much opportunity to meet the priests. But I believe you. Go on. I don't really see any reason why you would lie. If you are what you say, you can enter without giving a cent." He opened the gate and stepped back.

"No," Natcha said, "I didn't come for the ceremony."

The Millie Wooks guard closed the gate and shrugged his shoulders. "Well then. I don't really see why you would lie to me. But it's a pity to see a woman like you, ma'am, who doesn't participate in the ceremony. It's a pity for everyone, I think…"

"Maybe," Natcha said, "but not for me."

"It turns me on just to look at you, ma'am," the guard said. "Just to imagine…"

She shot a quick glance at him. Another rush of dizziness rose up in her.

"We're like that, ma'am," the guard said, more Millie Wooks than ever. "Like that, like the New God made us. No reason to be ashamed or shocked. Anyway, not here, not in this place of truth."

She walked away without responding, holding onto the wrought iron barrier with one hand. Her legs were weak, her body covered in cold, sticky sweat. The colors and shadows were spinning around and inside of her.

Close to her, the crowd was swaying on their feet, humming along sporadically to the melody of the recorded music, as far as there was any melody. Their faces were frozen, blissful, or rather tense, full of nervous tics. Several individuals had started undressing and the whirl of colors slapped weird ritual paintings on their skin.

Natcha moved forward like a robot. Her hand left a trail of dark sweat on the handrail of the barrier. Every step, though light, echoed inside her like a gong. The walls started spinning, warping like smoke screens. The ceiling bore down, down...

The ceiling slowly, unrelentingly descended. Any second now it was going to crush her, or at least leave her so little space that she would be unable to breathe. Sweat poured into her eyes and down the small of her back. The thin fabric of her tunic clung to her breasts and belly. She felt like her scalp was roasting. Her hair was itching like mad. But she resisted and drove back the fainting fit as best she could.

The priests were climbing onto the round podiums. There were three of them. One for each podium. They wore long white robes with bejeweled crosses embroidered on the chest. When they reached the top, they stretched out their arms together and together they shouted, "Faithful Ones! We receive you in the name of the New God, in the name of the Only God, who protects the country!"

"We come naked before the New God!" the audience yelled as the music got louder.

Natcha blinked to wipe the sweat out of her eyes. The podiums swayed. She tried hard again, tried to insulate herself in the midst of the crowd. Price was not one of the three priests.

All at once dizziness struck Natcha, mowed down her legs. She reached frantically for the iron barrier, gritting her teeth, streaming with sweat.

"You are naked!" the priest yelled. "Conscious of your imperfections, conscious of your weak mental stability, conscious of your fragility! That's how the New God made you, you and yours. That's how he receives you. To be strong and resist the temptations of the outward life, come and offer up your sins of the body and mind. Come and confess! Come and rid yourselves! Confess! Confess before everyone and before the New God. Come and confess!"

"Ma'am," a distant voice said. She looked up. Through a red, shimmering fog she made out the grimacing face of the guard.

"What's wrong?" he asked. He had followed her, but on the inside and not the outside of the enclosure, and now he was holding her up, through the barrier, his two giant, dry hands closed around her waist.

Her gut reaction made her jump. Hundreds of shouts arose from the crowd, mixed with the clamor of the priests. They made a tremendous racket. "I'm okay," Natcha said. "I'm... Let me go, it's nothing. A dizzy spell..."

She recoiled. The guard's hands let go and slid down her hips for a second. His mouth was twisted, his eyes half-closed and a trickle of sweat glistened on his upper lip.

"It's nothing," Natcha said. "I suffer from claustrophobia and that's why..."

"Churches are not recommended for claustrophobics," the guard said slowly.

"I know..."

In the audience the naked men and women were petting each other and moaning. There were men with men and women with women. Shrieks erupted everywhere, ripping through the music and noise. A fat woman with sagging breasts, her torso drowning under rolls of fat, ran at the barrier, holding her arms out to Natcha, howling, "Come! You! You, pretty girl, come! Come!"

The guard turned and shoved her violently back into the human tide. She fell. An indiscriminate cluster of males and females closed in on her.

"Those fat bitches are the worst," the guard said to Natcha.

She tried to smile—how could she smile?—and brought her hands up to her chest. Her heart was beating wildly.

"Offer up your vices without shame!" the priests bawled. "Offer up your possessions to be cured of them with the help of the New God! New God will forgive your vices and your neurotic tendencies! New God will forgive you because you are honest with yourselves, because you make an effort to become good citizens!"

"If you want to leave," the guard said, "I can help you. If you want..." His left hand was clinging onto the handrail of the barrier; the other was in his pants, shaking frantically.

Nausea, like a hot ball, was spinning around in Natcha's belly.

A man passed behind the guard along the barrier, on his knees, his face distorted by the glare from the lights. His belly was round and pale, his calves very thin. Holding his genitals in his hands, he moved forward, moaning. His eyes empty.

"Let me go!" Natcha screamed. "Leave me alone… I don't need you! I don't need anyone!" She ran down the outer aisle and fled.

It was long and painful. It was really awful.

That shrieking music, that noise… Those naked bodies of men and women spinning around. Those men and those women who were not men and women or even animals, who were worse than that. Wallowing, groggy, carried away by their basest instincts, truly naked, truly laid bare… Offering themselves to the New God such as they were in order to obtain forgiveness… and also to keep this debauchery from taking them over at some time in their life outside.

It was exhausting.

And then Natcha found herself at the other end of the room in front of a door to the private chambers. She was utterly unable to say how long it had taken her to cross the room. She opened the door and slammed it behind her, leaning against the cold hinge, eyes closed. Later she realized that she could hear herself breathing, that the surrounding racket was much softer.

She opened her eyes. The room was small, but on the opposite wall a large window opened onto the outside, the sun, the light… Except, she saw a man sitting at the only table in the room. And the man was looking at her. He was fat, with very wide shoulders, too wide for his little, round, bald head. He had a crown of gray hair around his skull, winding over his ears and around the nape of his neck.

"Excuse me," Natcha mumbled. "I didn't mean…"

"What are you doing here?" the priest thundered. "Don't you know that it's forbidden? What are the guards doing? They're all incompetent, damn it!"

Natcha looked at the sun outside. A shower! Ice-cold in the glassy shower at home... A really cold air shower, that's what she needed. But she was already seeing the sun. She was no longer completely closed in... and some strength came back to her.

The fat priest stood up. He was huge. "Leave, ma'am," he said in his booming voice. "You have nothing to do here. You have no right..."

"I'm sorry," Natcha said, "but you're mistaken. I'm the wife of a priest of this parish, of this church. I never would have come here if I didn't have the right."

The fat priest's face changed in a second. The furious spark that gleamed in his black eyes disappeared. "In that case, it's me who should apologize. I couldn't know, ma'am. I'm sorry. I've only been here for a short time. Exactly three weeks and I... I'm pleased to meet you."

Natcha smiled. Her legs were still weak, her forehead soaked.

"My name is Bertum," the fat man said. "You seem... would you like to sit down?"

He pointed to his chair. The only one in the room. But Natcha refused with a shake of her head.

"I didn't mean to disturb you," she said. "My condition prohibits me from entering a church. I suffer from claustrophobia. But now it's okay, it's passed..."

"Oh," Bertum said. "Shall I open the window?" He did not wait for an answer, just did it. A slight breeze, a little cool, entered the room.

"Thank you," Natcha said. "I wanted... You see, I wanted to see my husband. He's the priest Price Mallworth. I thought I'd meet him and..."

"You're Mrs. Mallworth? I'm delighted to meet you. Come to the window, Mrs. Mallworth, please."

She obeyed. She crossed the room and was inwardly glad to see that she was not too wobbly. She leaned on the windowsill.

Bertum's face darkened again. He said, "It's that… your husband… Priest Mallworth is not here. We were worried about him, too. Today was the day of his service and he didn't show up at the church. I've known him personally for only a little while, but according to our colleagues, he has the reputation of being a very serious priest and certainly punctual… Yes, we were worried."

Natcha's fingers clutched the windowsill. She felt herself turning pale. "New God! He isn't here? Where is he? How did you leave? When did he leave? Where is he? New God, help me!"

"Would you like a glass of water, Mrs. Mallworth?" Bertum fussed. Again without waiting for an answer he went to the dispenser in the wall and came back with a paper cup for Natcha. He watched her drink.

"Thank you," Natcha said, handing back the empty cup.

"Don't you worry now," Bertum said. "He could have run into some unforeseen difficulties…"

"But I am worried," Natcha said. "I think…" She hesitated, then said, "A little after he left, a strange man came down our street. He made some hostile gestures at our house… One of those dangerous madmen. Even his clothes were aggressive."

"You should inform the Protectors," Bertum said. "Just in case, you know. As a basic precaution…"

Where is he? This nice lie explains your fear, but it's only a lie, Natcha. Where could Price be? Where could a neurasthenic go in the middle of a fit when he does not even know what time he is living in?

"Thank you," she said. "Yes, I believe I'll inform the Protectors… thank you."

"You can inform them here, it would be more…"

"No thank you, Priest Bertum. I'll go home first and on the way back make sure no one's seen him. Sometimes people see things but they won't tell unless you ask them to."

"That's true. Leave through here, Mrs. Mallworth. You can avoid crossing the ceremony room. It's hard to deal with in this heat. And with the summer coming it's like they're possessed by the devil." He said all this with a smile on his face and an apology in his voice. He unlocked the little door in the back of the church and opened it.

Natcha smiled. As she was leaving Bertum said, "I didn't know Mallworth was married, you see. He talked to me about you and his plans for union with you. We only saw each other once, last week. I see he made up his mind… and I have to admit, now that I know you, that I can't understand why he was hesitating."

The knot burned and then froze, spun around like a wicked drill in Natcha's head. For a second she thought she was going to faint. Fall down right there, like a log.

"You weren't united in this church, were you?"

She heard herself respond, "No… no, not in this church… In parish 18… That's where I'm from."

"I'm happy for Mallworth. He seemed to me like a really nice guy. I'm happy to see he finally made up his mind. I think he was hesitating because of your genetic cards, is that it?"

"That's right," Natcha answered, like in a dream.

"You'll see," Bertum said, "all you need now is a little surgery… unless it's already been done?"

She was on the verge of screaming that it had already been done! That it had been done eight years ago and that she had already been united to Price for eight years! He had not made up his mind last week but eight years ago! *Eight years!*

Anyway, that is what she believed, what she had always believed…

She said, "It's done… it's done, Priest Bertum." And she whirled around and dashed off under the sun toward the street. Her tunic flew up high on her golden legs. She ran, ran with all her strength…

For a long moment Bertum stood there, gaping, wide-eyed, still with a bit of smile frozen on his lips.

CHAPTER V

Take your trips during the day and travel
on the State airtrains.
You can rent out weapons just by presenting your
health card at the booths in the underground lines.
Your security for $100.
Isn't your life worth $100?
Travel on the State airtrains.

For a long time Price ran helter-skelter and when he was too tired to run, he walked. His thoughts were so muddled that he crossed his entire parish and parish 15 as well, without knowing it. That means that he ran and walked for almost two hours.

In the first ten minutes he turned around a lot, worried about seeing the fat, sweaty guy and his friends pop up right behind him. But nothing of the sort happened. The streets were empty, or almost. They all looked the same with the rows of bungalows cut out of the same mold. Sometimes an automobile vehicle passed by silently in a great whoosh of air. The children, whom the white heat grouped together in the shade of the front porches, let loose a shrill cry or tinkling laughter every now and again while they played.

On his walk Price had tried hard to see clearly in the great chaos that was jarring his thoughts. But it was still too hot. Before an idea fully bloomed, it was already dead; the hint of an explanation peeked out and just as soon crumbled away, dismally. He felt clammy all over, physically and psychologically.

That is how he ended up, without knowing how, in front of the ticket booth of the airtrain station. And only then did he realize the ground he had covered. He became suddenly aware of the leaden fatigue knotting his legs. His head was still muddled. He dropped onto a bench in the station just under the map of the network. The booth was empty, split into two equal parts of shadow and sun. The token machines were in the sun, Price in the shadows. The ground was littered with cigarette butts and maniacs had covered the walls with a variety of pornographic inscriptions and drawings.

Distractedly, and for the hundredth time, Price told himself that he had missed the ceremony at the church, that the priests would be worried, that they had maybe tried to reach him at his bungalow and in that case Natcha, too, would be worried. Especially Natcha, in her condition. But what could he do?

Of course, go back home. And then? If he went back home, he would have to explain. And that was where everything would become more complicated. Explain what? How could he tell Natcha and the priests what had happened to him? How, especially to Natcha who already believed (he knew) that he was on the road to madness? How to explain to the others what he was unable to understand himself...

He could not deny it, he knew. He had never known how to lie well and he had no talent as an actor, no imagination... Try to deny or come up with God knows what—that was the last thing he could do. At some time or other it would break down and be worse than ever.

New God! Yes, he could do anything, but certainly not go back home and face Natcha in the condition he was in.

He saw again the face of that guy who called himself Sher. What was that crazy story all about? The guy was saying, yes, he said, "You're being cured. Reality is here and the other world is just a manifestation of the madness." Maybe those were not his exact words, but that was the gist of it.

The other world... So, this one... So, he was completely crazy right now, living in a kind of maniac's nightmare. It was not real, so...

Price groaned and dropped his head between his hands. Whether it was true or not, it was, in any case, precisely the kind of thing to drive you crazy! A huge, unfathomable abyss that he had better not lean over... But also an abyss that was sucking him in, sucking him in relentlessly. Viciously.

He jumped up and headed for the automatic token machines, searching his coat pockets. Sitting there on the bench, racking his brain was also something not to do. Not now. The best thing was to keep moving, to occupy his mind with something in particular, not trying to understand everything in a few seconds.

He got change for a five-dollar bill and bought a token for downtown Tucumcari. He did it without thinking and the destination he had in mind seemed to him the surest place. He could always change his mind during the trip if he came up with something better, if he managed to work out some kind of solution to his problem.

"New God! And what a problem!" he said out loud.

He made sure that there was no one in the immediate vicinity before rapping on the walls of the box, of the token machine, and stamping his foot on the ground. Good God! It was real, solid... But the trees, leaves, the wet ground of the *other side* were real and solid, too.

And his fa… that guy who called himself Lice was real enough, too.

The airtrain arrived silently, hanging on its rail like a big, blue toy. It stopped at the platform and Price slipped his token into the door. He got on, the door closed behind him, spitting back his token, and the train started moving again.

There were only three people in the car. A girl with pink hair, dressed in a long, yellow dress cut low all the way down to her waist and a wiry little man in leatherette shorts with a 12-year old boy. The boy was curled up in his seat like a cat. He had a huge head and snot was running onto his folded arm. Price picked a seat so that no matter where he looked he would not see the kid.

The suburbs started flying by before his eyes. A monotonous succession of blocks of bungalows, all identical and smeared together under the optical effect caused by the speed. The blurry vision soon made his migraine worse. He closed his eyes to be lulled by the gliding train.

He let five or six stations go by before opening his eyes again. Now there were a dozen people in the car. The airtrain was snaking through a deep canyon of buildings downtown. Everywhere were the same façades pierced by lighted bay windows. The sun had dropped to ground level by this time of the day and a carnival of neon signs was already casting thousands of brightly colored, blinking, flashing lights as far as the eye could see. There were lots of people on the different levels of sidewalks, stationary and moving. The city crowd, colorful and feverish. A crowd, a noise, movement that the suburb was not very used to.

The airtrain glided along for ten minutes or so in the midst of this hive of activity and then stopped at a station. Price got up and went to the exit, which relieved him of his token when it opened. He jumped onto the platform. His mind was still as muddled, without a hint of a solution in sight. He felt hollow, tired, stifled by the mugginess.

He went with the flow down the escalator and moving sidewalks, along the rolling roads that got lost in the city, cutting through blocks of houses and buildings. The crowd in the tunnels had thinned. In the stark white ramp lights, the faces looked carved out of chalky desert rock.

A man accosted Price on a rolling road, tried to sell him a pistol at half-price. Price refused. The man pulled out of his pocket a few rolls of film that he swore were "the most disgusting ever made." He wanted six dollars. Prices sent him firmly on his way. The man walked off insulting him.

Price followed the arrows "to go up", took another escalator and finally found himself in the open air. A few hundred feet from the goal he had instinctively set. The street was narrow and dark and most of the buildings dated back to the end of the 20th century. Only in the second row did new buildings rise up.

Price went up the street. Groups of individuals were hanging around on the sidewalks. There were some women, but very few. Price saw, as always, a few pairs of Protectors going this way and that, their long billy clubs slapping their legs at every step, their guns at their sides. Because of the whores of old and the hypno-prostitutes (H-Ps) of today, the street had kept a pretty bad reputation. However, like in the old days, those who sold sexual pleasure were tolerated by the government; the H-Ps were now recognized as being of public interest and were approved by the M.A.P.M.E. It was with society and the good old self-righteous public opinion—

which wanted to be and believed itself to be more royalist than the king—that the street, all the streets like this, had an unsavory reputation.

You had to be on the road to neurosis—and so a hair's breadth from rejection—to get the idea of consulting an H-P. You had to be already sick to consider paying for a mental pleasure that was totally fabricated by a third party. And what a third party! Were they so great, these professional voyeurs, these dream and pleasure brokers who knew how to do nothing but pour their own phantasms and their inner sludge into someone else's head? Could they be proud, really?

But you had to forget all about the fear and anxiety to talk like that…

Price regularly frequented an H-P on this street. He had spoken to Natcha about it. She knew. She was fully aware of his asthenic tendencies and she understood. He came for a bunch of reasons and one of those reasons was in direct relation with their genetic cards, with the fact that if they got married, the law would forbid them to have children. Of course Natcha had understood.

He stopped in front of number 47AZ. Could this really help him? In his present mental state, would the session bear fruit? He had no idea. None at all. He simply knew that in the deepest depths of the chaos he had thought of this place like one thinks of a refuge. And his feet had carried him here. It was a way of escaping, of relaxing. An attempt to see clearly. Whether or not it had positive results was another thing all together.

Price went up the porch, crossed the courtyard and entered the lobby of the establishment. A ruddy-faced receptionist welcomed him with a wet smile. "Mr. Price!"

He answered with a nod of his head and immediately asked, "Can Madame Leona see me?"

The receptionist checked the light table in front of her and gave Price a sorry look. "Mr. Price… I'm afraid that no. I don't see that you were expected and I…"

"That's right," Price said. "I wasn't expected. I didn't have time."

"I'm sorry, Mr. Price. Madame Leona is busy all day."

He, too, was sorry. He was used to Leona and she knew him thoroughly. It was always great with her. Very easy. He left the hypnosis tired but glad to have lived the wonderful moment.

"Who else?" he asked.

"Right away, if you want, there's Madame Sylvene. She's very good, you know. Really very good, at least as good as Leona. If you want my…"

"That's great," Price said. "Let's go with Madame Sylvene."

"You're absolutely right. 9th floor."

"You can put the session on my bill," Price said. "I don't have enough money on me."

"Okay," the receptionist said. "But only because it's you, Mr. Price."

"Thank you," Price said as he got in the elevator.

Madame Sylvene—he read the name on the silver medallion hanging between her breasts—welcomed him as he got out of the elevator. She was a tall, young woman with thick, curly, blond hair. Her face was triangular with dark green eyes caked with make-up. All she was wearing was white-lace shorts that stood out sharply against her tanned skin. Her office was exactly the same as Leona's. The pastel blue walls; the reclining chair in the middle and the other for the mistress of the place; the file pictures on one of the walls, the decorative panels…

"Welcome, Mr. Price," Sylvene said, "you've never come to see me before, right?"

"Never," Price said.

"Sit down," Sylvene invited.

He obeyed and sat in the chair in the middle of the room. She stretched out in her armchair. Her legs were very long, smooth and tanned. "I'm listening," she said. "Trust in me, Price. I'm here to help you."

He tried to relax, to push his fatigue and chaos far, far away. He began, "I'm 30 years old. I live with Natcha and I'm going to get married to her… if it's possible… (He described Natcha, spoke of their genetic cards that forbade them to procreate. Then he spoke of his parents, of his mother who had died when he was barely nine, of his father become abnormal and put in a State Center on the east coast among the hundreds or thousands of other Abnormals.) I would like the son that I will never have. I would like you to give me this son, Sylvene."

"Relax," Sylvene's distant voice said. "Watch the psychguidance screen."

He stared at the screen over his head. It was a black oval in the center of which a tiny bright point was spinning. Slow, gentle music surfaced, whose rhythm was tuned with the gyrating spot. He knew that everything was going to be all right and he was happy about it. Then he let himself be carried away on the waves of hypnosis, offered himself up to all the suggestions.

He did not recognize the house (Sylvene's creation could obviously not be the same as Leona's) but he knew that it was his. It was a long bungalow of natural wood with large bay windows because of Natcha's phobia. The house was built in the middle of a vast, green space, surrounded by thick hedges and a lush forest. The grass was new, soft and delightfully moist under his feet.

The child ran out of the house. He was laughing. Here again, the child looked nothing like the son usually offered by Leona. Price was inwardly aware of this, but it did not bother him. The child was Price's son. He was eight years old. His face was round, full of health, framed by a thicket of crazy hair. His name was Price Junior but he was used to being called Junior P.

Junior P rushed into the arms of Price, who was swinging in a hammock in the cool shade of two giant birch trees. The shock tipped over the hammock and the father and child collapsed to the ground, tangled up, in fits of laughter. Junior P was the first to get up and start running again. He shouted, "You can't catch me! You can't catch me!"

Price smiled. This little man who looked so much like him was his son. The continuation of his life, the last leg of the relay, the extreme limit at the end of a hundred-million-year old memory.

"I'm going to catch you!" Price yelled. He ran full speed behind the boy who let out a piercing cry that turned straight into a long roar of laughter. For a few minutes they chased each other like that until Price ran out of breath and fell to the ground. Junior P went up to him, red and disheveled, still shaking all over with crazy laughter, and fell into his father's arms.

"You know I had you," Price said with extraordinary dishonesty.

Junior P dried a joyful tear and then stared into Price's eyes. He could change without any transition whatsoever from the most uncontrollable hilarity to the utmost seriousness. He said, "You'll never die, will you, Price?"

"I'll never die," Price said.

"And Natcha either," Natcha said. They both turned around. Natcha was there, smiling. She was wearing a long, embroidered tunic; her blond hair was blowing gently in the breeze. She had the body and face of Sylvene, but it was Natcha.

"Natcha will not die," Price said. "Nor anyone. Ever!"

He looked up... and Natcha's eyes were no longer there. Instead there was a man in his forties with gray hair. The man said, "My name is Lice and not Anton Vallmach Mallworth. Why do you want to be my son, Price?"

Price felt himself dry up. Dry and icy. "No!" he screamed in the night.

It was absolutely impossible. He did not want it! Not now! How could he defend himself? He was under hypnosis and he knew it... Could it be that Sylvene was behind the hoax? No, no, of course not. But how could he defend himself?

He hesitated a long time before opening his eyes and then finally decided to.

He was lying on a soft bed. The room he was in was bathed in a soft half-light. It looked circular or oval; anyway Price could not make out any trace of an angle in the walls. He tried to sit up, then realized that his wrists and ankles were locked in metal shackles fixed onto the edges of the bed. He was bare-chested and wore only light pants.

"Why am I here?" he wondered aloud. And the sound of his voice surprised him.

He tried to remember. It was black; it was nothing-ness. It was, in his head, like a very long, empty tunnel, deserted, whose tiny end opened onto a small point of daylight. And in this point there was an impression, a name. TUCUMCARI.

He remembered Tucumcari, but no longer knew what it meant. He searched for it. The harder he searched, the smaller the point of light at the end of the tunnel became. He stopped searching.

He felt nothing. Except, maybe, a little, dull anxiety rising inside of him. The anxiety was linked to Tucum-cari.

He lifted his head as far as he could and looked around. A few feet from the couch was a kind of arm-chair with a large, reclining back topped by a string of electrodes bundled together and connected to a big box. He told himself, "They" did something to me. That's why I don't remember.

"They"… What was behind that?

A door opened at this very moment, somewhere in the wall. Two people, dressed in identical white suits approached Price. Two women. Their faces were very square, their hair short and light. Their noses grew out of the middle of their foreheads. It was weird.

One of them leaned over Price and smiled. She said something that he did not understand. She smiled again, then turned to her companion and looked at her for a few seconds. She ended up nodding her head, turning back to Price and taking off the shackles that were imprisoning his wrists and ankles.

He felt himself suddenly drowning in dreadful fear. He remembered Tucumcari, parish 16, Natcha. He re-membered his world, the year 2534, his country. He remembered what had already happened to him once before.

Then he jumped up, shoved aside the first woman with the weird nose and ran toward the second just as she was opening the door. A long, silent corridor opened up before him. He dove in.

"How do you feel?" Sylvene asked.

She was leaning over him, with a hint of real worry in her big, green, heavily made up eyes. Her silver pendant was swinging slowly.

Price let out a long sigh. He sat up. His sweat-soaked clothes clung to his body.

"How do you feel?" Sylvene repeated.

It was none too good. He stammered, "What happened?"

Sylvene straightened up and sighed, too. "I'd really like to know. That's the first time that's happened to me with a client."

"Was I… was I here the whole time?" Price asked. Barely out of his mouth and he regretted what could be a very dangerous question.

Sylvene answered, "Yeah! For whatever it means to be here… I've been fighting with this for two hours… You were here, sure, in body. There (she tapped his forehead), you were gone. I don't know how or why… It started out fine."

"That's right," Price said. "I remember. You did very well…"

"Okay, but afterward… the black hole. It was impossible to reach you in any way… What happened, for you?"

He closed his eyes and instantly saw the weird faces of the two women. "I don't know," he lied. "I don't know. A blank... I'm sorry..."

"You don't have to apologize."

He got up. He was in a hurry to do only one thing—leave this place and be alone. If he was going to fall apart and become truly crazy, he wanted it to happen someplace other than an H-P's room.

"I'm sorry," he repeated. "I'm going. You did your best... Thanks."

She went with him as far as the elevator, gazing on him with a funny look. She told him, "You should see a psycho-counselor. This kind of thing isn't normal."

"That's what I'm going to do. That's what I'm doing right now."

Alone, in the elevator, he cried.

CHAPTER VI

Drink Wayne lemon juice
(guaranteed by the government,
authorized by the M.A.P.M.E.)
Wayne lemon juice.
The only natural drink that has both nutritional
and therapeutic qualities.
Wayne lemon juice has a sensible dose
of antidepressants.

In the end, she was acting stupid. She should not have panicked like that. If she had not suffered through the church ceremony before, she would not have panicked. She was sure of that now. All the same, for a little while, she was really wondering if Price might not be right… and if she were not the one affected. But Bertum had admitted to her: he was new, so he could not know anything. Except what Price told him during their one and only conversation.

Anyway, the danger was real. She had proof that Price was saying crazy things and he could say them to anyone. He could, in one sentence, denounce himself, if the other did not know him.

Price was crazy.

He had woken up that morning in a full-blown mental crisis. They had made love and then he had left. But where did he go?

She was tired. Her sweat-soaked hair stuck to her cheeks, hung all over her forehead. Her legs were heavy, her lower back felt wrapped in lead. Every new step took tremendous effort.

At first Natcha had gone back to the bungalow. Price was not there. She left again and wandered aimlessly through the streets of parish 16. She questioned children and old men sharing the shade in front of the houses, but no one had seen Price. Then, after several hours of walking, she headed for downtown Tucumcari.

When Price went to the city, it was when he was going through a depressive period. And where do you go when you are in a state of mental fatigue? You try to forget, you search for a remedy that will help you endure life, that will spin your head for a little while, in dreams. You walk down the mean streets to visit an H-P.

That was the case with Price and Natcha knew it. He did not have a child and never would. As long as he was united with her, he would never be a father. So, for a few hours an H-P on some "mean" street in Tucumcari would give him the feeling. The girls—or guys—by means of hypnotic suggestions would provide him with this reality that Natcha could never give him.

The maternal fiber had never been very highly developed in her. Maybe her childhood memories were too bitter. Whatever the case, Natcha had never felt the need to create or bring a child into the world. Nevertheless, she fully understood and accepted the fact that Price, as opposed to her, might feel this need and thus feel somewhat frustrated. They did not talk about it, or rarely, but she knew and so she let him visit the H-P pleasure brokers.

In the present situation it was flagrant: Price was in an unusual state of depression. If he had come to the city, he must have, logically, headed for one of these mean streets. If he was in the city… This was, of course, only hypothetical, but at least she had a relatively solid base in the infernal chaos that was scrambling her brains. The slightest lead could be the good one and turn something up. The slightest hope…

In Tucumcari there were a good 50 streets whose buildings housed H-P "clinics". And Natcha started going through them one by one. She entered the establishments and asked the receptionists if a man answering to the name of Price Mallworth (whom she described) had been in. They inevitably said no, that no one of that name had been seen that day, that it was the first time they had even heard the name and that the description did not remind them of anyone at all. And it was absolutely impossible to know if the responses were sincere or if they were given out of some purely professional policy of discretion.

Night came, bearing down on her fatigue and desperation. The night and the neon lights transformed the streets like cheap make-up transforms a face and from a sweet smile comes a scowl… The night: a different realm, a world apart.

Natcha shivered. She was no longer counting the streets, the climbing up and scrambling down, the number of questions asked on the edge of mad hope, or the answers, always the same.

She had fallen into this underground airtrain station and, for a few minutes, on the bench, listened to the fatigue spread through every one of her muscles, every nerve. She knew that a train would come, that she would get on this train and go three stations farther down to run through a new street and ask the same questions again and again. Maybe she also knew, deep down inside, that the questions would find no answers.

There were around thirty people in the station, but she paid no attention to them. Nor did she notice the group who, for a few minutes, had followed her silently and now, like her, was waiting.

With a long dull hiss the train sprang out of the dark tunnel and stopped exactly between the station markers. Passengers got off. Natcha stood up. The people up front were already getting on the train. She wanted to squeeze through, but the three individuals in front of her, shoulder to shoulder, did not budge. They were planted there like cement posts and obviously had no intention of taking the train.

"Excuse me," Natcha said. "Please…" They did not budge an inch.

She tried to go around them on the right, ran into a tall, thin guy with a really bony face, who looked at her, grinning. A hideous grin.

She spun on her heels. To the left there was a broad-shouldered, baby-faced girl. Same grin.

"I have to take the train! Be ki…" No, they had no intention of being kind.

An icy wave ran through her belly. In a second she felt utterly discouraged, exhausted, overwhelmed. "No," she mumbled, "not this… not this, *as well!*"

And then, just as she was about to scream, the train shut its doors and took off. She stood there, in the empty station, surrounded by these five characters. Not scared—not yet—simply worn out. The three individuals who had blocked her way turned around to face her. They were grinning too. They had very long hair and bushy beards. Their clothes were faded and threadbare.

The tallest of the beards stepped forward, pressing up against Natcha. He stank to high heaven of sweat. Stretching his grin he said, "*As well* as what, babe?"

Natcha backed away but her calves bumped into the edge of the bench. "Leave me alone," she gasped. "I didn't do anything to you. I'll scream and you…"

"So shut your trap, little bitch," the beard said calmly. "What good would it do you to scream? We've got 15 minutes, minimum, to get cozy here together. 15 minutes before the next batch of assholes turns up for the next train."

He paused. His grin was still as big, but a hard, metal flame gleamed in his pale eyes. "15 minutes… and even the Protectors don't dare step into the underground at night. You see, we're getting cozy! We can do things during this time…"

He raised his hand, which closed around Natcha's right breast. A horrible nausea rose up in her. Someone let loose a shivering laugh. The other hand of the beard was holding a knife. He laid the blade against Natcha's breast, said, "All the time in the world. We could all jump you and not worry at all about being disturbed, if you fancy that? Jump you all over the place and even Marry can find a whole bunch of things to do to you. Funny things. I can cut off your butt cheeks and make you eat them and you can yell as loud as you want, it won't change a thing, honey."

"Let me go," Natcha stammered. "I'm… I'm claustrophobic and if I stay here too long…"

"Shit! A claustro," the chubby girl hurled. The tall, thin guy burst out laughing.

"Please," Natcha begged.

One of the beard's partners spoke pensively, "Marry loves claustros. Men, women, dogs, cats. Guess where she puts them? Nothing turns her on more than when they start wiggling around…"

"Please," Natcha murmured. Her forehead was drenched in sweat. The walls of the tunnel, the ceiling and the station started warping grotesquely.

"Well, okay," the beard said dryly. He pulled away his knife, let his arms hang at his sides and said, "We could do all that to you and worse if we were thugs, little claustro. But you're in luck, we're not scum. We don't want to hurt you. We don't want to hurt anyone."

She dropped onto the bench. They did nothing to stop her. She heard a voice, very far away, say, "Hey, Miles, is she really losing it or what?"

New God, yes! She was really "losing it"! Her mouth was dry and waves of heat pulsed down her neck. She opened her eyes. They were all there, watching her. "Why did you stop me from getting on the train," she asked in a fuzzy voice. "What did I do to you?"

"Nothing," the beard called Miles said. "It was you or someone else. We were following you for a little while on the street…"

"You're Abnormals! You can deny it, but you're all Abnormals!"

"We don't deny it, little bitch. I said we're not scum. Not aggressive. Not killers or sadists or anything like that. That's what I said… But you're right, we're totally Abnormal. That's what our dear government decreed and that's what the M.A.P.M.E. confirmed double quick to protect this dear government."

Natcha's eyes widened. A rush of real fear infested her. "You're…"

"Yes," Miles said. "That's it exactly. Just got to see your face to know that you understand and the government campaigns have borne their fruits. They decreed that our way of thinking was a psychotic manifestation. They classified us among the Abnormals and not just any ones: the most dangerous. And it's true that folks like us can be dangerous: dangerous for the monopolies, dangerous for the F.U.S.A., for the religion, for everything!... but certainly not for the individuals, certainly not for the people."

He was warming up, getting louder and louder. "The government doesn't give a damn about the people. And especially not the individual, the human being. They're at the controls of the machine and the machine is theirs and they're the only ones to profit from it. All they see in the individual, in the people, are the cogs and wheels of the machine... So, sure, from this perspective we can be dangerous: proof, it's out of fear that they classified us among the crazies. A dreadful fear to see our ideas reach every level of society and wake up the sleeping consciences. Fear! But it's not over! They're going to shit in their pants they'll be so scared! So, they launched their barrage of propaganda... For all the poor jerks, for all the poor exploited, for all the poor sleepers. It was really necessary to defend them against us fast, to sink them deeper into the fear and the phobias and the panphobia, to crush them under the weight of new, fresh terrors to control them better! All the "warped maniacs", all the "anarchopsychopaths" are dangerous paranoiacs, crazy in the full meaning of the word... And what does it mean, huh, "anarchopsychopath", "warped maniac"? Because we chose to awaken some old ideologies that were crushed by the Single Party, because we unearthed these ancient ideologies from past ages when it was not yet forbidden to have your own ideas... because we think that fascism is not the will of God but is shit instead... and besides, we also think that God floats on the same level and was never good for anything but to benefit certain parties, certain classes, to the detriment of too many others… Because we got it in mind to believe in man—the Machine kicked us out!"

He stopped, out of breath.

Natcha stood there, agape, with nothing to say.

The tall thin man said, "Hey, Miles! What makes you think you have to give a speech?"

"We have to spread our ideas," Miles said. "Take advantage of every opportunity. They have to know that we're not what the government says. That we're not murderers or madmen, but simply individuals who don't agree with the one and only ideology anymore." He turned to Natcha again. "What we want is your money. That's all. We've been reduced to that so we don't smash up or give up. To eat and be able to keep going. We're outside society, you know, gorgeous? They won't let us work, in any way whatsoever, to keep us down. They won't let us do anything. But we don't want their work anyway. Not the work that benefits them… When we've fucked everything up, work will be something else!"

"I have very little money," Natcha said feebly.

She had listened to the torrent of words without really understanding everything. In truth, she only wanted one thing: to get out of there. To breathe fresh air, to escape this awful, enclosed space… Curiously, she was no longer scared of them. So much so that she dared to tell them, "You say that you care about the individual, about the human person… but it's a human person, an individual who you want to rob."

Miles smiled. "We have no choice, sweetie. It's the start. Soon, in spite of the segregation, in spite of the Protectors, we won't attack the cogs and wheels anymore, but the brain of the Machine! That'll be a big party! And there won't be a handful of us, but thousands!

Blacks, Yellows and Reds with us! The great tidal wave, angel! Not only in our fucked up country, but on the other side of the ocean, too. What do you know about the countries on the other side of the ocean, huh? Nothing! The government decided once and for all that they were pathetic, uninteresting, just plain not human, since they're not Chosen Ones from the F.U.S.A. They have their 50% crazies on the other side of the ocean and the governments are pretty much the same assholes as ours. But they also have their pariahs who are fed up, who want another life. Who want to get out of this damn rut they've been stuck in by all the politics of a few profiteers! It's going to go up in smoke, gorgeous... In the meantime, we need your money. And just for that we can get really nasty. But it's not theft. It's a trade: now, if you want, you can look around with a different eye."

Look at the world with a different eye... Since the morning she had been looking at the world with a different eye. Since she knew that she had to denounce Price's madness.

A crazy idea crossed her mind. A really crazy idea...

She stuck her hand into her tunic's belly pouch and took out a flat purse that she handed to Miles. While she opened it to check the contents—pretty slim pickings—she said, "My husband's in the city. He's a priest, but that's not important. He's suffering from some mental confusion, maybe neurasthenia, and he's past the neurotic stage. I'm afraid... I've been looking for him since this morning... Can you help me?"

Miles and the others had the same stunned look on their faces. After a minute one of Miles' bearded partners spit out, "That's what I call having some nerve..."

Miles smiled again and said, "Even if we wanted to—and maybe we would, who knows—we can't. Because we don't trust you, gorgeous. We can't trust you, get it? Not right away, not just like that." He snapped his fingers.

"But I swear to you …"

"Don't swear anything. I said we don't trust you. You have no idea of the traps we're constantly avoiding. Once outside, you could just scream to bring a whole regiment of fucking Protectors onto us. No... wait. I didn't say you would yell, I said you could. Even if there's just one chance in a million of it going down like that, we can't take the risk."

"Miles!" the tall, thin man said.

From the passageway came sounds of footsteps, voices.

"It's the next batch," Miles said. "We'll leave you, gorgeous. And thanks for the dough. You'll be able to say that the craziest crazies aren't what they believe, right? And, in a pinch, you can join us some day if it gets too much for you."

The first of the new wave of passengers came out. Miles dropped onto the bench next to Natcha. He whispered to her, "I've got a piece in my pocket. Any bullshit and you're a goner... Maybe in this crowd there are other folks with pieces and they wouldn't mind using them—that's also part of the anti-Dangerous-Crazies propaganda. But what's for sure is that it would make a big pile of cold meat... *Okay?*"

Natcha nodded.

The station gradually filled up. Miles' partners were spread out so they could control the whole platform. They all had their hands in their pockets.

"Here," Miles held out his closed fist to Natcha. She opened her hand and received two crumpled ten-dollar bills. "It's not much, but it can help if you're really looking for that speaker husband of yours... We keep the rest."

"Thanks," Natcha said.

The train whistled into the station and stopped. Miles stood up slowly. He spoke again, "We don't exploit. We don't loot... At least not everyone, not just anyone. As much as you can, take it easy."

He walked off, melting into the wave of travelers. Natcha closed her eyes, clutching the two bills in her hand. When she opened her eyelids, the station platform was deserted; the train had left.

She got up and staggered toward the escalators at the end of the passageway that led out to the open air.

She knew that she had no more strength to continue. To run through new streets, to enter new tunnels, to take new trains... And run the risk of meeting new gangs of Abnor... of those people voluntarily on the fringes, whom the M.A.P.M.E. had classified among the Abnormals. No, she could not go on.

She collapsed on the first bench outside the station. The night was cool but sticky on her wet skin. Lead bars were banging together in her head. She waited.

What could she do? Videophone the bungalow again? Her last try was at least half an hour ago, just before entering the bowels of this station. And the screen had remained desperately blank, black.

Price was lost and she knew it. It was not just a bitter, very bitter hypothesis, but a certainty. A dreadful certainty. The hope that she had methodically maintained for too long was dead, killed by this awful day.

The neurosis had grown too fast. It had become a downright psychosis and Price, distraught, had taken the plunge. Price was an Abnormal wandering around the city at random. He could make a huge mess.

Their union had lasted eight years. Eight peaceful, happy years. Too happy and that was what made the break so cruel. But what could she do?

She saw the Protectors approaching. There were three of them, swinging their billy clubs, and the people walking in the opposite direction moved aside as they passed by.

She stood up. Absent-mindedly she told herself that they looked even more frightening than the gang of rejects who had stolen her money. They were, however, clean, shaven, combed and well dressed in impeccable uniforms.

"Gentlemen," she said.

They jumped as if she had attacked them and encircled her. "Ma'am," one of them said, who looked a little more open than the others.

She said, "My name is Natcha Mallworth. My husband is Price Mallworth. He's a priest of the New Religion in the church of parish 16." She paused, took a deep breath of fresh air. Her legs were trembling; a huge void gaped open in her stomach.

"Well?" the Protector said.

Natcha said, "My husband left our bungalow at noon for the church ceremony, but he didn't go to the church and since then he's disappeared. He was suffering... he was suffering from asthenia and his condition had gotten the better of him, lately. He confuses time. He has memory lapses. He..."

"Yes?" the Protector said softly.

"I think that, now… I think he's crazy. I think he's an Abnormal. He must be found, understand?"

"Of course," the Protector said, "We'll help you, ma'am. We'll find him for you."

CHAPTER VII

The Fascist Union of the States of America settled
the chosen people as solid as a rock, once and for all.
Be proud to be Americans in the year 2534!
Poster on the wall:
I've been settled on my ass for 30 years
and I'm no prouder for it.
Graffiti under the poster:

"The city! New God! Help me... the city. Tucum-cari. That's really the name of the city, I'm sure of it. There's the desert not too far away. The white and red desert with the buildings of the solar energy plant. Tu-cumcari. Tucumcari is a city in the F.U.S.A. The F.U.S.A. is my country. I like F.U.S.A. more than "Fas-cist Union of the States of America". I like it more. Why?

"I'm a priest of the New Religion. I'm a "Speaker of the Enlightened Catho" as they say. Is that really it? What use am I? Good God! What's happening to me? I know very well that I'm not crazy! I know it. I'm sure of it. It's all about me, anyway. And I'm still capable of judging, right?

"I don't know what's happening to me. It's huge. It's like nothing else and yet, there must be some expla-nation or other... Who can I talk to? Natcha? I'm able to talk to Natcha about everything, always have been... but *this*... She thinks I'm suffering, I know it. Well, by the New God, how could she believe me in this condition?

It's impossible. No, I can't talk to Natcha about everything. Not since she got sick...

"Should I go see a psycho-counselor? Those guys explain everything. Understand everything. Yes, but they explain and understand by automatically establishing a relation between two concepts: healthy mental balance and mental imbalance. That's all. For them the word "abnormal" conjures up precise images... And that's not the abnormal I'm thinking about. It's not that. I'm living something abnormal, but it has nothing to do with madness. I'm not crazy...

"Like everyone else, I know I'm neurotic. I know I'm asthenic. But that's all! That has nothing to do with what's been happening to me the last few days. The last few days? New God! No, since this morning. No. Since noon. How can one afternoon seem so long?

"If I visit a psycho-counselor and if I tell him my story—these unbelievable resurgences into another world—he'll judge me crazy. He won't try to go farther, to explain the phenomenon outside of psychiatry. He'll see absolutely nothing at all that can be explained on a material, physical basis and totally outside of my mental universe.

"Madness... fear of madness... That's also a common, popular phobia... The first phobia. The psycho-counselors see Abnormals everywhere. Everyone knows that. That's what they're supposed to do and that's what they do...

"By the New God, that last time... I stayed there, physically present in that girl's chair. I was there. I was really there and then... and then I was somewhere else at the same time. It wasn't like the first part of the induced dream. It wasn't at all like that. I was physically sitting in the chair and simultaneously I was physically present in that world, on that bed… The women with weird noses were physically present. I bumped into one of them when I escaped. I felt the impact and she yelled and…

"Who will explain that to me?

"Split personalities. Yes, that exists, too. But I'm sure it's not that either. No, it's not that! It's not… *it can't be that!*

"And the first time… The rain, those smells. That guy who called himself Sher and who explained to me… He said that the real world was nothing but a mental projection of the inner world of a sick person. Therefore, I'm sick now. I'm somewhere and I'm inventing what's around me. I'm inventing Tucumcari, the F.U.S.A., everything I know… I also invented this world's past, the first United States and before that the Indians and even before that… I invented everything.

"That's not possible.

"If I invented the past, I also invent the future? I possess the future inside me… Who knows if the projections in this other universe are not, for me, dreams, like premonitions? It's stupid, of course… Right now, being sick like I am, I could also have invented Sher and the explanation he gave me. I invented Natcha. But why did I create her sick as well? Why would I want our union not to be able to produce children? Am I a masochist? Sado-masochist?

"I want to be happy. Why would I have invented this world populated by unhappy and crazy people?

"New God! Have pity… I'm really becoming crazy. I'm falling… I don't know anymore. No, it's not possible and Sher is a creature from another universe into which I fell by some unknown set of circumstances… His explanation is wrong. Maybe he believes it, but he's wrong…

"There's also my father. He said that he was called Lice. He said he didn't know me, that he only had a son who was three-years old. That's how old I was when he quit reality, when he was locked up, swallowed up all of a sudden by schizophrenia... That could tie up with Sher's theory. Inevitably, in that world, everything has to be coherent... in a certain way. Or else...

"The mentally ill of this world have their own universe that the Normals are incapable of imagining. It's likely... Could it be? So, in fact, I'm becoming crazy. I'm gradually becoming crazy and catch a glimpse of that other world... *Their world*. Their world that, for them, is totally normal, of course, and the one they left is, on the contrary, comparable to a sickness they were cured of...

"If Sher was right, in spite of everything?"

He did not see the night coming. It was not important. Time was passing and Price was standing there, motionless. All around him the city bustled, pulsed, blinked its hundred thousand electric lights. People lived and passed away. They went wherever; they were whoever. Maybe they did not exist.

For more than an hour, Price racked his brain to find a way to get to the east coast. The airtrain or an airplane was the first solutions that came to mind, of course, and he rejected them in a second. He needed money for an airtrain or airplane. A lot of money... more than he had on him. No question of putting the whole cost of the trip on his credit account. The transport companies demanded cash payment to drastically reduce any attempt at fraud. And forgetting about conscious fraud, there were all those cases of neurotics who could look honest.

There was also no question of Price going back home to get the money needed for it. He could not enter the bungalow. Not yet...

He searched and sought, flipped and flopped the problem in his head to no avail; there was always, in the end, the same dead-end.

He even imagined stealing a private car. Yes, the thought crossed his mind! It was completely crazy, not to mention how risky it would be, about the serious punishment when he was caught—because he would be caught. He had never been in a private car and it would be almost impossible for him to drive.

And then, as he was walking by a public video-phone, the solution suddenly dawned on his muddled mind. New God! It was so simple... Why move physically. Why make a trip in person when he could so easily just call the coast on the videophone. Mentally scolding his stupid self for not thinking of this solution sooner, he put a dollar in the booth's automatic door. The door opened, let him enter and shut tight behind him.

It was hot and muggy in the closed booth. The ventilators, cut into the side windows, were not working. In less than 30 seconds, Price's forehead was covered in sweat. He checked the price chart, had to do it over and over before finally understanding that a 15-minute call to Savannah came to 1,000 dollars. Good. He had enough on him and once it was spent, he would still have 2,600 dollars and change.

He dialed the number of the Center. Colored zigzags crossed the screen and exploded in every direction. When the three musical notes chimed, Price slipped the money into the machine's silver slot. He bent his knees a little to be at the right height in front of the screen.

The screen turned pale, flooded with a pulsating pink light. Then it cleared up and the luminescence stabilized. A man's lean face, reddish eyes and close-cropped white hair appeared.

"Hello, sir," the man said. "The Savannah Care Center for Abnormals is at your service." He spoke strangely, with a clipped voice: between each word the right corner of his mouth twisted up.

"Hello," Price said. "I would like…"

"Speak louder," the shorthaired man said.

"Hello. I would like to speak to a patient."

"Speak to?" The man's big red eyes became huge. He was a real albino.

"No, not exactly," Price said. "I would like to pay a visit to a patient."

"You seem to be suffering," the man said. "I figure you're at a public phone, right? Where are you calling from?"

"I'm in a phone booth, that's true. I'm calling from Tucumcari."

"By God!" the albino said. "And you want to visit a patient? Get your money ready for that wretched device. I hate those machines… Are you suffering?"

"No," Price answered. "Tired is all. Can I have my visit?"

"We'll see about that," the man said. "Your name?"

"Price. Price Mallworth."

"Price Mallworth," the man repeated, his eyes lowered onto something off screen.

"I'm a priest of the New Religion," Price said. "I live in Tucumcari, suburb 3, parish 16."

"Tucumcari… suburb 3… parish… Parish?"

"16. Parish 16, sir."

"Parish 16," the albino said.

In the booth the heat was more and more stifling. Price felt sweat pouring down his back and under his arms.

"A visit costs 4,000 dollars," the man said, looking up. "Can I see your health card?"

"Here it is," Price put the card up to the screen and said, "You can take the amount of the visit out of my credit account. F.U.S.A. Bank, account number 456 768 54 Y T H 13."

"Could you repeat that?"

Price repeated.

"Okay," the man said. "I believe we know you, Mr. Mallworth."

"Yes," Price said. "I want to see my father: Mr. Anton Mallworth. Cell 4567654, level 654."

"That's it, yes," the man said. "Hold on, I'll transfer you to the inside line. If you don't want to get cut off, keep an eye on your counter, Mr. Mallworth."

"Don't worry," Price sighed. His palms were sticky and he could not stop wiping them on his pants. The beads of sweat running down his back were cold.

Various white stripes crossed the screen. A new image appeared. A man was sitting in the middle of an empty room. He was wearing a jacket and light pants. His knees were crossed, his arms dangling with his hands on his thighs, palms turned up, fingers curled up.

A bitter lump formed in Price's throat. The spy-camera zoomed in on the man's face. A square face, deeply grooved, with very white hair. The eyelids were opened over two perfectly empty, colorless eyes. A kind of nervous tic regularly twitched his right nostril, raising his upper lip.

"How... how is he?" Price asked.

The off-screen voice of the albino answered, "Stable condition. Just like it's been for years. It's like that, generally, for all the acute schizophrenics. Your father is definitely suffering, Mr. Mallworth, you know that. Totally disconnected. He doesn't know who he is anymore. He doesn't even know that he's got a human body."

"How can you know?" Price questioned.

"Excuse me?"

"How can you know if he's disconnected from everything, if he doesn't know anymore…"

"But Mr. Mallworth, schizophrenia has been known for a long time…"

But you're not schizophrenic yourself, Price thought. He was on the verge of saying it.

"We could cut one of his limbs clean off," the albino's voice resumed. "His nervous system might register pain, but it wouldn't communicate it to his conscience."

"Please…"

"It's only to give you an idea, Mr. Mallworth."

Price swallowed, wiped his forehead on the sleeve of his coat. On the screen his father's empty eyes stared at him, right though him…

"Has he moved these last few days? Has he left that room?"

There was a moment of silence and then, "I guess you must be joking, Mr. Mall…"

The image and sound were abruptly cut off. A white light, in the shape of a four-pointed star grew and grew and then dissolved in the middle of the screen.

Price noticed that he was still holding the second 1,000-dollar bill meant to continue the visit. And the crumpled bill in his hand trembled. He stuck it in his pocket and for a long moment stared at the opaque screen on which the dancing lights from the street were reflected.

You must be joking, Mr. Mallworth? No, unfortunately for him, Mr. Mallworth was not joking.

He turned around and put a wet finger on the exit button. In the gray box of the automatic lock, the coin taken when he had entered the booth clinked and finished the second part of its journey. The door slid open.

Price found himself in the street, in the noise, in the false half-light haunted by the red pulses of the neon signs. He found himself among people. He started walking.

The videophone visit to his father's cell had not helped him at all. What was he expecting? At worst the visit just deepened the inner chaos that was brewing and boiling on the fragile borders of his reason.

He was walking. Now he could go home. Take refuge in his bungalow, see Natcha again, tell her everything, tell her what he believed, what had happened to him. Too bad if she thought he was crazy. Too bad if it risked making her condition worse... He could not be lost and alone anymore.

He stopped at the first airtrain station he came upon. 20 people were waiting. Price was on the very edge of the platform when the train stopped. The door was right in front of him. But Price did not get on the train.

He was squatting on the moss in the thick bushes on the side of the road. On the road, the three blue vehicles were stopped one behind the other. Two men in helmets got out and calmly walked over. Price knew that he could not escape them for long.

He was very tired.

The Protectors had taken her to their car and asked her to get in the back. It was the first time in her life that she had sat in this kind of vehicle. She appreciated the soft seat more than anything.

The Protectors dropped her off in front of her bungalow. During the drive they had taken the time to ask her for more information about Price and she gave it to them. They took off in their long black car after promising her they would act swiftly.

The empty house closed in on her like a trap. She walked through all the rooms, driven by a last drop of mad hope... A last crazy hope, really...

She plopped on the bed, absolutely exhausted, and had to force herself not to drift off. She knew that if she lay down, the physical fatigue and desperation would carry her away all at once on a great big black wave of sleep. So, she stood up, took off her shoes and her dress, and headed for the bathroom. She took a fresh, humid air shower and lingered under the regenerating jets. Then she left the room and put on some lounge clothes.

As the shower had dispelled some of her fatigue, it had also awakened her hunger. She realized that she had eaten nothing all day, so she took out a fake-steak sandwich and a bottle of Wayne lemon juice from the refrigerator. She drank the tasteless lemon juice and chewed up two bites of the sandwich, which she barely swallowed. As quickly as it had come, her appetite suddenly vanished.

Natcha went back into the living room and, after hemming and hawing, finally sat before the videophone. She hesitated again and for a long time, for a very long time, stared without blinking at the black screen. Then, as if someone had thrown water on her, she made up her mind and dialed the number, her accurate finger not missing a button.

The emaciated face of psycho-counselor Emeerlink appeared on the screen. His bald scalp glistened. In the background she saw part of the magnificent aquarium that held pride of place in the center of his living room. Colored fish sparkled in the clear water. You had to be in the psycho-counselor caste to be allowed such a luxury.

"Natcha!" Emeerlink exclaimed. "To what do I owe the pleasure?" The cheerful tone was in absolute contrast with his serious face. It had been many years now since Natcha had worked for Emeerlink and she could not remember him smiling once.

"It's not very much pleasure, I'm afraid," Natcha said.

"Uh huh?" Emeerlink responded. And he waited.

Natcha took a deep breath, exhaled, and then said, "It's about Price, sir."

Emeerlink's left eyebrow rose. The right dropped. But he said nothing. He knew Price, saw him regularly during the mandatory consultations. He was the one who had detected his asthenic tendencies, who had advised him on his choice of sleeping pills and stimulants, who, after all, had given him the address of Madame Leona in the "mean" streets of Tucumcari.

Natcha had the sudden impression that what she was about to reveal to the psycho-counselor would not surprise him in the least. Maybe he knew Price better than she knew him. All the psycho-counselors are like that. They just needed a few mandatory visits to probe the depths of your soul and become aware of the particular jungle hiding in you. They are capable of foreseeing the most incredible growth spurts of this jungle. As much as they can they try to prevent and cure, of course. But, above all, they wait... They wait because they are incapable of doing more; they do not have enough material means or sufficient intellectual capacities. They are the lighthouses around which vast fleets of lost ships gather. Lighthouses far too scarce whose light is oddly lacking in strength, despite all their efforts. And the lost ships are growing in number...

"I'm listening, Natcha," Emeerlink finally said softly. His eyebrows had balanced out again over his blue-gray eyes.

Natcha said, "Price left me at noon. He was supposed to go the church, but he didn't. I looked for him all day long, couldn't find him, and finally asked for the Protectors' help. They're continuing the search at the moment..."

Emeerlink passed two fingers slowly over his lips, as if to dry his mouth. He said, "You're worried?"

She nodded. "He was in a crisis when he left me. For a few days he hasn't been too well. Really not well. He was tired, in full mental confusion. Before, he used to confuse time for only a few minutes, but then... it lasted. He was living eight years in the past, wondering if we could get married because of our genetic incompatibility... I think he crossed the border between asthenia and neurasthenia, sir. Acute neurasthenia..."

Emeerlink nodded. The luminous fish were dancing in the water behind him. "That's possible," he said. "But he could also have been the victim of some unexpected difficulty. You can't be sure of anything, Natcha..."

She smiled weakly. "Thank you for saying so, sir. But unfortunately I don't believe I'm mistaken... If the Protectors find him alive, he'll have to enter a Care Center. I would like it to be in your service, sir. And here, in

Tucumcari... I could care for him and... that's why I decided to disturb you..."

For a few long seconds, Emeerlink stared back at Natcha without flinching. Then, finally, nodding his head, "You know how overcrowded the Services are, Natcha. But still, I'll personally intervene to work things out as you want. Besides, his position as priest makes him a priority. Stay calm, Natcha."

She thanked Emeerlink and said goodbye. He repeated one more time, "Stay calm, Natcha and don't think that you're disturbing me." Then he cut off communication.

Natcha found herself alone in front of the empty screen. It was done; it was said.

For Natcha, for the Protectors who were busy with the search, for Emeerlink, Price Mallworth no longer belonged to the healthy society of the F.U.S.A. From now on he was one of the rejects, on the same level as the "dangerous" anarchopsychopaths who truly wanted to destroy the privileges of class that he was going to enjoy. So, he was going to enjoy it? No, *he* would not enjoy it at all. He would be an Abnormal like the millions of others, an outcast like the millions of others. The privilege would help Natcha. Only Natcha...

She did not even have the strength to wipe away the tears running down her cheeks.

She was still in front of the videophone when it rang, half an hour later. She accepted the call and the helmeted face of a Protector appeared. "Mrs. Mallworth?"

"Yes."

"We've found your husband, Mrs. Mallworth."

A hot ball rose up and exploded in her chest. "How... how is he?"

"Alive," the Protector said. "But maybe it'd be better if he were dead... Mrs. Mallworth! Hey, Mrs. Mallworth!"

The room had started spinning fast and then the blackness fell. And Natcha collapsed to the floor. On the cradle of her disheveled hair, her pretty face with bloodless lips was as pale as delicate ivory, transparent.

"Mrs. Mallworth! Hey!" the Protector called out once or twice. Then he swore and grumbled something incomprehensible before cutting off the call.

The empty house gently folded its silence around Natcha.

CHAPTER VIII

Your country has the lowest percentage of
Abnormals in the world!
The highest number of Care Centers!
The Abnormals who are dear to us will be
kept alive with the greatest care!
The Abnormals of the F.U.S.A. are
the best treated in the world!
Don't wait for one of your parents or your friends
to fall into psychosis, reserve a place for them in
one of our Centers at the first sign of sickness!
Do it for your personal well-being!

Treyca was getting old. The days passed and every evening he appreciated more and more the tranquility of his private home nestled in the heart of the 5th district of the forest-city. He could no longer spend those long, tiring days at work; long and tiring, but also so passionate! As was the case a few years ago.

Fatigue woke up early and went to bed late in him.

However, the fatigue was only physical. Although it had pervaded his whole body, it did not have the least hold on his morale and Treyca's days, though necessarily shorter, were by no means less passionate.

At the age of 15, he had received from the Training the title of Seeker-Guard. At 20 he was the One and Only Leader of the city squad. 250 men obeyed him, like so many arms that he could throw out simultaneously in every direction. The number of Strangers they intercepted defied the most exacting memory. And when it came to memory, Treyca had no equal, but he was unable to remember the exact number of his captures. The Service Books were there, he just had to open them.

Treyca got up from his desk hanging in the center of the bubble room. He drifted over to the large, round bay window and looked out, thoughtfully, upon the magnificent evening reddening the landscape. The trees, rising straight up like flames of stone, cast long, purple shadows on the lawns. Behind the bright, flowering hedges, the pyramidal pavilions of the Training were lined up.

A soft sigh streamed through Treyca's thin lips. Even though they inevitably reminded him of his increasing old age, Treyca loved the evenings. The red evenings, haunted by the listless flight of a few drunken birds; the evenings, sometimes, turbaned in long stoles of fog; the calm and peaceful evenings tentatively beginning the first ramblings of the night.

In these moments there were always the flashbacks. Not really an assessment, certainly not! Gusts of dense memories, portions of past times that rose up to the surface. And it was never unpleasant, quite the contrary…

Treyca had known exactly how to use his life. He had abandoned it completely to seeking and studying the Strangers. It had been passionate. It was always passionate, even though positive results were practically nonexistent. They crept into the mystery, on tiptoes… Someday, someone would find out, someone would know, someone would understand and the black veil would be rent asunder… The long chain of sustained efforts, patiently forged by generations of Seekers, would finally bear fruit, thanks to all of them. One link of this chain would hold the name of Treyca forever. He was the one who had managed to establish contact with the Strangers and who had instilled in them the necessary rudiments of the language of men. Of course, it was not perfect. To understand and speak the language of men, the Strangers lost their entire memory at the same time, or else it was a new tactic on their part? A new defense?

One day, yes, someone would benefit from all these links in the chain and he would find out, he would understand...

The vocaphone rang on Treyca's desk and the One and Only Leader jumped instinctively. He walked briskly back to the hanging furniture and turned on the listening.

"Hello, O and O," a nasally voice said. "We've found him."

"Shmmirt?" Treyca said. "I was waiting for your call. How is he?"

"He's as good as can be expected," Shmmirt's voice said. "He didn't put up a fight. Right now he's in our vehicle. Should we take him to the pavilions or do you want to see him now?"

Treyca let a couple of seconds of quick reflection tick off before deciding. "Bring him here immediately."

"Okay," the nasally voice said. "See you soon."

"Right," Treyca said.

And he cut off communication. He remained standing and thoughtful for a moment and then went back to the round bay window.

His last memory was an odd mix of total despondency with a certain amount of relief and it was, in a way, a memory that continued into the present moment. Plus a great curiosity all mixed up with growing anxiety.

His last memory... yes. Beyond that was nothing-ness. Nothing, the void and its strange, sickly smell that was not inhaled physically, for which the sense of smell was not necessary. He would have given half his life to know what this void was hiding. But could he allow himself to stake half his life?

The men who had found him, who were now taking him with them, did not look like him. They were differ-ent—the basis of comparison being, of course, totally subjective. (Maybe he should have said, *I am different* from these men?)

There were four of them in the vehicle's "cab". The others climbed on board, too, and must have been at the commands. The cab was oval, with a comfortable bench ringing around it at mid-height.

He sat on the bench and the four men sat across from him. They did not say a word and no expression could be read on their smooth, stony faces. They sat still, hands on knees, strapped into their white uniforms. They watched him.

I'm not like them, he told himself. I don't have the same face... I don't have that nose stuck high up on my forehead. My eyeballs don't have that mobility that makes them independent of each other... But that's a perfectly understandable necessity, with that bony, prominent, nasal bar that runs up between the eyes.

He also asked himself, Why am I here? Where are they taking me? And what country is this? He was sorry he could not remember anything.

The cab was completely opaque so it was impossi-ble to have any idea of the outside. The vehicle drove or maybe flew; anyway, it moved—he was sure of that. As for knowing in what direction... toward what goal...

He asked, "Where are we going? What do you want with me?"

The four faces remained like marble.

"Who are you?" he asked further.

This time one of the men broke a thin smile and in a deep voice answered, "And you, who are you?"

The question surprised him. He kept his mouth open for a second without being able to make a sound. A sudden wave of slimy sadness washed over him. He ended up looking down without saying anything.

"You don't know who you are?" the man continued.

He did not answer. Silence, like heavy water rising, filled the cab again, filled it up completely…

All four stood up in perfect unison. The one who had just spoken made a gesture, inviting him to get up, too. He obeyed. It was not easy to stand up on the curved floor of the cab, so he had to spread his legs to get better balance for the upcoming jolt of stopping. There was no jolt. At the end of the cab the airlock slid open. Two of the men in white uniforms stepped out. He did the same and the other two followed.

The room they were in was huge and brightly lit. The air felt cool. He searched in vain on the walls for a trace of the access that allowed the vehicle to enter the place. They were smooth, uniform, pinkish. The floor was covered with a hard, gray protective screed. In the walls and ceiling—but where did the walls end and the ceiling begin?—bright windows were embedded to spread light. The only particularity in the utterly sober décor: a relatively big, cylindrical pillar springing up in the center of the room, connecting the floor directly to the ceiling.

They headed for this pillar and stopped in front of it. One of the men typed on a colored keyboard molded into the wall of the cylinder and immediately, without a sound, a panel slid open, revealing a rectangular opening.

"Go on," one of the men said.

He entered the cylinder. Two guardian angels went with him and the panel closed behind them. They stayed in this "tube" for a few seconds but nothing happened. Apparently. Then the panel slid open again.

"Step out," a man said.

He stepped out. The panel whispered back into housing.

He was now in a round room, a kind of ball cut off by the floor, with huge glass walls opening onto the outside and the red evening. The furnishings were few and far between. The only thing that really stood out was the long desk in the middle, hanging from the ceiling by three steel wires.

Behind the desk was a man. A man who got up, who came over to him, smiling, with his hand held out, saying, "Good evening. My name is Treyca. And you?"

It was Price.

It was his body, his face, but a puppet body with the strings cut, a face with eyes reflecting nothing but the void.

Since the moment when the Protectors had brought him to the bungalow until now, Price had not flinched or twitched in the slightest to jostle his frozen features. He was led and guided blind, walked when he was dragged, sat when they plopped him down.

Right now he was lying on a rollaway stretcher, his arms resting along his body. In his pale face, the cheeks were strangely hollow, the eyes like burned out light bulbs staring at the bare ceiling. Natcha walked next to the stretcher being pushed by a male nurse in a white coat. The fatigue in her had changed and become an almost total absence of sensations. She was a gaping hole that walked with constant pangs of the most frenzied disorientation deep down inside.

Near the end of the long corridor, Emeerlink appeared, his face a little tenser than usual. The nurse pushing the stretcher stopped. For a few seconds Emeerlink stood leaning over Price, scrutinizing his stony face. Then he straightened up and looked at Natcha.

"You should get some rest, Natcha," he fired off in one breath. "We'll take care of it."

"Do you think that electroshock could…"

"I can't say anything," Emeerlink said. "I can't promise you anything, of course… and you know that."

He nodded to the nurse who started pushing the stretcher to the very end of the corridor. Double doors slid open onto a room flooded with harsh light, then closed on the white-coated man and the stretcher.

The sour taste of sticky heat rose up in Natcha's throat.

"Rest," Emeerlink said. "Sit down here." He led her to a bench and helped her as she dropped onto the seat. Natcha looked at him again and he quickly straightened up, averted his eyes.

He said, "Where did they find him?"

"There were some people who reported him," Natcha said. "He was in an airtrain station. He was coming back home, I'm sure of it. He was coming back…"

Emeerlink said nothing. For a second he looked at her with, it seemed, a great deal of compassion deep in his eyes. He did nothing to try to comfort her or stop her from crying.

She spoke again, "The people said that he was about to get on the train. He was… anyway, he looked normal, according to what they said, and that's what the Protectors told me. And then…" She nodded her head several times in silence.

"Yes?" Emeerlink asked softly.

"And then he was stuck there, all of a sudden. With no warning. He became this… this kind of dead puppet, this human robot. He became *this*!"

"Right," Emeerlink said. "I'm going to see… Don't move, Natcha. Stay here and wait calmly. I won't be long."

He paused and then asked, "Are you hungry? Or maybe thirsty?"

Natcha refused, shaking her head. "Thank you, sir. I don't need anything."

"Wait for me," Emeerlink said. He entered the room that had swallowed Price and his male nurse a few minutes earlier.

The corridor was empty, silent. There was only Natcha on the bench, with her face wrinkled by tears and tiredness.

"Are you hungry? Or maybe thirsty?" She told herself that she would never be hungry or thirsty again. Never, until the habit came back or the need, of course.

No, she needed nothing. Nothing except Price in perfect mental health. Price with whom she had lived for eight years. Price, the companion, the accomplice. Price who now was dead without being so, here and gone at the same time…

"New God!" she murmured. "Bring him back to consciousness! Bring him back!"

It was stupid. The gods were not created to fulfill prayers; they teased them out like cowards and that's all.

Natcha's shoulders sagged. She buried her face in her hands and waited.

Of course, she guessed. It only took one look at Emeerlink's face. One single look and the crazy hope vanished. Swept away in a split second.

Emeerlink nodded his head slowly and said, "Schizophrenia."

The word, like a sharp claw, gripped Natcha's brain and twisted, crushed, ripped. Her heart raced in her chest and every beat echoed loudly, throbbed in her temples and between her breasts. She was like an island of stone in the center of a fluttering universe that was spinning, spinning...

From very far away, coming out of some chaotic horizon, Emeerlink's voice was saying, "We were afraid of this, Natcha. You know as well as I do."

It was true that she was afraid. It was true that she knew. But right now... it was here, really here. Emeerlink had really pronounced the word.

She struggled, as if to physically drill a passage in the midst of her wild heartbeats. She asked, "Why? Why, sir?"

Emeerlink slowly shrugged his shoulders and sighed. He sat next to Natcha, crossed his hands. For a moment he looked at his tangled fingers. Finally he said, "Price was suffering. For a very long time. At first unconsciously, then consciously, which unleashed the neurosis, the asthenia, and then the neurasthenia and its cohort of symptoms and manifestations. The mental confusion grew recently until the thin line separating him from madness suddenly snapped."

"Why? But why did he have to suffer?"

Emeerlink cast a sad glance on the young woman and then, once again, contemplated his crossed fingers. "His hereditary baggage was very fragile, Natcha. His father was a schizophrenic. He became abnormal when Price was only three-years old. His mother died when he was nine. In other kids this left no mark. For example, in your case... But Price was cruelly affected by the lack of tenderness, maybe by that lack of support that parents represent, especially in this world of ours where enemy No. 1 is mental disturbance. He suffered, yes, suffered from never having been a truly free child with the possibility of relying on real parents who bear your responsibilities during the time of awakening."

"He wanted so badly to have a child," Natcha said.

"Yes. It was a kind of transfer. He wanted a child to find himself again through the little being. He wanted to be the strong, dependable father, mentally speaking, that he never knew, that he couldn't have. He hated his own father to the core of his being. He hated him because he went mad. He also hated madness, all the neuroses, all the phobias. And then it was this hatred that compelled him to transfer his own anxieties and his own neurosis onto his circle of friends, onto you, when he unconsciously felt the first signs: he wasn't the one affected, it was the others. He was strong, he was great."

He paused, uncrossed his fingers and then recrossed them right away. He continued, "When he met you, Natcha, it was his salvation. You were pretty, healthy and strong. You were a mother for him like you would be for his children. You were the ideal sexual partner also, with no flaws or complexes or deviations whatsoever. You were a rock and also the image of that father who had abandoned him so young. You were God. But your genetic cards were not compatible. It was certainly a very big shock for him. You can be sure—he never held a grudge against you. He could never hold it against you. To put his anger and disillusionment on you would be killing once again the father and mother he never had, it would be toppling the idol he had erected, crossing out his only reason for living. He blamed himself and those who had given birth to him… That's also the reason for his wandering around when he confused time and why he thought he was living at that time right before your union. His subconscious had chosen that time for him when he could still hope…"

"But if I'd been someone else," Natcha said. "If my parents, mine…"

"No, you can't say that. Price's parents alone were enough to prohibit procreation. I guarantee you… He knew it. I advised him to visit the H-Ps. He did it and it gave him a certain amount of relief. He could invent the son he didn't have and would never have. He could, thanks to the hypnotic creations, identify himself with the father and son at the same time. Of course, this therapy was a last resort and in the end maybe it was a mistake on my part… Price was no longer up to supporting this solitude of mind in which he found himself sinking deeper and deeper every day, with that part of himself forever ripped out, which nobody could ever give back to him. The sessions of H-P treatment, even if they were a temporary relief, left a bigger heartache in him afterward. He would have wanted to live forever in the dream, in *that dream*. And he couldn't. He couldn't escape the world he lived in, materially speaking. He couldn't, for example, abandon you, you who were everything, you who were the world recreated. It was a huge conflict, colossal, with no solution. With no solution except one… And it was once again his unconscious that dictated it to him. Yes, the refuge in dream… it was the all-out withdrawal into himself. It was the asthenia, then the next phase to finally throw himself into the abyss of the long sleep. It was a total withdrawal which, in spite of everything, allowed his mind to keep living. And to live like he'd wanted to for so long…"

He stopped talking, but continued to watch his hands for a minute.

"Do you think…" Natcha asked, "Do you think he'll ever come out of this unconsciousness?"

Emeerlink lowered his eyes again. He stared at the ground between his feet and answered, "I hope so, Natcha. With all my heart, I hope so… But I don't think so. With schizophrenia, the number of cures is less than 0.1%."

"Thank you, sir," Natcha said.

She looked up. Her eyes were red but dry. She furiously tried to keep her chin from trembling. She asked, "Can I see him?"

"For as long as you like… and as long as it won't get in the way of our work, of course. From now on you can stay in one of the pavilions directly attached to our establishment. I'll take care of it."

"Thank you," Natcha repeated.

"I assure you," Emeerlink said, "there's nothing to thank me for… I assure you."

CHAPTER IX

Soft madness, dark madness
Madness like a rowboat on quaking earth,
Madness like a hideous mother's womb,
with bad blood,
with the bad blood of a mother at sea,
who moans and howls and spits.
With the hot womb, the deep womb, the womb
closed to all, the womb of iron and steel.
Madness like an upright tree under the rain of
blood and sharp glass fangs; madness,
my viscous repose, my bygone heart...
from "Furipariah" by Bersch
(underground poet, 1999-2067)

He shook Treyca's outstretched hand. It was cold and dry.

"I don't know," he said. "I don't know who I am or what my name is."

He had trouble getting used to these men's eyes, these damn eyes split down the middle by the bridge of the nose. Yet, it seemed to him that Treyca's were friendly. Or if not friendly, at least considerate. He felt this like something nice.

Treyca was rather small and wiry, all cold and dry like his hand. His hair was thin and yellow, his face clawed by the wrinkles of time. He was probably pretty old. However, under all this apparent and wholly physical coldness, there emanated from him an intangible scent of a kind of openness.

Treyca smiled and asked, "Really, you don't know?" And, without waiting for answer, still smiling, he grabbed him by the arm and led him to the desk. He pressed a button on the furniture's keyboard, which brought two soft lumps out of the floor.

"Sit down," he said, pointing to one of the squirmy forms. "Don't be afraid, they're just chairs."

To prove his point, Treyca plopped down on one of the masses, which welcomed him by molding around the shape of his body. Price did the same and found it quite pleasant, in these seats that supported his whole body without putting any pressure on it and without him even feeling any contact.

"Are you thirsty? Would you like to eat something?" Treyca asked politely.

"No, thank you." He was not thirsty or hungry and he said so.

"Would you like anything at all?"

"I would like," he said, "to know who I am and where I am. And why and how it is that I'm not made exactly like you... I mean my eyes and nose... my facial features..."

Treyca's smile grew bigger. "This curiosity does you honor and delights me," he said. "The Strangers in your situation and who have this attitude are relatively rare."

His eyes widened. He did not try to hide his surprise. "Strangers in my situation... So, I'm not alone?"

"You're not alone, no," Treyca said. After a brief pause, he added, "Unfortunately for everyone..."

"I don't understand."

Treyca found his smile again and said, "I'll try to explain it to you, Stranger. That's why you were brought here. Trust me."

"I trust you," Price responded. It was true. Anway, he could hardly do otherwise… But really, sincerely, he trusted him. He could not explain why. He really liked the ball-room where he was; it was pleasant and relaxing. He also liked the bay windows a lot, letting him look outside. And the outside was pretty: it was made of lawns and trees with red-brown leaves that drifted along in the wind.

He looked at Treyca, who nodded and said, "I believe you're telling the truth. I truly believe we can do some good work."

"I hope so," he said.

Treyca reached out to the desk and pressed another button. A folder lifted slowly out of the desk and Treyca took a sheet of opaque plastic that he held out. Price took the sheet and examined it. Weird signs, which he did not recognize, were lined up apparently in no order whatsoever. They had been written by a trembling hand, it seemed, using some kind of red marker, and formed this drawing:

PRICE MALLWORTH
PRIEST NATCHA NEW RELIGION
TUCUMCARI SON H-P NOT NATCHA
SICK
NATCHA POOR NATCHA

He stared at the mysterious signs for a long time, turned the sheet around in his hands, examining it from different angles. All the signs together formed a kind of zigzag—that's all he could get out of it.

He looked up and immediately met Treyca's eyes. "Well?" Treyca said.

"I don't understand… this drawing, is it supposed to mean something to me?"

Treyca sighed slowly, took the sheet and for a few long seconds his eyes wandered over it. He said, "It's not a drawing. They're signs, letters, and you wrote them yourself when we asked you to. You talked, too, and I believe that these signs translated some of the words of the language you were speaking, before..."

"Before? Before what? How could I have written this? I don't know you. I've never met you."

Treyca nodded his head slowly. We've already met. You don't remember now... I'll explain. But first..." He paused, tapped the sheet with his fingertip and continued, "I believe that you were saying your name is Price—I think my pronunciation is correct. Price... Do you remember?"

"I've never in my life heard that name... But it's possible. I don't remember."

"Do you like the name? Would you mind if we kept calling you that?"

He closed his eyes and repeated in his mind, Price, Price, several times. He said, "Sure, it's a nice name."

"So, I'll call you Price. You're Price."

"I'm Price," Price said.

Treyca seemed satisfied, as if he had just accomplished a kind of feat. He stood up, put the sheet back in the folder on the desk, took a few steps and stopped abruptly. He turned to Price and asked, "What part of the world do you come from?"

The question was sharp, direct, like a punch. Price answered without thinking, "I don't know, sir. I don't even know where on the planet I am and..."

"What?" Treyca said. "Repeat word for word what you just said."

"I... I said I don't know where on the planet I am..."

"There you go!" Treyca yelled. "*Planet*. Explain this word to me. What does it mean? What's its definition? Why do you remember this word?"

The flood of questions was somewhat confusing to Price's mind. Treyca had come closer to him, his cheeks flush with excitement. How could he explain it to him? The word had jumped out. It was there, hidden away in some dark corner of Price's consciousness. He said, "A planet is the world. It's our world. We live on a planet... What do you want me to say?"

"Does this world have a name?"

"Maybe. I don't know... Of course... but I can't remember."

"What does a planet look like?" Treyca interrogated feverishly.

"But... it's a mass of solid matter that... it's a kind of globe, suspended in space and it moves around a sun. Space is full of suns and planets and..."

"Okay," Treyca said with another sigh. He lowered his eyes and contemplated the fingernails of his right hand for a moment—as if there was a treasure hidden underneath them. His eyes were serious when they met Price's again. He said, "Forget all that, Price. Everything you just told me. It's simply a product of your imagination, a remnant of the fantasy caused by the adaptation sessions that we made you undergo and that remained imprinted on your memory. A little like a particularly memorable dream."

"No!" Price said. "I assure you..."

"You are hardly in a state to be sure of anything whatsoever, I assure you... This particular concept of the universe was pure invention on your part, pure fantasy. Space, planets, none of that exists. And believe me, if this "construction" had even a chance of existing, our men of science would have looked into it long ago… During your treatment, we gave you drugs, some of which occasionally have unfortunate hallucinatory effects. It's these aberrant memories you keep. Your unconscious fabricated them and in those moments of dream no conscious barrier was erected. The mechanism of your reasoning judgment was asleep, non-existent. That's why you confuse these hallucinatory reveries with reality."

He stopped talking, leaned over Price (who looked dazed) and put a friendly hand on his shoulder. "Don't be scared. You'll accept it faster than you think."

"But then," Price said, "then, the world…"

"The world," Treyca straightened up, "the world is immense. No one knows its limits and no one can know. It has nothing to do with this figuration of planets that you give it… It is unique and boundless. Above is the sky and below the earth. The sky, like the earth, has no limits. This unique world where men live is called Isha."

"Isha," Price repeated.

The world was unique and immense. It was One. Everywhere. Always…

"I would like to drink something, please," Price said.

"Certainly."

Treyca reached out and tapped on the desk keyboard. A rack with two cups rose out of the top. Treyca offered one to Price, kept the other for himself and went to sit back down in the lumpchair. The drink was a pretty orange color. It was refreshing and tasted nice.

"The world is called Isha," Price said pensively.

Treyca nodded and said, "Isha. That's the name we gave it, in fact. But maybe other peoples living in the world call it something else. In our language we call it Isha."

"Other peoples?" Price was surprised. "There are people other than you in the world?"

"Of course. There are, at least, yours, Price. Except, where could you have come from?"

Price took another gulp of the liquid without answering. Treyca watched him for a minute, then let his eyes wander back to the contents of his cup. After a short silence he said, "You see, Price, as great as our technical means are, we are still far from being able to know the world in its entirety. Moreover, I can state with conviction that we will never know it, I believe. It's too vast for us puny little men... but you, Price, you come from one of those countries. One of those countries that are out of reach, but that exist... somewhere, beyond the invisible borders of Time."

"How do you know that these countries exist?

Treyca smiled. "Once again, you are the living proof. I'm going to tell you a story, Price. You're not the first Stranger. For centuries upon centuries your kind have been coming among the people of Isha. We have proof and testimony in our archives, going back a long time... You were very few, in ancient times. But the number has grown over the years. Grown an awful lot, to the point where the people of Isha now consider you a danger. And I believe that the people are right. There are too many of you among us... so many that we can imagine a kind of invasion."

"An invasion? But I..."

"Listen to me, Price. Let me tell you truth. Yes, we're afraid of an invasion. We don't understand it and it could be that you don't understand it either. But the facts are there. There are millions of you among us. No one knows how you've managed to cross the huge distances that separate your world from the country of Isha, but you have. You're here. Some Seekers credit you with strange, inexplicable powers... For centuries we've hunted you relentlessly. We've captured you. There are women and children among you. Your language is unknown... I myself am a Seeker and I've spent my life trying to find a solution, to shed some light..."

"Have you?"

"You seem sincerely interested, Price, I'm happy about that, really... But no, I haven't. I have, let's say "made a step forward". If we can persevere in any way, it's thanks to my work. Yes, I am behind this treatment that you underwent and thanks to that we have implanted our language. Except, this treatment isn't perfect..."

"Memory loss..."

"That's right," Treyca admitted. "The subjects under going treatment do actually learn our language, but they wake up afterward as if the induced sleep had erased their memories. So far there have been no exceptions. Except, maybe, you."

"Me?" Price said. "But I assure you that I don't remember anything and that..."

"And yet there are those signs that you wrote during the induced sleep and certain words you uttered that made us think that those signs might represent elements of your world... Your name, for example. There are also some false memories fabricated by your unconscious. I'm talking about that weird idea of the world represented by a sphere in the void, etc. As crazy as they are, these aberrant pictures still have some foundation. A real foundation. These images might also be symbols that we have to decipher..."

He stopped, waiting for a reaction from Price that did not come. Price just put his empty cup on the rack.

"Another?" Treyca asked.

"No, thank you." He thought for a minute and then, "It's weird. My mind is empty. I'm here and I accept what you tell me. I feel like I have to accept it. I need to cling onto something, you understand, if I want to get out of this void. I don't understand. Isha is immense, as you say, and I come from the other end... I don't know how or why. I want to go back, Treyca. To go back home..."

"What?"

"I don't know... I don't even know why. And yet, I feel like the solution is in that country I can't remember."

"We're going to do everything we can to get you to remember again, Price. It'll be your salvation."

"What do you do with the Strangers you capture?"

Treyca shrugged his shoulders slightly. He looked a little troubled, for half a second. "Okay, I shouldn't hide it from you. I told you, you're too many and it's become really dangerous for our people. If we understood this invasion... but the facts elude us and defy all logic. That's where the real danger lies, perhaps... Oh, you don't do any harm. You're here, that's all. Everywhere. Really everywhere... Your reactions are unpredictable and inexplicable—you yourself escaped immediately after waking up from the treatment. It was almost pure luck that we found you again. And since then, even though we were expecting the worst, you haven't shown the least hostility toward us."

"Should I have?"

"No, of course not. You're safer here than out there. The anti-Stranger campaign is growing stronger, frighteningly serious... Soon, I'm afraid, we won't bother arresting you, we'll kill you on the spot. We're already teaching this to our women and children..."

Price turned pale. "You can't kill men like that, for no reason..."

Treyca, once again, looked surprised. "Why not? There is a reason. I told you. There are too many of you and we're scared. Scared because we don't understand... We'll all die anyway."

"But you'll be judged for your crimes!"

"They won't be crimes. Self-defense."

Price shifted in his lumpchair. "But come on! You don't know anything. Maybe we're really friendly. Maybe we only want to live in harmony with you!"

"*Maybe*, yes. And we're not sure. And there are more and more of you. You're squeezing in everywhere, you want food, you sing, you bother our women. You don't give anything, you take. That's how it's been for centuries and we've put up with it for centuries... We're tired of it, Price. Can't you understand this?"

"I... I guess so, maybe."

"I'm sure you can understand."

Price did not answer. He sat back in the lumpchair again. After a minute he asked, "And the ones you captured, the ones you treated... what do you do with them?"

"Some." Treyca said, "don't support the treatment too well. They're hostile and kind of crazy. They've got only one thing in mind: escape. Others react a little better, which means they accept us. But we can't get anything out of them."

"What do you do with them?"

"We can't keep them..."

"So you get rid of them, don't you?"

"They don't suffer. The passage from life to death is not important…"

"For you! But for them?"

"Why would it be important? They leave nothing behind them that they might regret. They're only living in the present… They're already without…"

"But if they enjoy living in the present? What makes you think you can judge them so decisively? What makes you think you can play with the life and death of a living being like that?"

Treyca tilted his head to the side. "Your reaction is interesting, Price. In your opinion, my way of thinking is revolting, horrible? And yet life and death belong to living beings, don't they?"

"Life and death belong to God! Don't you know that?"

Treyca jumped. A little glimmer of joy flashed in his eyes. "God? Tell me… Can you say what it is?"

Price's eyes were bulging. He had really pronounced the word "god". It was almost as if some kind of gust of wind had blown through his head, rattling his mind. Amidst the flurries, forgotten words came back, exploded in a brief illumination.

"You said," Treyca repeated softly, "that life and death belonged to God. What is "God"? Or who is it? Is it the name of your people? The name of your country?"

Price's head swiveled slowly. "I don't know… I don't know… It's above man, I think… I don't know… Who created Isha?"

"Excuse me?"

"Who created Isha?"

"What makes you ask such a question?"

"I don't know… It seems to me that it has something to do with what I'm looking for. I believe…"

"The world *is*," Treyca said. "Living beings are on top and they participate in its development. They form a part of the creation and the life of the world. Why does anyone have to have *created* the world?"

Price let his head fall back. He raised his hands and put them on his forehead, over his eyes.

"You're tired," Treyca remarked. "We'll stop for now and you can rest… I think that we're going to do good work together, you and I. Maybe we'll be able to clear up the mystery."

He stood up. Price stood up, too. His legs were a little weak.

Treyca went to him and gave him a gentle tap on the shoulder. He said, "Think about it, maybe your health and safety are here. You have no business trying to escape. Outside, in the next few days, there will be a reign of death over the Strangers."

Somewhat by reflex, Price nodded.

Treyca played again on the desk keyboard and a guard in a white uniform rushed into the round room. "Take this man to his rest room," Treyca said.

"Yes, sir," the guard said.

And Price followed him.

"See you soon," Treyca shouted.

"See you soon, Price answered.

CHAPTER X

A man dreams that he is a butterfly.
When he wakes up, he does not remember
if he is a man who dreamed that he was a butterfly
or if he is a butterfly who is dreaming that he is a man.
(Mystical doctrine of the Tao.
Origins lost in the mists of time.)

Price met Treyca a number of times. The man was nice and seemed to be sincerely interested in Price's fate. The meetings took place in the round room of the bubble house; Price never met Treyca anywhere else. When the "work" session ended, he was led back to his rest room located in an oval building adjoining Treyca's house.

Price had nothing to complain about. He was well treated, properly fed, taken care of, almost pampered. He was neither cold nor hot; he could do whatever he wanted during his rest time. He had the choice between doing absolutely nothing or working on different games of manual and mental dexterity. He preferred reading and devouring the documentary works that provided him with a little knowledge about the country of Isha.

Yes, he was well treated. Yes, all he had to do was say the word and a guard would immediately do his best to grant his wish.

And yet... yet, deep down inside, Price's desire to escape was rising and growing stronger and stronger. Every day more caustic, it quickly became all he could think about so that he had to force himself, with all his might, to concentrate when working with Treyca.

He did not express this desire to escape, this need becoming more and more critical every day. He wanted to leave the safety and luxury and calm for an uncertain world where (Treyca constantly repeated to him) he would be risking his life every second. He had a crazy desire to go back to his distant land beyond the borders of Isha, where he came from, according to Treyca. That was what he wanted, even though he knew it was crazy.

The work sessions with Treyca produced no positive results. At least, that was the impression Price had. All the efforts spent trying to find some clue in the depths of the abyss of his buried memory were fruitless. Behind him was emptiness and his past life was summed up in a few words pronounced by Treyca, and still, it was a hypothetical life.

Strangely, this did not bother Price. The nothingness had vaguely alarmed him at first, but he got used to it very quickly. He continued to participate graciously in Treyca's investigations, mostly to indulge him. Maybe also, more or less unconsciously, to prolong his life. Didn't Treyca lead him to believe that when he had nothing more to get from a subject, they would kill him, just like that? He did not particularly want to be killed.

He knew almost nothing about Isha, except what he read in the documentary books. And here again it was weird: he could take a lively interest in a book, while he was reading it, but a few days later he had only a few confused memories, a few sketchy ideas in the thick fog that clouded his mind. He accepted this as normal.

What interested him was not Isha, it was the countries beyond Isha, those countries that "must have existed" but that no one knew about. His country, perhaps...

Over the course of a few days—but how many exactly? Four, five, six?—he saw Treyca age very clearly.

And this was another oddity. As if time did not flow in the same way for the Seeker of Isha and him. And then one morning the guard informed him that Treyca was dead. This saddened him, but he was especially worried about his own fate.

His worry was not completely unfounded. The new Seeker who replaced Treyca and moved into the bubble-house was a tall, thin man with a perfectly smooth skull and a severe face, his eyes constantly on the move. His name was Rardoll. At their first contact Price knew the good times were over…

"For months now," Rardoll said, "Treyca has been busy getting what he called "interesting" information from your memory."

"You're obviously mistaken," Price said. "It hasn't been months, but only a few days…"

"Well now!" Rardoll scowled. "You doubt the truth of what I'm saying? That's a pretty bold attitude for a Stranger, don't you think?"

"I don't see what's bold…"

"Be quiet, Stranger! I am a Seeker of Isha and you owe me respect and obedience. Be quiet when I'm speaking. It seems to me that Treyca got you into some nasty habits. I don't deny his knowledge, but he was very old and the methods he'd been using lately are, for me, very unorthodox. I'm probably telling you nothing you don't know when I say that this "interesting" infor-mation is, in fact, practically worthless. Treyca was an optimist, which fed him with insane hopes. I don't share his views, Stranger, and I'm warning you, if, in the com-ing days, you and I don't produce some positive results, I'll be forced to get rid of you. Like hundreds of others of your kind, you're a burden on Isha. Do you under-stand me, Stranger?"

"Certainly," Price said. "Can I ask a question?"

Rardoll narrowed his eyes and hesitated for a few seconds. Finally he agreed by nodding.

"How," Price asked, "do you figure you will some day understand where we come from and how we got here? How are you going to understand if you stop searching?"

A worried smile flashed across the Seeker's lips. He said, "Do you think this question bothers me? On the contrary, it reveals your twisted mind. You believe that your enigmatic presence in the country of Isha is a weapon that you can still use… Well! Those times are over, Stranger. We're not looking to understand any-more—it's a waste of time. And when we understand, it might be too late. We can't take the risk anymore. So, we've decided to take action. The Leaders as well as the people. For the last few days the Strangers have been hunted down mercilessly and killed by the people. That's the only way to strike down the danger. Are you satisfied? Do you understand now that it's really in your best interest to make an effort? That you are strongly advised to produce some positive results in the next few days?"

"I understand," Price said.

That evening the guard came in and put the dinner on the table in the middle of the room. He took off his helmet as he always did and sat in the other chair, watching Price eat and talking with him. He was a nice man but careless because of Price's good behavior.

When Price got up and with a swift hand plunged the knife into his throat, the guard looked utterly sur-prised and hiccupped violently. Price took the knife out and the man slid down in his chair, collapsing onto the floor while a mighty geyser of blood sprang from his gaping throat. Without even looking at him Price rushed out of the room. He went the same way he had taken so often, which led to the bubble-house, but he veered off at one point and came out in the park.

It was night, refreshingly cool. Price glided among the smells and shadows, his heart swollen with excitement, until he found himself, a few minutes later, out in the countryside. He walked. The trees were tall, majestic, tranquil. The rows of thick bushes offered all kinds of hiding places.

And Price was walking. He was happy. He was walking toward that inviolate land, toward that inaccessible country of his. And, in spite of the enormous distance, he would get there...

What else can be said?

That, at one moment, fatigue and sleep overtook him. That he slept in the forest, fell asleep all curled up.

The light of the new morning awoke him. He stood up and started walking again.

And that is how, after three or four hours of easy walking, Price arrived at the country that was his own.

It looked almost exactly the same. Maybe it was still even the country of Isha... Who knows? The forest had simply parted and several round houses, like gigantic dewdrops, sprouted up in the clearing. All around the round houses were people. There were children.

Price went to them.

To one of them.

A child around eight years old, with tousled, light-colored hair and a triangular, freckled face. He was standing in the middle of a space that could have been a road and he was not moving, he was watching Price approach. The others got out the way fast. Some screamed.

But Price did not hear the screams. He did not see the people run. He was walking toward the motionless child who looked so much like him and a tremendous rush of joy flooded over him, carried him away, rolled him in its red waves…

He had arrived in the unknown country, he was sure of it. He knew it.

He was only a few feet away when the child brought out the gun he was holding behind his back, and pointed it at Price, and fired. It was like a scythe shearing off his legs. He saw the houses spinning, the forest, the child's face. No pain, nothing. Just this little nothing of a hole in the middle of his chest and the red splatter that burst through his back. He fell down.

A deep, dark shadow spread over the great spinning. He screamed, without knowing it, but aware, terribly aware, for a fraction of a second, of what the country of Isha really was… demented.

And it was too late. It was over.

The people who had fled came back again. They surrounded the child. "Mama," he yelled toward a pale-faced woman. "Look! I got one! I got one! All by myself!"

"Don't stay there," the woman said, "you're going to walk in the blood and get it everywhere. It's disgusting."

He child stepped back and repeated, "I'm the one who got him. It's me!"

"He yelled something," someone said, "but I didn't understand."

"Yeah," another one said, "but we never understand what they say."

"Excuse me!" the first retorted. "Some are treated and know our language. This one must have known. Just look at his clothes. He came from the Seekers' Center."

"What did he yell?" the mama asked.

"I don't really know," the child said. "Something like "natcha" I think."

"Natcha?" the first individual was surprised.

"You see," the second said. "It doesn't mean anything."

"We have to contact the Watch," the mama said. "So they can get rid of him for us... Don't just stand there, children, go and play somewhere else."

The children obeyed, pouting, slowly dragging their feet away.

Price's blood flowed in fits and starts and flooded a small patch of green grass.

She got off the airtrain and regretted once again having chosen, a few years before, to live in the bungalow in the suburb. At her age the daily trips between the suburb and the Center were grueling. Not to mention the more than insufficient security measures...

There had been new writing painted on the sidewalk and on the walls of the M.A.P.M.E. Center. She read them distractedly, noticing one really big one that claimed: THE WHOLE WORLD WANTS TO LIVE FREE AND UNITED. She nodded her head.

The scribbles were becoming bolder and bolder. Barely one year ago they were happy to write their slogans on the walls of the underground tunnels of the airtrain. Now they had no fear of "officers" right in the heart of Tucumcari. If only they had kept themselves to writing... They were openly moving into action, multi-

plying the raids against the State institutions, the churches, pillaging and stealing, sometimes massacring.

The news updates from the government were terribly short. After some bitter warnings and the deploy-
ment of the Protector force, they tried to shrug off this
"flare-up" of madness. But was it really the right method?

The "Crazies" had their own pirate radios and their
news shows did not stop at a few empty phrases. Year
after year their movement was expanding, not only in the
country but everywhere in the world, among the mysterious people unknown to the F.U.S.A., but who lived
under the same totalitarian regimes, if you believed the
revelations of the "Crazies".

Natcha remembered the meeting in the airtrain station. It was in the evening… Yes, the evening when she
was searching for Price. That was 24 years ago now…
She remembered the dirty, bearded young gang who had
surrounded her to steal her money. They still called
themselves anarchopsychotics at that time and they
wanted something else; they refused society and the
government, the Enlightened Church, everything… They
wanted something else—to live as they pleased. The tall
bearded man had told her, "You'll see, sweetie, we're
going to fuck everything up and we'll make the rich
bastards pay." Something along those lines…

She did not believe him, at the time. But the sentence had hounded her for the rest of her life. Was it still
a long way off, the day when "they" would make the
rich bastards pay?

She entered the Center, crossed the cold lobby
where large, tinted bay windows kept out the sun, and
went to the elevator. She was no longer afraid of elevators or enclosed spaces. Medical Professor Emeerlink

(New God rest his soul) had cured her of the claustrophobia. For ten long years he had been a wonderful husband…

On the 32nd floor, Natcha stepped out of the elevator, went down the corridor and stopped in front of a door on which her name was inscribed, followed by: Medical Professor 135. She entered. The blonde secretary welcomed her by standing up.

"Don't bother, Millie," Natcha said.

"I'd like to wish you a good day," Millie said.

"Thanks."

Natcha sat behind her desk. She was sweating profusely under her arms. 20 years ago she was thin and supple like Millie. 20 years… and you became a fat woman who sweats and smells.

"Looks like the scribblers are everywhere, doesn't it?" she said.

"That's true," Millie said. "I saw that."

"What do you think, Millie, personally?"

Millie blushed, looked away and said, "I don't think anything, ma'am. What should I think?"

Natcha smiled feebly. "Nothing. You're right. Excuse me for asking, Millie."

The young lady stood up, walked over and handed her a list. "Our losses last night, ma'am."

"Thanks. Were there many?"

"No… not too many… But…"

"But what?"

The secretary did not answer. She looked embarrassed. Natcha took the list and saw that the first name to appear was Price Mallworth. "New God!" she shouted.

"I didn't know how to…"

"That's okay, Millie, that's okay," Natcha sighed.

He was lying on a one of the metal tables, naked and stiff, pale. He, too, had aged. His body was dry and bony, the crook of his elbow blue and puffy from the intravenous needles. His cheeks were sunken, his lips cracked open over the reddish cavity of his mouth. One of his eyelids was not completely closed and his murky eye glistened under the lashes.

"Price," Natcha murmured.

He did not answer. Never would again. He had not been answering for 24 years already. 24 years on that bed, in that cell. Isolated, lost, withdrawn from the world. Living some inner adventure, swept away by death without ever revealing anything of his secret…

Price Mallworth, whom she had loved. For whom she had resisted for 14 years before finally laying down her arms and remarrying, before becoming Mrs. Emeerlink.

Price Mallworth, who had abandoned her, who had left her alone, without totally dying… A dry body now, on a table in the morgue. A construction of flesh and bone and organs that would soon rot.

Nothing anymore.

She felt strangely empty. Empty and yet too heavy. Cautiously reaching out a trembling finger, she tried to lower the dead man's eyelid, but could not. The thin line of the cold, rigid eye kept staring at her.

Footsteps from behind made her jump. A nurse came up. "I was on duty, ma'am…"

"When did it happen?" Natcha asked.

"At three this morning. He was in bed as usual. As always. All of a sudden he sat up and screamed.

"He screamed?"

"Yes, ma'am. Twice. The first time I thought I heard something like "icha" but then he screamed again.

It wasn't "icha" but "Natcha". He screamed out your name, ma'am. Then he fell back. I ran over... he was dead."

A long moment later, the nurse asked, "Can I do something for you, ma'am?"

"No... no," Natcha rasped. "Thank you."

The nurse left.

A little later Natcha Emeerlink also left the room.

The thin line of dead eye filtered through Price Mallworth's lid stared at the white ceiling.

"That's them," Elio communicates. He stops near the two Creator-Candidates and Alam stops as well.

"But which of the two?" Alam asks.

"Difficult to say, although personally... I worked hard trying to figure it out."

"Too bad," Alam communicates. "One of the two has to be stopped and in both cases their creations were not lacking in interest, don't you think?"

"Absolutely... But we're here to verify and prevent cheating, as far as possible. That a Creator sometimes enters the dream of another by accident is understandable, but that he do it intentionally and interfere with a creation that is not his own, and then use the "loot" for himself, well that's not acceptable. Two "performances" are irreparably damaged because of one thief. And the spectators suffer for it."

"That's true," Alam agrees. "Do you have any idea of who's guilty? I think that in our present case... I think both of them."

"Yes, I have an idea. What's worse for them is that they're just Creator-Candidates. And because of one of them, both of their creations will be deleted... I think that Creator-Candidate Two is guilty."

"Why?"

"For many reasons that I gleaned from studying his dream... I'll tell you."

"I'd like that, yes."

And Elio communicates: "It was already strange that two Creators arrived at such similar vital projections. I mean the humans. Both created colorful characters and used them as support for the main personage. I think that here, already, Creator Two had made a quick foray into Creator One's dream. I admit that the construction of a universe such as Creator Two imagined displays great qualities. That wonderful idea of planets, solar systems, that outrageous construction starting from the infinitely small and the bond of force and energy existing between everything... yes, I think it's wonderful. That planet Earth, the appearance of Life in the world, its evolution... I'm delighted with it all. While Creator-Candidate One was happy with a single, flat world, huge and limitless..."

"Maybe he was acting on the safe side," Alam expresses.

"That's highly likely. He controlled his imaginative forces while Creator Two burned through most of them at the beginning to build the foundations of his world. Which drove him to cheat later and enter his colleague's dream. And that's why he sent spy-characters into the Isha universe of Creator One. Some characters, at the beginning, whom he "disconnected", somehow, from his own creation and threw into Isha. During this lapse of time—and there's another nice idea: Time—during this lapse of time when the subject-spies were elsewhere, he had to isolate them in their own universe. To make them just simply disappear posed too many problems for the logical sequence of events, especially in the context of the particular rules and laws he had created. That's why Creator Two invented madness for his spies... Like that he sheltered them, in a way, from the laws he had created in his universe... But he completely ignored the fact that the sudden and constant "apparitions" of his subjects could cause such damage in the universe invented by his colleague. That's how the first disruptions happened and from that we got the first complaints from the spectators who were following the development of Creator One's creation."

"Yes, I see," Alam agrees. "It's really too bad. Like you said, the work of this cheater was praiseworthy, at the start. I, too, liked the Earth and the other planets. We've never witnessed a conception of this kind... worlds floating in incommensurable space..."

"Never before, that's true... Maybe he stole the idea of humans... but, we can't be sure. He reached a stage of harmless, personal repose during which he could have "recharged"... It's true, his civilizations were launched and they moved on their own, on the immutable rails laid out at the start. All he had to do was intervene from time to time, when he wanted to, to guide such and such subject, to initiate some event or another... That idea of different races wasn't bad either. It allowed a myriad of new developments that I'm sure he never dreamed of. He just had to let it go. There was another good idea: I mean the people's need for knowledge. That led them toward a goal. Inventions like emotional and sexual relationships, etc, among others, were marvelous. And then the wars, the cataclysms... that distracted the spectators, once in a while. As far as that, I mean the wars, his subjects were gifted... And it was a sensational idea to have created them imperfect, that is, to establish from the start the rules and laws and taboos against which the subjects tended to rebel instinctively. The fundamental nature of the subject not being made for those shackles and the shackles being more or less necessary for the smooth continuity of the story—that offered such incredible possibilities for conflict..."

"And the idea of God, too..."

"True! A stroke of genius. A kind of joke in which Creator Two brought himself into play... A beautiful achievement. He let himself be interpreted differently by the different peoples of his dream... Yes, really, there were a lot of good things. Too bad he had those incursions into the other's dream. Because Creator Two felt the danger right away. But the error was committed and there was no turning back. It had left traces. He felt the danger, foresaw it. He probably knows it right now like he knows the inevitable outcome it is destined to... There was nothing more he could do, since he didn't know how to pace himself, his imagination, at the beginning. He ran out of more and more resources... He kept using those "spies". He was quickly overwhelmed by them. His world became a world of apathetic, useless madmen. And the world of Isha was invaded by the real, living Strangers, but really "strangers"... And then all his civilizations were affected. Madmen, sick men... Of course there were the doctors, but operating as balanced men, how could they cure subjects suffering from a problem willed by him, the Creator? How? To allow them to discover the innermost mechanisms of life was also to reveal his identity to them!"

"Didn't he try?"

"That's true... I've picked up some traces. Like an attempted suicide, in a way, at times when he was particularly devoid of imagination. Then he instilled certain suggestions in the subjects. Scientists, researchers... and those little replicas of himself who are artists and writers... but the researchers whom he put on this track were talking against the established system, this system that was, in a way, also a self-defense for Creator Two. They were never taken seriously. Not to mention the artists and the writers of imaginative and "unreal" stories... But you're right, he did make a few attempts to get his creations to find out his "Truth". And some subjects *practically found it. Far too few, anyway, to get anything going."*

"What are we going to do?" Alam communicates.

"Wake the two of them up. Interrupt and destroy their creations. There won't be any more Humanity or Isha. That's all we can do... There's really too much chaos in both worlds: one from the madmen and the other from the Strangers. If we let it go, Isha will soon turn into a huge carnage out of control of Creator One's will and then Humanity, the Earth, a world peopled by sick men tearing each other to pieces in spite of a handful of balanced subjects... We have to wake them up and stop their dreams. They'll each remain Creator-Candidates. Maybe they'll be authorized to prove themselves again. Creator One will certainly be able to since he was looted. Creator Two, well, his unbridled imagination at the start of the story might earn him some indulgence..."

"He knows that," Alam communicates. "He knows everything."

"Maybe."

"For sure," Alam communicates. "I'm wondering about these subjects in which he showed certain things concerning the Truth. I'm thinking about a mystical doctrine of one of his peoples in which they said, among other things: A man dreams that he is a butterfly. When he wakes up, he does not remember if he is a man who dreamed that he was a butterfly or if he is a butterfly who is dreaming that he is a man... That's pretty clear."

"I remember that."

"One day, one of the created subjects used these words to write a book in which he spoke about Isha and Humanity..."

"Was it an important work?"

*"No. A book they call fiction, meant to entertain...
which means that it did not have much influence... It was
called* But What If Butterflies Cheat? *And Creator Two
used this author to manipulate time, to dive into the future, the future of his creation, of course. To predict the
moment we're living now, right here. To predict this
sentence, also. He predicted everything, including our
words. He predicted this conversation we're having and
he even predicted that we would talk about this, that we
would notice this."*

*Silence falls over them, interrupting the conversa-
tion.*

Then Elio: "It's true..."

*"And what if we ourselves," Alam communicates
slowly, "what if we were being thought up, created by...
by others?"*

"Come on, that's ridiculous."

*"And what if we were being thought up, created
by... by him, Creator Two? What's more, by his own
creation? By that man in the dream who imagined he
was created by us, or who wrote his book pretending to
imagine it?"*

Another silence breaks the communication.

*Alam resumes, "I'll communicate the last lines of
the book. They are:*

"I'll communicate the last lines of the book. They
are:

"Can we wake up Creator Two?" Alam asked. "For
our own safety?"

"Come on, that's ridiculous."

"And what if we were being thought up, created by
him, Creator Two? What's more, by his own creation?

290

By that man in the dream who imagined he was created by *us*, or who wrote his book pretending to imagine it?"

Another silence broke the communication.

Alam resumed, "I'll communicate the last lines of the book. They are:

"I'll communicate the last lines of the book. They are:

"Can we wake up Creator Two?" Alam asked. "For our own safety?"

"Come on, that's ridiculous."

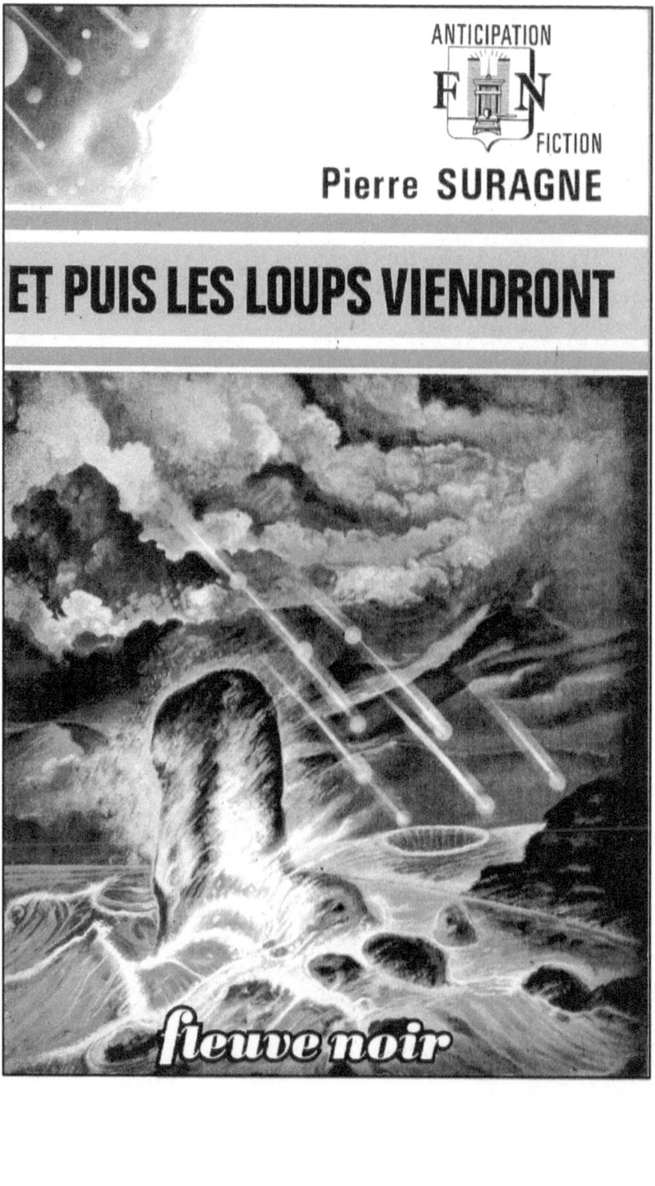

ANTICIPATION

FICTION

Pierre **SURAGNE**

ET PUIS LES LOUPS VIENDRONT

fleuve noir

Bibliography

Science fiction:
Une Autre Terre [*Another Earth*] (Arian Dhaye 1) (Hatier, 1972)
La Septième Saison [*The Seventh Season*] (*As Pierre Suragne*) (Fleuve Noir Anticipation (FNA) No.505, 1972)
Mal Iergo le Dernier [*Mal Iergo the Last*] (*As Pierre Suragne*) (FNA 519, 1972)
L'Enfant qui Marchait sur le Ciel [*The Child Who Walked On The Sky*] (*As Pierre Suragne*) (FNA 530, 1972)
La Nef des Dieux [*The Ship Of The Gods*] (*As Pierre Suragne*) (FNA 549, 1973)
Mecanic Jungle (*As Pierre Suragne*) (FNA 566, 1973)
L'Île aux Enragés [*The Rabid Island*] (Arian Dhaye 2) (Hatier, 1973)
Les Légendes de la Terre [*The Legends Of The Earth*] (GP, 1973)
Le Pays des Rivières sans Nom [*The Land Of The Nameless Rivers*] (GP, 1973)
Et puis les Loups Viendront [*And Then The Wolves Will Come*] (*As Pierre Suragne*) (FNA 577, 1973)
Mais si les Papillons Trichent? [*But What If Butterflies Cheat?*] (*As Pierre Suragne*) (FNA 612, 1974)
Le Dieu Truqué [*The Phony God*] (*As Pierre Suragne*) (FNA 625, 1974)
Ballade pour Presqu'un Homme [*Ballad For Almost A Man*] (*As Pierre Suragne*) (FNA 633, 1974)
Vendredi, Par Exemple [*Friday, For Example*] (*As Pierre Suragne*) (FNA 695, 1975)
Les Barreaux de l'Éden [*The Bars Of Eden*] (J'ai Lu (JL) No.728, 1977)
Foetus-Party (Présence du Futur (PdF) No.225, 1977)

293

présence du futur

pierre pelot

la guerre olympique

denoël

Le Sourire des Crabes [*The Smile Of The Crabs*] (Presses-Pocket (PP) No.5003, 1977)

La Cité au Bout de l'Espace [*The City At The End Of Space*] (*As Pierre Suragne*) (FNA 797, 1977)

Transit (Ailleurs & Demain No.47, 1977)

Delirium Circus (JL 773, 1977)

Canyon Street (PdF 265, 1978)

Le Sommeil du Chien [*The Sleep Of The Dog*] (Kesselring No.5, 1978)

La Rage dans le Troupeau [*The Rage In The Flock*] (PP 5060, 1979)

Virgules Téléguidées [*Remote-Controlled Commas*] (*As Pierre Suragne*) (FNA 970, 1980)

Blues pour Julie [*Blues for Julia*] (Ponte Mirone, 1980)

Parabellum Tango (JL 1048, 1980)

Le Ciel Bleu d'Irockee [*The Blue Sky Of Irockee*] (PP 5072, 1980)

La Guerre Olympique [*The Olympic War*] (PdF 297, 1980)

Dérapages [*Out Of Control*] (*As Pierre Suragne*) (FNA 999, 1980)

Kid Jesus (JL 1140, 1981)

Les Îles du Vacarme [*The Islands Of Clamor*] (PP 5096, 1981)

Les Mangeurs d'Argile [*The Clay Eaters*] (Hommes Sans Futur 1) (PP 5126, 1981)

Les Pieds dans la Tête [*The Feet In The Head*] (Dim. 48, 1982)

Nos Armes Sont De Miel [*Our Weapons Are Made Of Honey*] (JL 1305, 1982)

Mourir au Hasard [*To Die Randomly*] (PdF 339, 1982)

Saison de Rouille [*Rusty Season*] (Hommes Sans Futur 2) (PP 5135, 1982)

Soleils Hurlants [*Screaming Suns*] (Hommes Sans Futur 3) (PP 5157, 1983)

La Foudre au Ralenti [*The Slow-Motion Lightning*] (JL 1564, 1983)

Le Père de Feu [*The Fire-Father*] (Hommes Sans Futur 4) (PP 5173, 1984)

PIERRE PELOT

Delirium Circus

Le Chien Courrait sur l'Autoroute en Criant son Nom [*A Dog Was Running On The Highway Shouting Its Name*] (Hommes Sans Futur 5) (PP 5190, 1984)

Paradis Zéro [*Paradise Zero*] (Chromagnon Z 1) (FNA 1355, 1985)

Le Bruit des Autres [*The Sound Of Others*] (Chromagnon Z 2) (FNA 1369, 1985)

Ce Chasseur-Là [*That Hunter There*] (Hommes Sans Futur 6) (PP 5209, 1985)

Les Passagers du Mirage [*The Passengers Of The Mirage*] (Chromagnon Z 3) (FNA 1426, 1985)

Fou dans la Tête de Nazi Jones, Belladone et Compagnie [*Mad In the Head of Nazi Jones, Belladona & Co.*] (FNA 1463, 1986)

Les Conquérants Immobiles [*The Motionless Conquerors*] (Chromagnon Z 4) (FNA 1469, 1986)

Mémoires d'un Épouvantail Blessé au Combat [*Memories Of A Scarecrow Wounded In Action*] (Tony Burdern 1) (FNA 1482, 1986)

Observation du Virus en Temps de Paix [*Observation Of The Virus During Peace Time*] (Tony Burden 2) (FNA 1495, 1986)

Alabama Un.Neuf.Six.Six [*Alabama 1.9.9.6*] (Tony Burden 3) (FNA 1553, 1987)

Sécession Bis (Tony Burden 4) (FNA 1565, 1987)

Offensive du Virus sous le Champ de Bataille [*Offensive Of The Virus On The Battlefield*] (Tony Burden 5) (FNA 1580, 1987)

Une Jeune Fille au Sourire Fragile [*A Young Girl With A Fragile Smile*] (Siry SF No.6, 1988)

Le Présent du Fou [*The Madman's Gift*] (Raconteurs 1) (FNA 1732, 1990)

Les Forains du Bord du Gouffre [*The Carnival On The Edge Of The Abyss*] (Raconteurs 2) (FNA 1737, 1990)

Le Ciel sous la Pierre [*The Sky Under The Stone*] (Raconteurs 3) (FNA 1743, 1990)

Pierre Suragne

LA PEAU
DE L'ORAGE

ANGOISSE

FLEUVE NOIR

Les Faucheurs de Temps [*The Time Reapers*] (Raconteurs 4) (FNA 1750, 1990)

La Nuit du Sagittaire [*The Night Of Sagittarius*] (PP 5338, 1990)

L'Expédition Perdue [*The Lost Expedition*] (Nathan, 1994)

Messager des Tempêtes Lointaines [*Messenger Of The Far Storms*] (PdF 566, 1996)

Horror:

La Peau de l'Orage [*The Skin Of The Storm*] (*As Pierre Suragne*) (Fleuve Noir Angoisse (FNAG) No.235, 1973)

Duz (*As Pierre Suragne*) (FNAG 243, 1973)

Je suis la Brume [*I Am The Mist*] (*As Pierre Suragne*) (FNAG 251, 1974)

Suicide (*As Pierre Suragne*) (Fleuve Noir Super-Luxe (FNSL) No.1, 1974)

Une Si Profonde Nuit [*Such A Deep Night*] (*As Pierre Suragne*) (FNSL 8, 1975)

Brouillards [*Fog*] (*As Pierre Suragne*) (FNSL 13, 1975)

Elle Était Une Fois [*She Was Upon A Time*] (*As Pierre Suragne*) (FNSL 25, 1976)

Le Septième Vivant [*The Seventh Living*] (*As Pierre Suragne*) (FNSL 27, 1976)

La Forêt Muette [*The Silent Forest*] (Albin Michel, 1982)

Purgatoire [*Purgatory*] (Fleuve Noir Gore (FNG) No.34, 1986)

Aux Chiens Écrasés [*The Run-Over Dogs*] (FNG 59, 1987)

Une Autre Saison comme le Printemps [*Another Season Like Spring*] (Denoël, 1995)

La Fille de la Hache-Croix [*The Girl from Hache-Croix*] (Magnard, 1998)

Outback (Club Van Helsing) (Baleine, 2008)

Fantasy:

Konnar le Barbant [*Konnar The Boring*] (Konnar 1) (Fiction Nos.320-321, 1981); revised as Le Fils du Grand Konnar [*The Son Of Great Konnar*] (FNA 1788, 1990)

ANTICIPATION

PIERRE PELOT

LE FILS DU GRAND KONNAR

Konnar et Compagnie – 1

FLEUVE NOIR
ANTICIPATION

Sur la Piste des Rollmops [*On The Trail Of The Rollmops*] (Konnar 2) (FNA 1796, 1990)
Rollmops Dream (Konnar 3) (FNA 1802, 1991)
Gilbert le Barbant - Le Retour [*Gilbert The Boring - The Return*] (Konnar 4) (FNA 1811, 1991)
Ultimes Aventures en Territoires Fourbes [*Last Adventures In Deceitful Lands*] (Konnar 5) (FNA 1831, 1991)
Le Pacte des Loups [*The Brotherhood of the Wolf*] (novelization of the eponymous film) (Payot Rivages, 2001)
Brocéliande (novelization) (Payot Rivages, 2002)

Prehistoric Novels:
Qui Regarde la Montagne au Loin? [*Who Looks At The Farthest Mountain?*] (Sous le Vent du Monde 1) (Denoël, 1997)
Le Nom Perdu du Soleil [*The Lost Name of the Sun*] (Sous le Vent du Monde 2) (Denoël, 1998)
Debout dans le Ventre Blanc du Silence [*Up In The White Belly Of Silence*] (Sous le Vent du Monde 3) (Denoël, 1999)
Le Jour de l'Enfant-Tueur [*The Day Of the Killer Child*] (Ahorn 1) (Seuil, 1999)
L'Ombre de la Louve [*The Shadow of the She-Wolf*] (Ahorn 2) Seuil, 2000)
Avant la Fin du Ciel [*Before the Ends of the Sky*] (Sous le Vent du Monde 4) (Denoël, 2000)
Ceux qui parlent au bord de la Pierre [*Those Who Speak Over The Edge of the Stone*] (Sous le Vent du Monde 5) (Denoël, 2001)

Misc. Genre:
Les Larmes de la Jungle [*The Tears Of The Jungle*] (Rageot, 1991)
Le Chant de l'Homme Mort [*The Song Of The Dead Man*] (Matthew Garden 1) (Fleuve Noir Aventures (FNAV), 1995)
Après le Bout du Monde [*After The Edge Of The World*] (FNAV, 1996)
Les Pirates du Graal [*The Grail Pirates*] (Matthew Garden 2) (Fleuve Noir SF (FNSF) No.53, 1998)

SCIENCE-FICTION
Pierre Pelot

SOLEILS
HURLANTS

Presses
Pocket

SF & FANTASY

Henri Allorge. *The Great Cataclysm*
Guy d'Armen. *Doc Ardan: The City of Gold and Lepers*
G.-J. Arnaud. *The Ice Company*
Charles Asselineau. *The Double Life*
Cyprien Bérard. *The Vampire Lord Ruthwen*
Aloysius Bertrand. *Gaspard de la Nuit*
Richard Bessière. *The Gardens of the Apocalypse*
Albert Bleunard. *Ever Smaller*
Félix Bodin. *The Novel of the Future*
Alphonse Brown. *City of Glass*
André Caroff. *The Terror of Madame Atomos; Miss Atomos; The Return of Madame Atomos; The Mistake of Madame Atomos; The Monsters of Madame Atomos*
Félicien Champsaur. *The Human Arrow*
Didier de Chousy. *Ignis*
Captain Danrit. *Undersea Odyssey*
C. I. Defontenay. *Star (Psi Cassiopeia)*
Charles Derennes. *The People of the Pole*
Georges Dodds (anthologist). *The Missing Link*
Harry Dickson. *The Heir of Dracula*
Jules Dornay. *Lord Ruthven Begins*
Alfred Driou. *The Adventures of a Parisian Aeronaut*
Sâr Dubnotal *vs. Jack the Ripper*
Alexandre Dumas. *The Return of Lord Ruthven*
Renée Dunan. *Baal*
J.-C. Dunyach. *The Night Orchid; The Thieves of Silence*
Henri Duvernois. *The Man Who Found Himself*
Achille Eyraud. *Voyage to Venus*
Henri Falk. *The Age of Lead*
Paul Féval. *Anne of the Isles; Knightshade; Revenants; Vampire City; The Vampire Countess; The Wandering Jew's Daughter*
Paul Féval, *fils. Felifax, the Tiger-Man*
Charles de Fieux. *Lamékis*
Arnould Galopin. *Doctor Omega*; *Doctor Omega & The Shadowmen*
G.L. Gick. *Harry Dickson and the Werewolf of Rutherford Grange*
Edmond Haraucourt. *Illusions of Immortality*
Nathalie Henneberg. *The Green Gods*
V. Hugo, P. Foucher & P. Meurice. *The Hunchback of Notre-Dame*
Michel Jeury. *Chronolysis*

Gustave Kahn. *The Tale of Gold and Silence*
Gérard Klein. *The Mote in Time's Eye*
Jean de La Hire. *Enter the Nyctalope; The Nyctalope on Mars; The Nyctalope vs. Lucifer; The Nyctalope Steps In; Night of the Nyctalope*
Etienne-Léon de Lamothe-Langon. *The Virgin Vampire*
André Laurie. *Spiridon*
Gabriel de Lautrec. *The Vengeance of the Oval Portrait*
Georges Le Faure & Henri de Graffigny. *The Extraordinary Adventures of a Russian Scientist Across the Solar System* (2 vols.)
Gustave Le Rouge. *The Vampires of Mars The Dominion of the World* (w/Gustave Guitton) (4 vols.)
Jules Lermina. *Mysteryville; Panic in Paris; To-Ho and the Gold Destroyers; The Secret of Zippelius*
Jean-Marc & Randy Lofficier. *Edgar Allan Poe on Mars; The Katrina Protocol; Pacifica; Robonocchio; Tales of the Shadowmen 1-8*
Xavier Mauméjean. *The League of Heroes*
Joseph Méry. *The Tower of Destiny*
Hippolyte Mettais. *The Year 5865*
José Moselli. *Illa's End*
John-Antoine Nau. *Enemy Force*
Marie Nizet. *Captain Vampire*
C. Nodier, A. Beraud & Toussaint-Merle. *Frankenstein*
Henri de Parville. *An Inhabitant of the Planet Mars*
Gaston de Pawlowski. *Journey to the Land of the 4th Dimension*
Georges Pellerin. *The World in 2000 Years*
Pierre Pelot. *The Child Who Walked on the Sky*
J. Polidori, C. Nodier, E. Scribe. *Lord Ruthven the Vampire*
P.-A. Ponson du Terrail. *The Vampire and the Devil's Son*
Henri de Régnier. *A Surfeit of Mirrors*
Maurice Renard. *The Blue Peril; Doctor Lerne; The Doctored Man; A Man Among the Microbes; The Master of Light*
Jean Richepin. *The Wing*
Albert Robida. *The Adventures of Saturnin Farandoul; The Clock of the Centuries; Chalet in the Sky*
J.-H. Rosny Aîné. *Helgvor of the Blue River; The Givreuse Enigma; The Mysterious Force; The Navigators of Space; Vamireh; The World of the Variants; The Young Vampire*
Marcel Rouff. *Journey to the Inverted World*
Han Ryner. *The Superhumans*
Brian Stableford. *The New Faust at the Tragicomique;The Empire of the Necromancers (The Shadow of Frankenstein; Frankenstein and*

the Vampire Countess; Frankenstein in London); Sherlock Holmes &
The Vampires of Eternity; The Stones of Camelot; The Wayward
Muse. (anthologist) *The Germans on Venus; News from the Moon;*
The Supreme Progress; The World Above the World; Nemoville;
Investigations of the Future
Jacques Spitz. *The Eye of Purgatory*
Kurt Steiner. *Ortog*
Eugène Thébault. *Radio-Terror*
C.-F. Tiphaigne de La Roche. *Amilec*
Théo Varlet. *The Xenobiotic Invasion; Timeslip Troopers* (w/André
Blandin); *The Martian Epic* (w/Octave Joncquel)
Paul Vibert. *The Mysterious Fluid*
Villiers de l'Isle-Adam. *The Scaffold; The Vampire Soul*
Philippe Ward. *Artahe*
Philippe Ward & Sylvie Miller. *The Song of Montségur*

MYSTERIES & THRILLERS

M. Allain & P. Souvestre. *The Daughter of Fantômas*
A. Anicet-Bourgeois, Lucien Dabril. *Rocambole*
A. Bernède. *Judex* (w/Louis Feuillade)
A. Bisson & G. Livet. *Nick Carter vs. Fantômas*
V. Darlay & H. de Gorsse. *Lupin vs. Holmes: The Stage Play*
Paul Féval. *Gentlemen of the Night; John Devil; The Black Coats*
('Salem Street; The Invisible Weapon; The Parisian Jungle; The
Companions of the Treasure; Heart of Steel; The Cadet Gang; The
Sword-Swallower)
Emile Gaboriau. *Monsieur Lecoq*
Steve Leadley. *Sherlock Holmes: The Circle of Blood*
Maurice Leblanc. *Arsène Lupin vs. Countess Cagliostro; Lupin vs.*
Holmes (The Blonde Phantom; The Hollow Needle); The Many Faces
of Arsène Lupin
Gaston Leroux. *Chéri-Bibi; The Phantom of the Opera; Rouletabille*
& the Mystery of the Yellow Room
Richard Marsh. *The Complete Adventures of Judith Lee*
William Patrick Maynard. *The Terror of Fu Manchu; The Destiny of*
Fu Manchu
Frank J. Morlock. *Sherlock Holmes: The Grand Horizontals; Sher-*
lock Holmes vs Jack the Ripper
Antonin Reschal. *The Adventures of Miss Boston*
P. de Wattyne & Y. Walter. *Sherlock Holmes vs. Fantômas*

David White. *Fantômas in America*

SCREENPLAYS

Mike Baron. *The Iron Triangle*
Emma Bull & Will Shetterly. *Nightspeeder; War for the Oaks*
Gerry Conway & Roy Thomas. *Doc Dynamo*
Steve Englehart. *Majorca*
James Hudnall. *The Devastator*
Jean-Marc & Randy Lofficier. *Royal Flush*
J.-M. & R. Lofficier & Marc Agapit. *Despair*
J.-M. & R. Lofficier & Joël Houssin. *City*
Andrew Paquette. *Peripheral Vision*
R. Thomas, J. Hendler & L. Sprague de Camp. *Rivers of Time*

NON-FICTION

Stephen R. Bissette. *Blur 1-5. Green Mountain Cinema 1; Teen Angels*
Win Scott Eckert. *Crossovers* (2 vols.)
Jean-Marc & Randy Lofficier. *Shadowmen* (2 vols.)
Randy Lofficier. *Over Here*

HEXAGON COMICS

Franco Frescura & Luciano Bernasconi. *Wampus*
Franco Frescura & Giorgio Trevisan. *CLASH*
L. Bernasconi, J.-M. Lofficier & Juan Roncagliolo Berger. *Phenix*
Claude Legrand, J.-M. Lofficier & L. Bernasconi. *Kabur*
Franco Oneta. *Zembla*
L. Buffolente, Lofficier & J.-J. Dzialowski. *Strangers: Homicron*
Danilo Grossi. *Strangers: Jaydee*
Claude Legrand & Luciano Bernasconi. *Strangers: Starlock*

ART BOOKS

Jean-Pierre Normand. *Science Fiction Illustrations*
Raven Okeefe. *Raven's L'il Critters*
Randy Lofficier & Raven OKeefe. *If Your Possum Go Daylight...*
Daniele Serra. *Illusions*

www.ingramcontent.com/pod-product-compliance
Lightning Source LLC
Chambersburg PA
CBHW030343020726
47493CB00003B/667